NIGHTHAWKS

CHILDREN OF NOSTRADAMUS, BOOK 1

JEREMY FLAGG

NIGHTHAWKS

Limitless Publishing, LLC
Kailua, HI 96734
www.limitlesspublishing.com

Formatting: Limitless Publishing

ISBN-13: 978-1-68058-523-0
ISBN-10: 1-68058-523-1

Dedication

This book is dedicated to the kids who wanted to become heroes and the superheroes they became.

And to Nick Leonard—if only we knew then how amazing life would be now. Thank you for co-authoring my imagination as a kid.

Chapter One

February 13th, 1992 11:32AM

She sat at her desk, silent, running her hands along the smooth surface. In such a large room, filled with historic monuments to one of the greatest nations, it was the desk that always captivated her. Her fingers rested on a spot where the varnish had worn thin and she could feel the memories etched beneath her fingertips. Decades earlier, a man had sat at this desk and helped fortify the nation. His hands had rested in that exact spot, beginning the weathering of the mammoth structure. Years later, a less virtuous man would place his mistress on the desk and ravish her in an attempt to exact revenge on a bitter bride.

She let out a sigh as the memories wove themselves into her thoughts. An image flashed across her mind, a mistress being taken by her lover. With a startled gesture she pulled her hand away from the spot and pondered the realness of the images. They were always the same, and if she left

1

her hand there long enough, she would eventually begin to feel her brow sweat as she made stately decisions or her body tensed up in the throes of passion.

She reached for a crisp white glove on her desk and slid it over her delicate, aged hands, pulling them tight on her thin fingers. She rested her hand on the spot again and this time the memories were distant, as though if she focused, she might be able to remember. The gloves, while perfectly sculpted to her hands, were the thin layer of fabric between her right mind and losing herself to a distant past.

"Excuse me," came a young man's voice.

The woman turned in her chair and could see an intern standing at the door. "Please do come in," she said in a wispy voice.

"You asked to see me, Ms. Valentine?"

She could tell he was nervous in her presence. Despite her warm invitation, he waited at the door. He looked at her but averted his eyes to one of the various larger-than-life paintings that lined the walls.

She had grown accustomed to the averted gaze of the young people in the office. She waited patiently for him to test his bravery and enter. She rested her hands in her lap, one on the other, in the most delicate manner she could muster. In the years that she had worked there, she had learned to make herself the least threatening individual in the room.

He could see that she wasn't going to continue until he moved closer. He lowered his head, focusing on his feet, and took several steps in her direction, but left at least ten paces between them.

"Don't be afraid, son," she said with a slight smile. "I won't bite."

He tried to speak but his voice was caught in his throat. He adjusted his pristine tie, loosening it slightly, and tried again. "I apologize, Ms. Valentine," he said quietly, "it's just that…" He trailed off.

"You're new here," she said calmly, "and you've never been around somebody like me."

"Did you just…"

"The sweat on your forehead," she said with the slightest laugh. "I've been here for a while, Mr. Davis. A lady doesn't get to my age without learning to be observant."

"I'm sorry, ma'am," he said, his southern accent slipping into his speech.

"Please, call me Eleanor," she said with a slight nod of her head. "And please don't be nervous."

He let out a deep breath and she could see his entire body relax. She wondered if he had been expecting a scary old woman, or perhaps somebody who resembled a villain in a children's book. She often felt that she should be insulted, but dismissed it. She was fond of the interns and their prim and proper ways.

"You asked me to come to your office Ms. Va—" He paused. "Eleanor."

"Oh yes," she said, standing slowly as if not to startle the young man. "I need you to deliver several letters."

She was well aware his eyes followed her closely as she walked toward one of the large paintings on the wall. She pulled the painting away from the wall, arcing it outward like a door to reveal one of the most well-guarded safes on the premises. She found it humorous the painting hid the safe since everybody knew it was there. She punched a few numbers on the keypad and leaned forward against the safe as a blue line scanned her eyes.

Finally she turned to look at him. "The code changes daily," she explained. "The numbers are randomly generated and only I know the code."

"But what if…" The smile on her face stopped him mid-sentence. Eleanor couldn't hear his thoughts, but she couldn't ignore the waves of nostalgia washing over him as he compared her to his grandmother. She would give him that same smile, which revealed nearly a century of wisdom but the temper to keep the knowledge to herself.

"Thank you," she said, pulling the handle of the safe open.

"Did you just…"

"Yes, I did," she said.

She pulled out a handful of envelopes from the safe and then returned it and the painting to their original places. She walked toward him. "I need these to be mailed."

He raised an eyebrow at the request. "Why not ask the mail clerk, Ms. Valentine?"

"Eleanor," she corrected. "And because you were the one who had to mail them."

He didn't argue. She was well aware people in the lounge would whisper about her cryptic words. She knew he would do the same, telling them about his experience with the psychic.

She was within arms' length of him and she held

up the envelopes. "There will be trials and tribulations, Mr. Davis," she said matter-of-factly, "but it is extremely important that these be mailed."

"They're all postmarked for…" He looked at her soft smile.

"I know," she said calmly, "but I must repeat this. It is of grave importance that you deliver these by hand today."

He nodded as she placed the envelopes in his outstretched hand. She closed his fingers around the envelopes and stared at him without blinking. "What is it you want to ask me, Mr. Davis?"

He averted his eyes. "This is the first time I've ever met a…"

"I know," she said. "Be calm, Mr. Davis. I am merely an old lady, doing her best to make the world a better place."

He looked back at the envelopes. "What is in them?"

"That is only for the individuals meant to read them," she said.

He took several deep breaths and met her eyes again. It wasn't often, but with the young man standing before her, she felt every day of her age. His youthful exuberance contrasted with her tired eyes. Standing before her was a young man with a lifetime ahead of him, and she had several lifetimes slowly fading from her rearview mirror. For a moment she smiled, and she knew her crow's feet and laugh lines were deepened, the price for living a full life

"They say you can…" He paused. "You know."

She nodded.

"Can you…"

His voice trailed off as she placed her hand on his. She could feel his body stiffen at the benign gesture. She could feel his muscles twitch and then eventually relax. She stared into his eyes, not blinking.

Like the spot on her desk, she ran her fingers across the tops of his knuckles. Unlike the desk, she could feel her thoughts moving forward. The hair on her neck reacted as if she were running and she could almost feel the breeze wash across her skin.

Her mind was filled with images of the young man in front of her. She could see him as an adult, with children of his own and a wife, and even standing at the grave of his beloved. She let her mind become overwhelmed with the flashing vignettes of his future and finally she gripped his hand a bit tighter, giving clarity to her visions. She could see him and his father visiting a sickly, bald woman in a hospital bed.

She closed her eyes and took a steadying breath. She opened them to the sensation of tears running down her cheeks. She looked at the boy in front of her, his eyes quivering, afraid of what he might hear.

"Are you sure?" she asked. "Of anything I can tell you, this is what you want?"

He sniffed deeply, nodding his head.

"Mr. Davis," she said quietly, "your mom will be okay."

He began crying.

He pulled her in close and wrapped his arms around her small frame. "Thank you," he sobbed.

She hugged him back and his sense of relief washed over her. She could see the images come back to her. Unlike before, the picture was clear, projected as if she were standing in that moment. She could see him embracing his little sister, telling her that their mother was going to survive. When his sister asked how he knew, he replied, "An angel told me."

He pulled back, looking at her. "Why did you ask?" He wiped away the tears. "You knew, didn't you?"

She nodded.

He straightened himself and smoothed out his tie. He looked at the envelopes and back at her. "I'll go right now, Eleanor."

"Thank you, Mr. Davis," she said softly. "Take care."

She watched as the young man turned and walked out of her office and down the hall. She took off her glove and wiped the tears from her eyes, careful to avoid her makeup. She slid the glove back on and went back to her massive desk.

Sitting down in the chair, she reached for the bottom left drawer and opened it slowly. She pulled a wooden box from the drawer and rested it on the top of her desk. She closed her eyes for a moment and then opened it, revealing the small handgun inside. She could feel the history of the gun as she looked at it.

She quickly picked it up and put it into her purse. She closed the box and returned it to the drawer, and then closed the clasp on her purse. She had been taught how to handle a gun when she first arrived and had even been given special permission to keep one in her office. While she could handle herself, she hated having to touch the piece of metal.

Eleanor took a deep breath and stood up, pressing the blazer of her powder blue dress suit against her body, smoothing out the wrinkles. Pushing a loose strand of white hair behind her ear, she picked up her purse and draped it over her shoulder. Looking down at her white gloves, she clenched her fist and made her way to the door.

As she worked her way through the winding halls, she began to think about the events leading to this moment. She had become increasingly alarmed by the actions of her boss over the last few months. It was nothing the woman did or said, but her mannerisms were ever so changed. The simple way she looked at Eleanor over the edge of her mug while she sipped her morning coffee had felt off.

At first she had brushed it off as the stress of the job. Even Cecilia's husband was unaware of the changes. Eleanor had subtly brought it up over afternoon tea and he was completely dumbfounded. However, over the past few months she had been experiencing changes herself.

Eleanor Valentine was one of the most trusted associates of her boss. Her insight into the world had made her indispensable. For the last eight years she had been treated like family, and when she chose to speak, her boss listened to her words. She would like to think that she was doing her duty to all of mankind.

Orphaned at a young age, Eleanor felt it funny

that only in her twilight years she would finally be able to refer to somebody nearly half her age as family. She could sense the guards in the hallway as she walked toward the infamous doorway. Two men stood there in black suits with earpieces nestled firmly in their ears.

"Ms. Valentine," one man said, "how are you today?"

"Quite fine, Mr. Connors," she said with a smile.

He put his finger to his ear and waited for the next command to be fed to him. She had grown so accustomed to the burly men she kept company with. She knew that her twilight years made them see her as harmless, never as a threat in the building. While the guards were explicitly told not to banter with their charges, she could often find them in their private break room talking. On more than a few occasions she had brought them her infamous chocolate chip cookies.

"You can go in," the massive man said.

"Thank you," she said as she took a step forward.

"Wait, Ms. Valentine," he said, pointing to her clutch. "I will need to check your purse. I apologize for the inconvenience."

"For you, anything," she said, holding out the bag.

As he reached for the clasp, she could sense the alarm as he saw the glint of metal in her handbag. She quickly spoke firmly in her head, *"Everything is all set, Ms. Valentine."*

"Everything is all set, Ms. Valentine."

She found it unsettling how easily her body had acclimated to the sensation of pushing her will onto another human being. Her heartrate had barely elevated. She took another steadying breath and reached out for her purse.

"Have a splendid day," she said, aware that he handed the bag back to her in a manner that would avoid physical contact.

"You too, Mr. Jacobs," she said to the other guard.

Mr. Connors reached for the doorknob and opened the door for Eleanor. She gave a slight nod of her head as she passed through and waited for them to shut it behind her. She took several steps until she was in one of the most recognizable rooms in the civilized world.

She understood the pomp and circumstance, and that every object in the office was there for either historical or public relations reasons. She could accept nearly all the décor, but each time she saw the ugly carpet imprinted with a large eagle, she shivered a bit. She had mentioned it time and time again, but alas, to change even that had the potential of creating an international incident.

"Eleanor," said the woman behind the desk, "I'm glad to see you."

"Likewise, Madame President," Eleanor said with a minor curtsey.

She waved her hand in dismissal. "Only for a few more months, and then I can spend my time at charity events and talking about the glory days."

Eleanor sat down on the couch. "Shall we begin with pleasure or business?"

The president let out a long sigh. "Pleasure will have to wait, my friend," she said. "There are monumental decisions to be made today."

"We shall save the world first," Eleanor jested. "Then we can talk of this retirement."

The president was forty years her junior, her hair only beginning to show the faintest of white. In her suit, she was as intimidating as any man Eleanor had ever watched. She stood up and moved to the couch with several stacks of papers in dark folders. "Before we begin, I wanted to let you know that the young girl we discovered has been given a new home."

Eleanor sat up straight. "Really? You convinced them to take her out of the program?"

The president nodded. "I believe in the program, Eleanor. These mentalists have so much potential for the world. But a young girl should be given a choice. She'll be approached when her powers begin to flare, but until then, she has been given to a couple who work in the Library of Congress."

"Thank you, Cecilia."

"I promised you that we wouldn't let this project become a scientific prison. I want them to contribute under their own free will. I only hope that her powers are able to be tempered."

"I agree," Eleanor stated. "It is such a shame what happened to that young boy."

They both took a moment of silence to commemorate the boy who died after he decided to use his gifts for something of a more sinister nature.

Eleanor pulled her gloves off, folding them and resting the article of clothing on the coffee table in front of them. She picked up the first stack of papers and looked at the sticky note that read

"Classified."

"I find it amusing that your classified folders are merely labeled with sticky notes. You would think with the number of these that cross your desk, there would be a business of making official labels."

Cecilia laughed. "I'm sure there are some of them around here."

Eleanor let her hand rest on the folder. She felt the cool paper against the tips of her fingers. A jolt that came with her gifts surged through her body. She never needed to see the contents of the folder; she would never have understood the contents. Her eyes were open on the room, but phantom images emerged across the office. She felt herself jump from one moment to the next. She could see the timeline connecting each of the moments, splintering into "what ifs" and "what could bes." Small lines of light tied each moment together. She began to choose and pick which ones she would follow. On several occasions she worked backward and then forward again.

The images washed away and a slight breeze touched her skin ever so lightly. In the matter of seconds in which she looked at the folder, she had witnessed thousands of possibilities.

"Do not sign it," she said flatly. "It will result in defunding thousands of hospitals around the country in the next decade. Tell them that you will only sign if they agree to massive health care reform."

"That will be quite the upset," said the president.

"Your popularity will drop, but you'll be potentially saving millions of people."

"Potentially?"

Eleanor nodded. "Too many decisions influence the future to predict the outcome. But this gives the best chance for that to never happen."

"Done," said the president, taking the folder and setting aside.

"Do you ever question what it is we do here?"

Cecilia shook her head without hesitation. "You are one of my dearest friends, a confidante and a genuinely good soul. I also find that nearly all your decisions are supported by data, a think tank of advisers, and my gut."

Eleanor took the younger woman's hand in hers. "Thank you," she said.

Before the president could respond to the contact, Eleanor's hair began to stand on end. She waited for the images to fill her vision, but she couldn't use her gift when she focused on her longtime friend.

"No future," she whispered.

Eleanor focused on the hand tightly gripped in hers. Instead of walking forward, she felt as if she was falling, moving backward. Where she couldn't foresee the future with Cecilia, she could recall the past.

It began with her movements this morning, and as Eleanor pushed harder, she could see events that had happened weeks ago. Finally she saw the woman standing at the door to this very office and what she saw shocked her.

Nothing.

Eleanor let go of the woman's hands. She had never felt such a dark and cold sensation envelop her body. She could feel it sinking into her bones.

"Who are you?"

Cecilia stood up, gasping at the sensation of having her entire life played out. "You're only a precog," she gasped.

Eleanor pushed away from her on the couch. While she had felt fine when she walked into the room, fear started to wash over her body. She grabbed her purse and continued to scoot back from the woman.

"You're not Cecilia," Eleanor said calmly.

The President swung her hand, her knuckles hitting Eleanor with enough force that it knocked spit from her mouth.

"How long have you been Psychometric? How long have you been able to see my past?"

"Long enough," Eleanor said, trying to keep her composure and not let the fear take control of her body.

"You will be…"

"No."

Cecilia froze in mid-sentence. Eleanor could sense the woman's muscles struggling against her will, but she stayed paralyzed.

Eleanor could sense the wildness in the woman in front of her. The fake president was right, these gifts were new to her. She had been able to see the future her entire life, but only in the last year had she been able to see the past and touch another person's mind. A year wasn't enough time for her to master these gifts.

"…kill you."

Eleanor grit her teeth as the woman resisted her compulsions. She could feel the headache beginning just behind her eyes. It would only be moments before the nosebleed followed, and if she was unlucky, she would pass out from the strain. Her frail body betrayed the immensity of her mind.

She reached into her purse and held up the gun, flipping off the safety. "You will not continue."

"We did everything…"

"To avoid this?" Eleanor could feel her mind losing its grip on the woman in front of her. "For humanity," she whispered.

Her finger squeezed the trigger and a loud bang sounded throughout the room.

The breeze rushed along her body and the images began to overwhelm her. The event in front of her was creating a new path into the future and her gift was attempting to show her the repercussions of what she had done. While she had spent months examining each possibility, hours spent in a trance trying to unravel destiny, she had known any attempt to foil the president would result in her demise. She realized that her actions were not the catalyst that her gifts had shown her. The dark future still obscured her visions. Her actions today would not lift the turmoil on the horizon.

Bang.

The bullet penetrated her chest, pushing through her lung and sending her small frame to the floor. The shadows of the future washed away and she was aware she was in the present, grasping the plush carpet, staring up at the ceiling of the Oval Office. The woman she had shot stood above her. The bullet hole in her white blouse was apparent, but where she should have been bleeding, there was nothing.

"I've won," said the president.

Eleanor could feel her vision beginning to slip. "Only the handmaiden of destiny," she whispered.

The president's brow rose at the ominous statement. "You can't do anything now," she said, leaning over her, pretending to cradle her dying friend.

"But I already have," whispered Eleanor.

***

"While there was an attempt on the president's life this afternoon, authorities are certain it was not the act of terrorists. The threat, an elderly Eleanor Valentine, had been invited to the White House as a guest to share afternoon tea with President Cecilia Joyce. Investigations are still underway as to how she acquired a weapon. Sources say the Secret Service agents reacted quickly and may have saved the president's life. We will provide more details as we hear from inside correspondents."

Chapter Two

May 16th, 2032 1:30PM

"What do you think?" he asked.

The short woman with neon pink hair placed the canvas against a white wall and took a few steps back. She examined it, walking back and forth, tilting her head. She stood so it was mere inches from her face. She opened her mouth to talk but hesitated, instead opting to make a clicking noise with her tongue ring.

He grunted at her delays. "Gretchen, you're killing me."

"It's like..." She turned to him. "It's totally awesome."

"Really?"

She hugged him, the spikes of her leather choker threatening to stab him in the chest. "That makes twenty, right? We finally have enough that you can have a show."

He hugged her back, lifting her off the ground and swinging her around. "It only took two years to finish them."

She felt her feet touch the ground again. She turned back to the painting, clutching his hand. "You told me you'd explain who she was once you finished. So spill it, who is the girl in the painting?"

Gretchen examined the young woman in the painting. "She can't be older than twenty, yet there's a maturity reflected in her eyes."

That was one of the very few typical traits about the subject. Covering nearly two thirds of her face, bones protruded from the skin. Where her forehead should have been, a large callused surface rose above the epidermis, the young woman deformed. The growths were more extreme in some places, ranging from an alteration to the look of her collarbone to the more pronounced spike growing from her shoulder. Conthan knew Gretchen understood his aesthetic and only she would comprehend his fascination with the woman's beauty. His compassion showed in the way he took care with each brush stroke. He suspected she wanted to inquire about his bond with his subject, but so far she had held her tongue.

"She's beautiful, Conthan," Gretchen said quietly.

"I know," he said.

She wrapped one arm around Conthan's black leather jacket, nestling herself against the side of his body. "How do you know her, Conthan?"

He squeezed her. "We used to go to school together." He took a step forward, staring at the bone-covered girl. "I met her my freshman year of high school after my foster folks split up. She was kind of my saving grace. She listened to me complain and complain about the divorce. All the while she would steal my notebooks and doodle all over them."

He let out a faint laugh at the memory. He reached out, almost touching the painting, remembering his best friend. "She was so unbelievably beautiful. She was the kind of girl you couldn't help but notice, especially when she smiled. Then one day she got called out of Social Studies class to the office. I remember it like it was yesterday. We were discussing the long-term implications of Nostradamus' predictions. Mr. Whittaker was wearing that ugly tweed jacket and Zack Quiggley was snoring two seats behind me. I found out later she had been reported to the Genesis Division."

"She didn't have the…" Gretchen paused, then tapped her forehead, gesturing to the girl's cheeks. "Growths?"

"Not yet," he said. "She had been reported as an anomaly because the school nurse had noticed she hadn't been sick since she was a small child. She met with the principal and they took her blood. I recall thinking she had been missing from class for so long. I had even started a doodle of her as a robot attacking the school."

"She came back positive?" Gretchen asked.

He nodded. "She was considered a Class III mutation. Benign, no active threat. That was her last day at school. She was required to go to a live-in research facility."

Conthan stared off into space, remembering the

super slick building she lived in. "It was kind of cool when I went to visit with her mom. She had her own bedroom and she had to go to school there with the other kids. Her room was covered in drawings of the other kids with her in classes. Sarah talked about them. She had friends at the facility. She told me about their abilities, and it almost sounded as if she was happy to be among her own people. I thought she would be in some evil laboratory, but for the most part, it was a nifty place."

"But…" Gretchen interjected.

"But it was still a research facility. About six months into being there, they had confirmed she was a Child of Nostradamus. Her body began to undergo mutagenesis. During the tests they found that she had an abnormal amount of calcium in her body and it began to show. She had a single pimple on her cheek as the bone pushed through her skin. When I saw her next, several spots of her face were covered in bone."

"Oh God," Gretchen gasped.

"She said it didn't hurt, but it wasn't comfortable either. The scientists said it would continue and could potentially prove fatal if her body couldn't find a way to expel the excess calcium. She slowly became a prisoner in her own body. But…" He paused for a moment. "She never stopped smiling."

"She's beautiful," said Gretchen, admiring the girl's sly grin.

Conthan smiled. "Yes, she is. One day I asked her if I could touch one. She wasn't ashamed and she laughed as I poked her cheek. If she was ever sad about being kept under house arrest in the facility, she never let it show. My junior year of high school I went to visit on my own. We were sitting in the common room watching television when she leaned over and kissed me. It hurt so much as the bone dug into my face. It was the first kiss for both of us."

"It was the last," Gretchen said, sensing the change in his tone.

"Her dorm turned into a Class II research facility. They started housing some pretty mean individuals there. Because she wasn't a threat, they moved her to a new research center on the edge of the Danger Zone."

"Seriously?"

"Yeah, I had hoped she would come back after a while. But the local facility closed. Now they were at the Danger Zone, supposedly it was big enough to house them all. The first place had treated her like a human, and there was talk about her being able to be integrated back into the mainstream. But once it became a Class II facility, it was like she became a prisoner, made guilty by fate."

"You've never seen it?"

"Once," he said, "I snuck to the facility. I had to make arrangements to see her almost a month in advance. Unlike the first place, this one looked like a prison. There were guards everywhere and the large mechs patrolled the building. When I got in, they gave me a radiation badge and let me see her."

He tried to hide the sadness in his voice. The image of his friend looking worn and defeated crept into his thoughts. "We had to sit on the opposite sides of glass, just like a prison. We talked quickly and I could see that she wasn't smiling. She didn't say anything bad, but it was obvious the facility had begun to change her."

"How can they survive the radiation from Ground Zero?"

"The Children of Nostradamus are more resilient than us. They don't get sick and apparently are immune to the radiation. The prison was so heavily guarded I can't imagine what kind of powered people were housed there."

"Did you see her again?"

He shook his head. "I tried over and over again, but I couldn't get approval to visit. I tried writing her letters, but they all came back unopened. I tried calling, but eventually I was told that her mutation had made her more dangerous and that she was being housed with the Class IIs."

"What happened?"

He shrugged. "I don't know. Nobody talks up there."

She squeezed his arm tightly. "Well, I'm sure she would appreciate what you're doing here."

"You don't think people will see it as a circus sideshow?"

She ran her hand over the shaved side of her head and pulled her shirt down, revealing her collarbone covered in tattoos. She smirked. "I'm pretty sure my clientele will approve."

He smiled at her. "When do you want to do the gallery opening?"

"Well," she dragged out, "I didn't want to make you nervous, but I knew you were bringing this by today."

"Gretchen," he said firmly.

"It's tomorrow."

Conthan's eyes widened in disbelief. "Are you serious? How are you going to get people here?"

She reached to the front counter and grabbed a flier. "I've been promoting it for the past couple of weeks."

"How did you know I'd finish?"

"Have a little faith," she said, batting her eyelashes. "I've been as excited for this as you have."

She gestured to the back of the gallery. The lobby was a small area, and through an archway there was a massive back room. The walls were painted a bright white and lights shone down from the ceiling, illuminating dozens of art pieces hanging on the walls. As he walked closer he could see his portraits, framed and mounted.

"I took a few liberties with hanging your work," she said. "I didn't think you would mind."

He walked up to the first oil painting and admired the dark hardwood frame. A small plaque next to it read:

'We find beauty in the heart and courage in the soul. To display these virtues is to overshadow the judgments of the bitter and callous.'
—Cecilia Joyce

He examined the painting of Sarah, her face turned away from the observer, playing a coy game of hide and seek. He couldn't help but smile at the mannerism of his best friend. He continued to the next and saw a pencil portrait of her sitting on a bench. He had always admired her while they waited for the bus, and looking at the bones protruding from her body, he couldn't help but see the beautiful girl hidden behind her own skeleton.

"We are featuring another artist as well. He's a former member of the Corps. His approach to expression is a bit more brutal than your oils, but it creates an atmosphere that I believe will juxtapose yours quite nicely. I believe we will also have a speaker to give a speech during the evening."

"All this for my work?"

She nodded. "I had some faith in you, mister. I told you that we'd make this happen."

He had turned to explore the work of the other artist when Gretchen pushed him toward the door. "It can wait," she said. "I'll see you tomorrow night. Look sharp. It's your debut, Mr. Cowan."

"You're sure of this?"

She gave him a final nudge out the door. "When you come back, you're going to have your mind blown."

He stood outside her gallery, a warm breeze hitting his face. He heard Gretchen slam the lock into place. He began to feel nervous. For the first time, his work was going to be seen by the public. The prospect thrilled him, but there was something melancholy associated with the event. His subject, his best friend, the girl he had admired for years, was locked in a cell somewhere, unable to see the beauty she inspired.

***

24

"This isn't a drill," she barked.

All six men reached down to their feet, grabbing their weapons. They checked their magazines and punched them back into the weapon. One of the men toward the back fumbled with his magazine. On the second attempt he managed to secure the magazine.

"We've got a rookie on board," she yelled.

"Fresh meat," they recited back to her in unison.

Each of the men held his weapon tightly to his chest. Tethers ran up from their backs and secured to the ceiling of the plane. The men closest to her shut their eyes tight, and as they opened them again, a dim red light shone in the back of their retinas. Each man turned on his optic implants. She didn't need to look closely to know they were linking into the central network and activating their other enhancements.

She tried to hide her distaste. She would tell her superior her squad was a well-oiled machine, moments like this made the saying all too true. She walked down the line, tugging on their tethers as she passed the soldiers. She reached the rookie and pulled at his line.

The man's face looked deathly ill as he realized his commanding officer was staring him in the eye. He brought his weapon against his chest like the soldier in front of him. He took a deep breath, trying to steady himself. He had run hundreds of live simulations before joining the Paladins a month ago. It was the first mission their commander had greenlighted.

"What do we do with fresh meat?"

"Feed it to the wolves, sir," they replied.

His eyes went wide as she punched the release above his head. A screeching filled the air as the lights began to flash red. The floor under the man-boy vanished and he was falling. All the soldiers reached up and hit their releases. The floor broke open underneath each of them, dropping them from the plane. The soldiers whooped and hollered as they fell from the aircraft.

"Paladins are in play," she said.

"We have visual confirmation," a voice replied in her earpiece.

"Mack, hover us," she said.

The commander turned around, walked through a small door, and slammed it behind her. As the room got dark, blinking lights fired to life. Holographic displays began to appear around her, six monitors suspended in space. Each of the monitors projected images from the optic cameras, showing the ground fast approaching the soldiers.

The largest screen showed the view of the streets several thousand feet below the jet, the scene littered with small parachutes.

"Murdock, Vazquez, take the roof. Sims, Belletone, take the alley on the west side. Our target is on the other side of the block. You know what this means, Vlad."

"Working the meat market," a voice chimed in over the comms.

"Keep the fresh meat alive."

She pressed spots on each of their screens. As she pinged their monitors, their eye pieces were lighting up, directing them where to land. The large hologram in front of her cast a faint red glow. She reached up, grabbed the hologram, and pulled her hands apart, zooming in on the street.

There was a car turned over in the middle of the street, the back of it engulfed in flames. She spun the image again and noted the several dozen people hiding behind vehicles and in doorways. In her earpiece, she heard each of her team touch down with a grunt.

"We have civilians at all points."

"Do we have a visual on the target?" asked Sims.

"Negative, the computers are running facial recognition and tracking the target's path," said a foreign voice in her ear.

She didn't like the people at Operations. She didn't like how they would jump in on her mission and take control. Her team trusted her with their lives. Several states away men in ties who had never seen combat were bogarting her mission whenever they felt it was appropriate. They wanted her expertise, until they didn't.

"Jasmine, we should have that within the next twenty seconds."

She leaned into the hologram and zoomed again until she could read the faces of several women huddled together, clutching each other in between two parked cars. They couldn't be much older than forty, their plastic bags in shambles as fresh fruit and packaged meat lay in the street. Each of the women was cowering, but all their eyes were pointed in the same direction, on a narrow doorway leading into a building.

"Murdock, Vazquez, follow the line of sight of

the civvies. I think we have our target."

Both Murdock and Vazquez zoomed in with her implants. Reaching 20x zoom, they were looking at the faces of the civilians. Murdock's ocular implant directed his eye to a small alcove nearby.

"I have visual on the man," said Murdock.

"Wait until computer confirms," replied a tech.

The man was wearing jeans and a t-shirt. He began to run, charging the vehicles where the women were hidden.

"Take your shot."

"No," said the tech.

"Murdock, take it."

A familiar *fwap fwap* sounded over the comms. The man staggered backward. Dark red circles began to show just above his heart. Jasmine held her breath to see what would happen next. The man reached up to touch his chest, covering his hand in blood. He began to scream.

Another man stepped out from the doorway, holding his hands up in the air like he was surrendering. Jasmine turned from the bleeding man to the other. "We have another player on the field."

"We have visual," said Belletone.

The new man turned to where Sims and Belletone were hidden, just around the corner of a building. He walked slowly, his eyes staying fixed on one of the cameras mounted to a traffic light. "He knows we're watching."

"Uploading his file."

Jasmine watched as information about the surrendering man flashed across her screen. Her team was processing the data being sent directly to their cortex implants, she didn't have the luxury. She didn't look at the file for more than a moment before she saw his previous address.

"Bellevue resident. Extremely dangerous."

She took a step back from the screen as she watched his arm begin to burn.

"Jasmine," Vlad yelled, "we have a mentalist!"

Before she could bark out a command, the first perp jumped behind a car parked on the side of the road. He lifted his foot, placed it on the trunk of the car, and kicked. As if it weighed nothing, the car impaled itself on the vehicle in front of it. The screams of the middle-aged women ended as they were crushed to death between the vehicles.

"Vlad and Rook, light him up. Vazquez, direct him away from the civvies."

The strong man grabbed another vehicle and ripped off the trunk. He held it up, blocking the shot from Vazquez. She could see the cameras for the other two men closing in on his position. She turned her attention to the second assailant, whose arms were completely engulfed in flame.

"Non-lethal only," said one of the technicians.

"Fuck you," she replied.

"Taking the shot." Murdock fired his gun at the man ablaze, sending a single bullet through the air. The pyrokinetic held up his hand, which was bright white, stopping the bullet's trajectory and sending it to the ground.

"Incoming," yelled Belletone.

Metal from the trunk flew over the pyro's head, sending the two soldiers to the ground in the alley. They scuttled backward until they were out of the line of sight of both targets. Belletone leaned around the corner, holding his gun up, ready to take a shot. As he pulled the trigger, a burst of fire engulfed his weapon, causing the magazine to explode.

"Belletone's down," yelled Sims as he watched his teammate fall.

Jasmine didn't like how the fight was going. Vlad walked by a vehicle, his gun raised. He pulled the trigger and several more bullets pierced the strong man. He was stronger than any of them, even with their enhancements. The bullets tore through his skin, but they appeared to do little other than make him angry.

"We have a drone with a synthetic at your destination in two minutes."

"I'm going," she said.

Flames spewed onto an overturned vehicle came to life and washed over Vlad. He backed away from the fire, letting loose a volley of bullets at the muscular target. The rookie took a small cylinder from his vest and shoved it into the barrel of his weapon. He fired it at the pyro. The man lifted his hands, raising the flames up like a wall, the intensity burning brighter as the ammunition struck it.

The world flashed white for a moment.

Jasmine threw open the door in the small room and crossed her hands over her chest as she jumped through one of the openings in the craft. Wind whipped past her body as she plummeted toward the ground below. With a well-rehearsed motion she turned around in the air until she was speeding headfirst toward the fight. There was yelling through her comm but the wind was making it difficult to make out the words. She heard the cry of "man down," and knew it was time to intervene.

She brought her hands to her waist and let the metal cuffs around her wrists graze her belt. A magnet clicked onto the bracelets. As the clank of metal on metal reverberated through her hands, she threw her arms out wide. Fabric pulled out from her belt, creating cloth wings between wrists and her waist.

She spun through the air as she approached the ground. She was falling a block from the fight. As the ground threatened to crash into her soft, vulnerable flesh, she arched her back. Flying parallel to the street only a few feet from the pavement, she sped toward the strong man threatening her team.

The strong man grabbed the car covered in the dead women's blood and took several steps into the road in the path of the flying woman. He pulled the car back and braced himself like a batter at home plate. "Kirk, we're almost done here," the man yelled to his fiery companion.

"We were here for money, not killing humans."

"Consider it a perk."

Jasmine's eyes watered from the wind but she could still see the punk preparing to clobber her with a SUV. She didn't have any weapons on her. She had no way to land this close to the ground without crashing against a wall. Her men had been prepared to take on a brute with super strength, but a pyrokinetic—a fire maker—that was beyond their pay grade. She had been trained to take on superpowered beings, but this was a first for her.

She concentrated on the platinum wrapped snugly around her wrists. As she thought of the cold metal, she could feel her skin pulling at the cuffs. To date, she couldn't accurately describe how her epidermis would reach out, study the metal, and begin to mimic it. She screamed as her powers learned the material. The pain washed through her body and it felt like the worst cramp imaginable as her skin became as dense as platinum.

The bad guys weren't the only ones with powers.

With the density came a shift in her weight. She sped toward the ground. She braced herself, slamming into the pavement and breaking through the surface of the street, sending rock in all directions as she continued skidding toward the man.

The man raised an eyebrow as the woman sent pavement flying into the air. His deep, hearty laugh was cut short when she sprang from the pavement and sailed through the air. Her fists were in front of her, speeding straight toward his face. He swung the door, knocking her into the wall.

"What the hell?"

Jasmine broke through the brick and landed in the kitchen of a small cafe. The pain started to leave her body as her muscles began to adapt, growing stronger to compensate for the new epidermis. She stood up, shaking her head. She made eye contact with the man, his expression wide in disbelief that she was still moving.

She began charging, jumping out of the kitchen

onto the street. She picked up speed, and as he swung the door again, she threw up her arm, deflecting the blow. Her fist connected with his face. He spun and fell to the ground. She knew he wasn't used to being the weaker fighter.

"You're the one who hunts her own kind."

She held her fist in the air. The statement stung more than any punch he could throw. Before she could react, heat washed over her skin. The pyro was walking closer, his hands held out, fire flooding the street. She grabbed the door and threw it at him.

The pyro rolled out of the way. She didn't flinch as the strong man slammed his fist into her chest. She took a step backward from the blow, her stance barely wavering. The man howled as he cradled his hand. It was the look of a man who had crushed every bone.

"We want them alive," said a voice in her ear.

She grit her teeth at the command. She was sent to stop these Children from wreaking havoc in the city. She was sent to terminate them if they were a threat. Now she was an errand girl, collecting samples for some ass in a lab coat. She grabbed the man's fist and squeezed, sending him to his knees as he screamed.

"Stop."

The pyro was standing close enough to her teammates that he could send the soldiers into a fiery grave without much more than a thought focused on his hands. She stepped behind the beefy, muscular man and wrapped her hands around his head. The pyro paused as she threatened to kill his associate. He looked down to his hands and the flame began to flare.

It was a tactical advantage. Killing the Child was a means to an end. As she spun the man's head, snapping his neck, all she could think about was the furious look on the researcher's face at home base. It was her team, her terms, and she wasn't going to be a lackey to some ruthless humans looking to poke and prod her kind.

She hurled the corpse at the pyro and charged the man as he jumped back from the body. Before she could connect her metallic fists with the man, a searing pain shot through her. Every muscle contracted at the same time, sending her to the ground. She screamed out in pain as her body began to convulse from the electrical current running through her body.

"She's down," said the man in her comm. "Synthetics are being deployed. Murdock, switch to suppression fire. We take the man alive."

"He's a pyro," said one of the soldiers.

"Alive," the man said in a tone that didn't leave room for negotiating.

Jasmine could make out the pyro from the corner of her eye. He was confused at what was happening. The instigator was dead and now he didn't know what to do. She watched his body jerk as a bullet connected with his collarbone. The fire vanished as the man cried out and toppled to the ground. He lay only a few feet from her on the ground. She could see his eyes shaking in fear. The last thing she remembered was the tears rolling down his cheek. The world went black as she gave in to the pain.

Chapter Three

March 20th, 1992 8:37AM

March 20th, 1992
Mr. Davis,

I knew curiosity would get the best of you. It was only a matter of time before you opened this letter. I know you are asking yourself many questions about the events that have unfolded since our final encounter. First I must thank you. You have unknowingly been part of a plan that will someday rectify a series of events sending the world into dark times. I ask that you remember me as you do your grandmother, and rest assured that the events transpiring are part of grander plan bestowed upon me by a higher power.

You are asking yourself, did I offer to

tell you about your mother as a kind gesture or as part of a plot to win your confidence? I am glad that your mother is doing well; enjoy the expression on her face as you tell her about the conception of your first child. He will be healthy and born into a loving family. But to alleviate your doubts, I cannot say whether my offer was or was not part of a master plan. I continue to question my gifts and if they reveal the possibilities of a people with free will or possibilities fate navigates for us.

As to what was contained in those letters you hesitantly mailed…They are the words of a woman uncertain about the future for the first time in many years. While you question what the future holds for you, I have always seen my future as a vivid movie played out in my mind. These ghosts of what might be have appeared since I was a child. However, I see possibilities disappearing into a void. There is a darkness on the horizon and I see it engulfing the world. What it brings, I cannot say. For once I understand how each of you leads your life. I am scared of the unknown. Where my powers are faltering, I will rely on my gifts of intuition and push forward.

Do not get caught up in the details. I have had a lifetime to understand time in a nonlinear fashion. And yes, I was aware you would be the last kind exchange I had with another individual. I am grateful it was with you, as I felt a kindred spirit in that single touch and know you have the heart of good man. I knew when and how I would die that day. I went knowing my actions were those of a woman trying to do right. I would not change my fate.

Be well, Mr. Davis. Once you realize your hopes and dreams, I assure you the world will react kindly.

With Regards,
Eleanor P. Valentine

Chapter Four

May 16th, 2032 4:30PM

She tried not to move; moving made the cuffs cinched around her wrists hurt. The straps crossing her breasts in an "X" kept her from shifting in her seat, but her arms were sore from being restrained for hours. The truck leaned to one side as it made another right turn. She knew where they were going, but she had no idea how close they were to their destination.

The Danger Zone.

As they drove, her skin crawled. She knew it was her imagination, but her skin crawled as if she could feel the radiation penetrating her body. The bomb had been detonated in Portland, Maine, but the fallout spread throughout New England. She could only think back to seeing pictures of Hiroshima as a teenager. The devastation must be immense. As the truck took another turn, she tried to push away the thoughts of her future.

She had been given a choice when they caught

her: avoid trial and be banished or potentially receive a death sentence. The blood covering her naked flesh and the gun clutched in her hand had been all the evidence they needed. Before the police arrived, she shifted her ripped blouse in an attempt to cover her bare breasts. As they stormed through the door she began to cry. She made no arguments when they asked her if she was guilty. She had killed the man and wouldn't hesitate to kill him again. If given the option, she would aim slightly to the right, missing his lung; that way she could watch him die slowly.

Her lawyer thought they would be able to plead it down to justified homicide, but she didn't dare risk spending time behind bars. After living with the man for two years, she decided she would rather take her chances beyond the Danger Zone. Her final years would be her own.

"There's enough of us," said the man next to her. "We can take them."

The man was large. He either spent more time at the gym than not, or his body had been augmented with technology. She couldn't tell just by looking at him. She could, however, tell that he had been in more than his share of fights. Scars littered his body, down the side of his arm, across his face, and she assumed they continued behind his clothes.

"We'll fight our way out."

He reminded her of her dead ex. He was fast to resort to fists. What he lacked in intellect, he made up in muscle. The brute next to her, however, didn't have any of his charm, which in her eyes made him far less dangerous. *Far more sinister is the bully who can make you smile*, she thought.

"They have guns."

The conversation continued. She focused on the small slit on the far side of the transport that let her see beyond the confines of the dingy vehicle. The sun shone through, giving the impression there was hope beyond these metal walls. She watched as one of the inmates whispered to his neighbor, pointing with his chin toward another bound man. She turned away from them as they schemed, ignoring their use of the word "freedom."

Another hour passed as she admired the blue of the sky. There were few clouds hanging in the air as they continued to drive. The sound of the vehicle's brakes snapped her back to reality, sending the occupants lurching to the side. They whispered furiously, trying to formulate a plan of escape. She tried not to imagine their bodies littering the ground as they attempted to do what had never been successful before.

The back of the vehicle opened and armed guards waited. The belts across her chest clicked and released, leaving her free to stand. She didn't dare move for fear of being shot. She winced as one inmate stood and took several steps toward the back of the vehicle. He waited patiently as a ramp was pulled from the vehicle, leading out into the brightness of day.

"Single file," yelled one of the soldiers.

"Any aggressive behavior will be met with deadly force," announced another.

She waited until the queue built up. She stood and began the shuffle forward. The bright light blinded her, leaving her squinting, trying to make out the world beyond the transport. When they had all stood, the line began to move forward. She watched as each prisoner held up their arms, letting the officer release the cuffs and then continuing forward.

As her eyes adjusted she saw the truck backed up to a gate. Metal wire lined the perimeter of the Danger Zone. Worn metal signs were posted everywhere, the radioactive symbol hanging as a warning to those daring to walk into the wasteland. As the prisoners passed through the gate, they were left on foot to make their way into the chaos left behind by a nuclear bomb.

"Keep moving," an officer yelled at her.

She stepped forward to the ramp. One of the officers waved his hand over the metal cuffs biting into her wrists and they opened. He threw them into a bin with the others. The fence was massive, twenty feet tall and stretching as far as the eye could see. Every so often there were towers. In the closest one, she could make out the weapons, massive guns pointed directly at her.

The guard gave her a shove forward. She stumbled down the ramp and fell to her knees as she reached the ground. She had expected decaying buildings and nothing but dead earth. She was surprised at the amount of grass beyond the fence, and what few buildings she could make out seemed relatively untouched.

She fell to her knees, the pebbles on the pavement poking through her pants into her skin. She tried to hold back a scream as she saw the ditches just beyond the fence. Her mind tried to process the scene, and then the smell assaulted her nostrils and the stench of rot and decay filled her lungs. She screamed as she realized the ditches were filled with hundreds of bodies in varying stages of decay. Bones poked through the taut flesh of dead bodies. Skeletons of those long since dead were scattered about the ground. She couldn't fathom the number of bodies—dozens, could be hundreds.

"Move along," a guard said, pulling her upward to her feet.

As she entered a gateway through the fence, another guard took her arm. She couldn't focus on him as she stared at the mass graves just beyond the behemoth metal structure. She could only assume they were going to kill her as she took her first steps into the wastelands. What she thought had been her salvation was a death sentence hidden from the general populace.

Electrified metal cables passed through between pillars, buzzing loud enough for her to hear. Tall monoliths reached up to the sky, wires strung through them, creating a barrier between her future home and the life she was leaving behind. Cameras swiveled on the cement structures, documenting the entire process. She couldn't imagine who was watching this event, watching the mass grave be filled with bodies.

They had told her during orientation she would be allowed to pass through the gate, and if she continued to the closest building, there would be minimal supplies. She would be left to her own devices to survive amongst the dredges of society. Her only companions would be killers, rapists, and those who spoke out against the government. They would be left to die.

A guard grabbed her by the wrist and set her arm on a small pedestal. The top of the device lit up and she hissed as her arm started to burn. As the soldier released her, she could see the number '279782' clearly engraved into her flesh. She looked down at the number on her arm. She was no longer a person. She was an Outlander.

She froze as the yelling began. She was no more than ten feet through the gate when the large, brutish man started barking commands at the other inmates. He incited them with screams of "We can take them!" and "Fight back!" She had barely turned. The first boom of gunfire filled the air. She saw the large man's head explode. The other dozen inmates rushing back through the gate knocked her to the side. Several ran in different directions, scurrying away from the fighting breaking out.

Gunfire filled the air. *Pop. Pop. Pop.*

It was precision firing. Each person charging the gate fell to the ground. She felt the spray of blood from a man near her as his torso exploded. As fast as the riot began, silence filled the air. The scurrying survivors ran away from the fence, further into the Danger Zone. Her feet were like cement blocks, anchored in place as the last body fell to the ground.

Nobody spoke. No soldiers dropped their weapons. Each remained ready if she attempted to charge the gate. She spent seconds staring blankly at the guards, but she felt as if hours were passing as she attempted to process the scene in front of her. So many murdered bodies, and she was left without injuries.

"Move along," came a soldier's voice.

She lifted her arm and examined the number on her forearm. She had no desire to return to the world she was leaving behind. Left to fend for herself among killers, she felt her chances of survival were better on this side of the fence. She turned around and took her first step toward the nearest building. She imagined the soldiers pushing the new dead into the ditch, a reminder of what would happen if they ever approached the fence again.

She replayed the events leading her to this place, watching her knife sink into her abusive husband. She thought of the blue sky through the slits. Of the smell of dead bodies. As the wind caressed her skin, the situation didn't feel so dire. She was alive. She was a survivor; this was another test to prove she could overcome any obstacle.

She paused to take a deep breath. Further in the distance, a group of survivors ran toward the building. They would reach any supplies before her. She would be left to do without. The knowledge that she was without shelter, food, or even water didn't diminish her outlook. She turned her gaze to the beautiful sky filled with red hues. The sun was beginning to set, turning the deep reds into purples.

She squinted for a moment, catching motion in the air. At first she thought it was a giant bird of some sort. Her jaw slowly dropped as she began to make out the person attached to the wings. She had heard rumors from the inmates before they began their transport, but assumed they were a hopeless person's method of coping. Seeing it flying through the air, she believed a god watched over her.

"It's true," she mumbled to herself. "There is an angel in the Outlands."

***

Conthan walked down the aisle of the liquor store, checking the inventory. He paused to see what brands of tequila were discounted. The small store's narrow rows were so close together he had difficulty seeing cheap booze at the bottom. He gave a slight laugh and decided if ever there was a time to splurge, it was now. He reached toward a bottle at eye height and put it in his basket.

He continued browsing through the alcohol and stopped occasionally to see the clerk staring at him. Conthan snickered. He might have a mouth that wouldn't stop running, but he was probably the least threatening person in the world. He was probably the only person who came into the store today that wouldn't rob it. He grabbed a couple six-packs of beer and added them to his stash, avoiding eye contact with the clerk.

Conthan reached the cashier and placed the bottles down on an empty space on the counter. As he set the bottles on the glass counter, the register scanned them, spitting out the price. He winced as he saw the price of the tequila. He didn't dare make a joke about getting robbed. The gruff-looking man behind the counter with three days' worth of stubble looked annoyed that he wasn't at home watching his stories.

Conthan placed his thumb down on the counter. A small smiling face appeared on the glass, confirming receipt of his payment. The moment purchase confirmation popped up, the gruff man's demeanor became more pleasant. He took the tequila, and placed it into a small plastic bag.

"Try it with some orange juice," he said. "It's like candy."

Conthan smiled and took the two bags from the man. He couldn't imagine working in a place like that, fearful of every person who walked into the store. The half a dozen cameras watching his every movement were more than enough to make him swear he would never have a retail job. Conthan placed the bags in the passenger seat of his car as he pondered the man's social life. Did he have friends? What were his hobbies?

"Kill me if I become that," he said out loud.

As he pulled out of the small parking lot, a ringing came from his car speakers. He looked to the passenger side of the windshield to see the word 'Sculptee' blinking on the screen. He pulled out into the afternoon traffic leading toward the studio.

"Answer."

The name disappeared on the windshield, replaced by an audio spectrum of the voice on the other side. "Conthan, where are you, man?"

"I'm heading to the studio. You need to meet me there," he said.

"Why the studio?"

"Dude." Conthan's smile stretched across his face. "The show is happening."

"You mean with Gretchen?"

"Yeah."

"Oh man," said the voice. "Okay, I'm calling everybody. We'll meet you over there."

"We're going to party," said Conthan, happy Sculptee understood how big a deal the show was going to be.

***

"Jesus fucking Christ, he did it," a man said, thrusting his glass into the air.

"Salut," they all said in unison.

"You asses act like it was never going to happen," Conthan said with a grin.

A girl ruffled his hair. "You draw enough pictures of pretty women and somebody's bound to notice."

"Trish, you've hurt his feelings." Sculptee said as Conthan pouted. "His work isn't about pretty women, it's about transcending the physical and embodying the beautiful held in each of our tattered and frayed souls."

The room paused.

"I call bullshit," said another.

Sculptee held his glass in the air. "In all seriousness, it couldn't have happened to a better man. You've been with us since the start. We wish you the best."

"Don't forget us in your fucking memoir," said another.

Conthan thrust his glass into the air, clanking with his fellow artists. They all slammed their booze. He sat down on a couch made from a repurposed bench seat of an old car and stared at the small fire in the middle of their gathering. The six of them had been his family since college. When they were close to graduating, they decided they couldn't stomach the idea of corporate jobs. Instead of working in small coffee shops and living the artist cliché, they pooled their money to buy a large warehouse in a rough side of town.

The three-story high corrugated metal walls were supported with massive metal girders leading to a metal roof. The decor was a mix of industrial and abandonment, something they had unanimously agreed was perfect. The group of artists had taken over a small corner of the football-sized structure. They had built makeshift walls out of plywood, offering a little bit of seclusion from each other.

Conthan had to admit that much of his success was because of the people in the room. They frequently gathered on their mismatched furniture and drank while discussing the finer parts of art and the less than savory aspects of society. During his first critique, Sculptee, a self-proclaimed master of plaster, told him point blank his female nudes were passé. Trish, an installation artist, and her boyfriend Rocks, who Conthan wasn't quite sure how to describe—something about taking apart cars and putting them back together in less traditional forms—had agreed. Yiyi, a street artist and fashion trending guru, had suggested he start looking for something edgier and less done to death. Ultimately it was Patches, a man obsessed with the descent of mankind and its ability to destroy the world around it, who suggested he revisit the drawings in his high school sketchbook.

"Who was the Child you were drawing? There was something dope about the way you captured the normalcy of her…" He thought for a moment, searching for the word to describe Sarah's growths. "You showed how awesome she is by avoiding the obvious controversy in your subject."

Gretchen was the last acquisition to their ragtag group of artists. Her father owned an extremely lucrative chain of hotels, and as a graduation gift, he bestowed an empty building to her. Instead of following in his footsteps, she decided to create a place artists could present their ideas to the world. As none of them had expected, she was very good at what she did.

Rock startled Conthan as he poured another shot. "If you're not wasted before the night, I didn't do my job, man."

Conthan held up the shot. "For art."

"Fuck art!" yelled Sculptee. "For the money!"

"Salut!" they all yelled, raising their glasses.

Yiyi plopped down on the couch next to Conthan. She blew the neon pink hair out of her eyes and took a swig straight from the bottle of vodka. "Glad one of us can pay the bills," she said, passing it to him.

"Fuck you," Rock howled at Yiyi. The man was chiseled, his muscles bordering on freakish. As a youth he had worked on cars with his dad, and somewhere along the way he found art. The muscles helped lift heavy things.

"Yiyi is the one with the clothing line at Macy's. I'm pretty sure I saw her flashing a platinum credit card earlier."

"That's not art," she replied, snatching the vodka back from Conthan. She took another gulp from the almost-empty bottle. "That's me selling my soul."

"I'd sell my soul for half," said Sculptee.

"If only you had one," came a voice from the steel door. Gretchen slammed it behind her and sauntered over to the group. "I need to interrupt this party to talk some business."

"Boo," Trish said. "If you kill my buzz, Gretch, I'm gonna slap the tattoo off your face."

Gretchen reached into her pocket, took out a small ball the size of a marble, and placed it in the air. She let go, leaving it hovering as she reached back into her pocket for her cell phone.

"Okay, first." She pressed a button. The ball shone, projecting an image of a man wearing a tuxedo. "We might have the most notorious art critic this side of the river attending the opening."

Conthan felt his stomach turn. "I'm going to be sick."

Yiyi scooted away from him. "Do not throw up on this dress."

"Yeah, kind of a big deal," Gretchen said, flipping through her phone. "But of course I can one up that."

The image changed to a video playing. A man was standing in front of several news cameras. "The audacity of these youngsters, creating a media spectacle around the Children of Nostradamus, treating them like false idols. These abominations are not things to be celebrated, they are to be condemned and removed from the chosen race."

"What is this?"

Gretchen held her finger up to Rock. "Just wait for it."

"We will be at this gallery tomorrow, showing the owner we will not tolerate the wickedness associated with the Children of Nostradamus. Our flock will demonstrate the error of worshipping false Gods."

Gretchen pressed the button. "Bitches, be impressed."

Conthan closed his eyes and took deep breaths. "I'm going to be sick."

Yiyi moved further away. "Gretchen, what are you going to do?"

"That's the beauty of it. I'm not doing a damned thing. Who do you think alerted our favorite Reverend?"

"Whoa," Trish said, leaning forward. She gestured toward the frozen image of the man on the screen. "He's going to harsh the vibe, Gretch. Man has a reputation with the Children, he can't be much a fan of the Fringe either."

Gretchen licked her lips as she pressed the next button on her phone. The video switched to a woman with hair straightened in a row of foot-long, jet black spikes. The woman had seven obvious piercings and the left side of her face was covered in tattoos. "The keepers of the caste system have waged war on a people whose differences are presented to us, both literally and figuratively, in the

Children of Nostradamus. Hate-mongering groups such as Humanity First have exploited and marginalized a segment of the population…"

"You didn't," said Trish.

"I'm with Trish." Rock reached out, putting his hand through the video and pausing the stream. "Pops always said you don't store the gasoline with the matches."

Conthan rocked back and forth on the couch. Yiyi patted him on the head, but he barely noticed as he focused on the fire in front of him. "I don't know about this," he said between quickened breaths.

Gretchen threw her arms in the air. "You act like I've never done this before." She held out her hand and the small sphere moved until it was firmly in her palm. She reached out and took the bottle from Yiyi and chugged until it was half empty. "What could possibly go wrong?"

Sculptee pointed at Gretchen. "You are so screwed now."

Conthan tried to keep his stomach from tying itself into tighter knots. His first show was already shaping up to be on the front page of the newspaper. He was nervous with the exposure, but now he would be at the epicenter of controversy. His friends would be there. Gretchen would be running the show. He took a deep breath. It could only go so bad. It was more likely he would run his mouth to a critic and screw himself in the art scene. He felt his stomach clench again.

***

Sarah knew the moment she opened her eyes this was a nightmare. She stood in the middle of her high school classroom. The colors were desaturated, leaving the room a variety of murky grays. The edges faded off into nothingness, an abyss of black.

It was the classroom she was called out of to be told she was a Child of Nostradamus. The desks were in the same rows, and books rested on top of them, apparently untouched for years. It was the room that haunted her dreams night in and night out. This was the room where her humanity was stolen from her.

"But so much more was given to you, Sarah."

It was him.

The dream didn't change, not until recently. Before she would try to escape the room, but the doors and windows were locked. Eventually she would be frozen by fear. Her pulse would race in terror and just as she thought she might wake, the door would open and two figures would escort her from the room. She would wake in a cold sweat, screaming at the top of her lungs.

Then *he* arrived.

His presence had taken away the fear of the nightmare. As she awoke from one dream into another, she could feel a moment of panic, but it passed. She knew she was asleep in a small cement room. She was lying on top of a sterile mattress, wearing a white prison uniform. The nightmare lost its power over her. However, as the dream became less frightening, the voice speaking to her became more direct.

His voice had started as a whisper, a sultry,

seductive voice she tried to ignore. She had feared her nightmare was uncovering new methods of terrifying her. The whisper grew louder, talking to her, befriending her in this horrific location.

"Who are you?" she asked.

"I am here to help you, Sarah."

She shook her head, trying to force herself to wake. She felt the pressure of hands resting on her shoulders, a presence pressing up against her backside. "I can help you, Sarah."

The word was faint, barely audible as she spoke it. "Yes."

The grip on her shoulders tightened as a black liquid crawled along her feet, enveloping her legs. She caught herself on the window frame as the darkness crept up her body. She pushed at it. She tried to shake it off, but it was clinging to her like a second skin, climbing her torso.

She stared out the window, surrendering to the icy grip. Outside there should have been a massive tree, and beyond that, the student parking lot. Instead of the familiar high school surroundings, an empty blackness dominated the view. Far off in the distance a small figure shone brightly, warding away the darkness. As she submitted to the voice, she watched the figure reveal itself, wings spread out wide. Her vision blurred until the angel vanished. Somewhere in the recesses of her mind, she felt at peace as the darkness consumed her completely.

Chapter Five

May 16th, 2032 9:02PM

She hugged the building as she scurried down the street. The sunlight had faded and the full moon was the only light along the side of the skyscrapers around her. Even with the diminishing light, she could make out the billowing smoke about a mile away. She had been walking since yesterday afternoon, and with little sleep, she found her eyes fighting to stay open.

She placed her hand on the glass of the building next to her. She examined the window and had to assume it was a business office of some sort. Inside would be cubicles. Offices had fridges, and if she was lucky, water coolers that hadn't run dry. Her belly grumbled at the thought of food. She hadn't eaten since the morning before they were loaded into the truck. She had decided to avoid the supply depot from orientation.

Reaching into the Snoopy backpack, she grabbed a small Tylenol bottle and opened the cap. She took two pills and chewed. Despite their bitter flavor, they would alleviate her headache and the act of chewing gave her stomach false hope. When the sun rose, she would have to make food a priority.

She approached the glass doors and noticed the massive white X's spray painted on them. She had found these throughout every city block she explored. She assumed it was a method of tracking buildings that were pillaged so as not to waste time later. Much to her dismay, it meant another place with no food and most likely no water.

"I wish I could find a library," she said aloud. She flinched as lightning flashed overhead. She counted like her grandmother had taught her. Two Mississippis later, thunder shook the ground. Her thoughts returned to the library. If she could find one, she bet it would have something that could help her. Her mother had told her everything she ever needed to know could be remedied with a trip to the library.

"I bet I could find a book about plants I could eat. Maybe a way to hunt."

She had found that scavenging was effective as long as she thought to look in awkward places. The backpack she discovered in the back of a minivan. Her hoodie she pulled out from under a bed in house just outside the city. The Tylenol and lighter were underneath one of the registers in the back of a small restaurant. She had hoped to find cans of food, but they were all gone. She began to notice these empty buildings were covered in giant white X's.

She was determined to survive.

The smoke was visible only a few city blocks away now. She hadn't seen another living person since last night. The smoke could be a natural fire, but she decided it was worth taking the chance to see if there were other people alive. The people on this side of the fence were criminals; she couldn't trust they would be like her, simply trying to survive. Her stomach growled. *They may have food*, she thought.

Lightning crashed again, quickly followed by a thunderous clap. She bolted across the street, staying low to the ground. As she reached the canopy of a drugstore covered in giant X's, she could hear a sound like pebbles smacking against the ground. The air changed as the sky opened up and the rain came down in in a deluge.

She stepped out into the wet and let it soak through her clothes. She pulled off the hoodie and let the rain saturate the cotton garment. She held it over her mouth and began to squeeze. She gulped. The rain tasted disgusting. It took her a moment to figure out that the bitterness could be caused by some sort of fallout. She enjoyed the reprieve while she could, but decided it would be best to wait until she could uncover what other residents did for drinking water.

Shoving the hoodie into her backpack, she pushed against the pharmacy door. A piece of wood covered the broken glass on the lower half of the enclosure. She began kicking, knocking the wood down, and then clearing the remaining glass. She crawled through the door into a dark room. She stood reaching out, guiding herself in the darkness behind the counter. She tripped and fell to one knee and froze, making sure nothing was broken.

She stayed on the floor, reaching around behind the counter to see if she could find any identifiable objects. She pulled out a plastic baggy from her backpack and fished around for the lighter. Flicking the flint several times, she had to blink at the brightness of the little flame. She hovered the light along the counter, looking for anything she could use. She had to hold back a cheer. She reached underneath, toward the back, and grabbed a bottle of Sprite and a bag of beef jerky.

"Thank you God," she whispered.

She listened for the crack on the seal as she opened the bottle. Lightning illuminated the entire store for a moment. She was shocked to see so many shelves completely emptied. Thunder followed, loud enough that it echoed in her chest. She took her first swig of Sprite. It was flat, and fairly disgusting, but as the liquid filled her stomach there was a satisfying sensation. She let out an, "Ahhhh," as she set the half-emptied bottle down.

Her attention turned to the package of jerky. She ripped the bag open and took her first bite. The hard, savory meat instantly brought saliva to her mouth. She rationed out the food, eating half of it now. She pressed the seal on the wrapper shut and stashed the rest in her backpack. She had no idea when she would find food again, so she didn't dare give into her instincts and eat it all. The Sprite she continued to sip on, savoring each drop of the liquid.

Lightning. Thunder.

She froze at the sound of an engine revving outside of the pharmacy. There was a light outside the glass doors and voices shouted back and forth. She cursed. She was in one of the most important resources on this side of the fence. If she were them, she would check the pharmacy despite the giant X. There was no point in being cautious when it came to having drugs to ward off disease.

"Stupid," she whispered to herself.

She dropped low to the ground and scurried toward the broken door. She peered through the shattered window and saw a pickup truck. One man was driving while another was in the back and a third walked alongside the slow-moving vehicle. The driver hit the brakes and pointed in different directions, barking at the other two. She fell backward as his finger ultimately pointed and held at the pharmacy door.

Lightning. Thunder.

There was more hollering and she jumped at the sound of gunfire. She pulled herself back to the window to see one of the men waving a small gun in the air. There were only two of them now, the third one nowhere to be found. She yelped as a body fell from the sky, landing on the roof of the truck. The two men screamed to get out of there. The driver slammed the gas, but before the truck could move, another figure dropped out of the sky, landing in front of it.

It was the angel.

The angel grabbed onto the front of the truck and leaned in, digging its feet into the pavement. The vehicle slowly pushed the figure backward as the men continued yelling. The angel jumped onto the hood and grabbed the man in the back. Wings open, it launched itself into the air for a few feet. It came down hard on the pavement, crushing the man into the ground. As the angel's feet touched the ground, it spun around, slinging the man back at the truck.

She gasped at the strength of it. She had seen augmented guys who didn't have the same impact the winged figure did. The wings were magnificent, she thought. As the lightning cracked again, she was amazed at the wingspan of the figure. The bright white feathers attached to the back, just like the pictures she had seen in Sunday school. She could make out the face and realized the angel was a female. She had assumed because of the ferocity of its actions it was a man.

She crawled through the hole in the door so she could get a better view. The angel was running back toward the truck. She leapt, sending herself airborne, and sailed into the back of the pickup truck. The truck turned the corner and vanished.

She stepped out from under the awning, her backpack slung over her shoulder. She could feel the rain soaking through her clothes again.

She waited, letting minutes pass by. She couldn't hear the truck over the sound of rain hitting the ground and waves of water gushing into the sewer grates. She didn't know if she should run or wait for the angel to return. The decision was made for her as the figure lowered itself in front of her. The wings flapped hard, slowing the woman's descent to the ground. She landed hard enough it put her down on one knee.

The angel stood. Lightning. Thunder. As her wings pulled in tight to her body, they seemed to vanish from sight. The moon cast just enough light that she could make out the collar of the robe, high enough to hide the winged figure's mouth.

"Twenty-seven," the angel said. The convict grabbed her arm, her fingers touching the carved numbers in her forearm. She had thought about her new identity and how the branding was like a signature to her new life. She had thought about calling herself by the number, but she had yet to say the words out loud.

"How did you…"

"We need to be away from here," the angel said. Before Twenty-Seven could ask why, the angel responded, "There are more of them on their way. You're not safe."

"Where do we go?"

The angel held out her hand. It was the first kind gesture Twenty-Seven had seen since entering the Danger Zone. "I have friends nearby that can provide asylum."

"What about them?" she said, pointing to the corpses on the ground.

"Their thoughts are far from pure."

"But…"

"Trust me," the angel said. Twenty-Seven took her by the hand. She had no idea why, but she trusted the figure in front of her. Trusting her meant survival. She squeezed the angel's hand. She would survive the Danger Zone.

***

He stood in the park across from the gallery, his last chance to turn around and avoid the scene unfolding in front of him. Across the street, the crowd gathered just outside Gretchen's art gallery. His shoulders tensed at the circus. He had expected a modest turnout—Gretchen had a knack for getting a crowd—but the scene before him was more a spectacle.

The crowd that collected outside of the building was frightening, screaming back and forth over several policemen. Some held picket signs while others pumped their fists in the air. One of the signs read 'Kill the Freaks,' hoisted high above the protestor's head. An angry man shouted into another man's face, his spit visible from several feet away.

Conthan took several steps closer. He could see there were police wedged between the two opposing sides. The other side was just as vocal, holding their own signs, 'God Loves All,' and chanting their own ridiculousness at the opposition. The police had donned their riot uniforms, helmets and tactical vests. Each of the officers held a shield, which they used to push the crowds apart.

He started to walk forward again when he saw two of the policemen wearing glasses instead of helmets. He could tell by their demeanor that they weren't there for riot patrol, they were there with a mission. He didn't need to see their badges to know they were part of the Corps. Beneath the exterior of normal human flesh was a labyrinth of wires and surgical implants, enhancing their abilities and making them borderline superhuman. Their eyes were enhanced, able to see in the dark and receive readouts fed to them by some unseen computer. He had watched a news feed last night that was acquired through the live feed of a Corps member's eyes. The man who was projecting the image had punched through a metal safety door.

"Gretchen, what have you gotten me into?"

He pushed his hands into his pockets and moved forward. He reached the crowd, astonished by how loud the bullhorns were. A flesh and blood officer helped him along, pushing people back as Conthan reached the building. The door was opened and he was shoved inside while the policeman went back to his job.

There were easily another two hundred people in the gallery. It wasn't exactly crammed, but it would take a while to navigate through the crowd to reach the back of the room.

"Name please?"

He turned to see the receptionist in the lobby. He looked at the young girl, her blue hair sticking straight up in spikes. Her body was covered in tattoos, a lion eating a dragon wrapped around the torso of a naked man and so many others.

"Your name, please?"

"Uh," he stammered, "Conthan."

"The Conthan?"

He raised an eyebrow. "Because there's more than one Conthan on the list?"

She gave him a dirty look and waved him in. "Gretchen will find you."

"What is going on?" he mumbled to himself.

He dodged his way through the crowd and lifted

a glass of champagne off a tray from one of the several servers circulating the room. He rounded a white wall in the middle of the gallery space and got his first chance to see one of the other painter's pieces. Conthan stared for a moment and then began to fall into his schooling. *Examine the work. Absorb the work. What did the artist want you to see? What did you feel?*

He explored the black vortex of paint on the two-by-two-foot canvas. He could see the liberal use of the palette knife and sloppy delivery of the medium. He felt dark looking at the piece, as if he were looking into an abyss. He leaned back and attempted to unravel the possible messages being delivered by the artist.

"Fascinating, isn't it?" asked a gentleman next to him.

"He has a unique style," said Conthan. "A bit awkward on the application of the medium, I feel."

The man gasped at the criticism. "The medium does not matter. This work is an examination of the soul of humanity. The artist is trying to explore our depths and reveal to us the dark nature that is burning the foundation of our society."

"Bullshit," commented Conthan. "Could you go find another elitist to talk to? I'm trying to enjoy art."

The guy swore several times under his breath and stomped away from the wall. Gretchen quickly took his place. "You realize you just pissed off Mr. Leboy, the art critic for the NY Times?"

Conthan shrugged. "That would explain why he doesn't know anything he's talking about. The guy wouldn't know art if it bit him on his ass."

"He put an offer on one of your pieces," she replied. "Willing to offer you twenty thousand for one painting."

"Uhm." Conthan thought for a moment. "No."

She let out a sigh and smacked her forehead. "You really are difficult sometimes, you know that?"

Conthan chuckled at the obvious. "You already told him no, didn't you?"

"Of course I said no," she grumbled. "I told him about all this integrity bullshit and what I wanted to say is 'No, he's the biggest bonehead I know. Of course he won't take your money.'"

"What's with the crowd outside?"

She stood on her toes to see out the massive windows that lined the front of the gallery. "I hired the police force. I figured that your work might bring out some of the crazies. I also had a suspicion that the haters were gonna hate. You can tell by the guest list that the people inside here are a bit more"—she paused—"endeared to your cause."

"I don't have a cause."

"Whether you know it or not, tonight you are the poster child for the Children of Nostradamus."

Shit, he thought.

"Did you notice the two Corps soldiers outside?"

"What the fuck," she said, seeing the two out-of-place officers. Things rarely bothered Gretchen. This was orchestrated by her, but the sight of the officers thoroughly irritated her.

"Not your idea, I take it?"

"I need to introduce the two of you to the crowd

and then I'll go outside and take care of the Corps."

Conthan laughed out loud as she walked away. He had no doubt in his mind that she, a tiny woman, was more than daring enough to go wrangle cybernetic humans. *The Corps should be fearful of that girl when she goes on the warpath*, he thought.

"Excuse me, everyone," came a booming voice over the speakers in the room.

He turned to see Gretchen standing on the stage with a microphone in her hand. "I'm glad everybody could make it this evening. Gallery Systems Incorporated is more than delighted to present two new up-and-coming artists. The first is a recent college graduate, Conthan…" She paused, looking at the card. "I don't even know his last name."

The crowd laughed in response.

"His work embodies the soul of the Children of Nostradamus, explored through the admiration for one individual. His precision with the pencil or the brush shows not only mastery of the medium, but allows him to be captivated by his muse, a young woman challenged by her mutation. He explores his affection for the subject and allows the viewer to feel the longing experienced by both the subject and the artist."

Conthan grumbled. He hated being analyzed. Most often critics would give some crap description of his work. He had already insulted one of the most renowned bullshitters of his generation. However, Gretchen was right about it all. He missed Sarah. Looking at his pictures over and over, he couldn't help but see beauty in her less-than-traditional features. His heart ached, and he wanted nothing more than to see his friend. Soon, he thought, soon he would see her.

"Our second artist is a veteran who has been painting for nearly four decades and recently has been keeping my doors open." Laughter. "Jed Zappens's more abstract approach to the subject of super humans explores a darker side of the culture. Having been classified a Class III himself, he has witnessed firsthand the dangers of not only his species, but the pain inflicted on them in the name of preservation."

"Holy shit," Conthan said out loud. "Now the guards make a lot more sense."

He worked his way toward the stage and finally caught Gretchen's eye. She looked down, and with the microphone still in hand, announced him. "Meet Conthan, ladies and gentlemen…and Jed Zappens."

The man next to Conthan raised his hand to the clapping crowd. Conthan could see the stereotypical artist. His black pants, black turtleneck and slicked-back hair made him not only a stereotype, but truly a douchebag.

"Nice to meet you," said Jed. "I really admire your work."

"Thanks," Conthan said, shaking the man's hand. "Yours isn't half bad either."

Conthan smiled, not at Jed but at the fact he had managed to say two sentences and not insult the guy for being pretentious and a prick. He chalked it up to growing older and maturing, something he'd most likely regret any moment.

"So," Conthan said, "you're a super human?"

"Not one to beat around the bush, are you?"

"I prefer my bushes not beaten."

"I am," he said. "Discovered it at fourteen."

Conthan attempted to do the math but lost track. "So what's your power?"

"Sizing me up?"

"I figure next we can whip them out on the table and have Gretchen measure."

Gretchen jumped in the middle. "Will you behave? I love you, really I do, but stop being a jerk."

"He's just curious," said the elder artist. "I'm a vocal mimic."

"A what?"

"My voice," he clarified. "I can quite literally do impressions of every person I've ever heard speak."

"Wow," Conthan said, "not exactly a pyro or that really strong guy."

"Could be worse," admitted the man. "I once met a kid whose mutation made him green."

"Really?"

"Yup, so at least I know I'm not at the bottom of the totem pole."

"Can you do it now?"

He held up a finger, gesturing for them to wait a moment. He began to roll down the collar of his shirt and revealed a thin black band on his neck. "I was collared when I left the program."

"Collared?"

"Being a Class III doesn't win me any points with the military. My abilities have been neutered and I have no way to use them."

"What if you take it off?"

Gretchen sighed. "Tact is not your strong suit. I'm going outside to make sure the Corps don't shoot anybody."

Jed tensed up at the name of the police force outside. He quickly relaxed his body, but it was obvious he was not thrilled at their presence. Conthan saw him out of the corner of his eye giving him an awkward glance. Conthan finally shrugged. "Not a fan?"

Jed put his hand to the collar. "I have an explosive device grafted into my neck," he said firmly. "Would you be a fan if you were a walking time bomb?"

"Noted," Conthan said.

The crowd froze as a pane of glass shattered in the front of the gallery. Conthan instinctively ducked and looked to his partner. "This isn't going to end well."

Jed shook his head. "It's a hotspot in here right now. If the Corps soldiers get involved, there is going to be a massacre."

"A hotspot?"

Jed rolled his eyes. "Do you think I'm the only powered guy here? Everybody in this room could be undocumented. The Corps is here to sniff all of you out. If they catch you, it's off to the facility."

"Dammit, Gretch," Conthan muttered. He looked to the man next to him and realized how dire it could be. "There's a back door. You can get out."

"What?"

"The humans are fine, let's get you out of here. At least this way you're less likely to pop your top."

"You're insufferable," Jed said.

"I've been told."

They watched as one of the Corps soldiers took a punch to the face. The man's head hardly moved from the impact. His hand shot out and grabbed his assailant. His grip tightened on the protester's neck and the man spasmed as electricity began to surge through the soldier's hand. "Your peaceful protest is now in violation of the law."

Conthan could see the crowd beginning to push away from the gallery lobby, lining the walls and sheltering themselves from the gaze of the Corps soldier. The cyborg's vision landed on Conthan and his companion and the officer froze. "Class III detected."

"Shit."

Conthan pushed Jed into the crowd. They began to work through the wall of bodies. "What if you waited?" Conthan asked. "Not like you did anything wrong."

"I was born wrong," Jed shouted back. "I'll be seen as part of a non-peaceful protest and in violation of the law."

"I'll pay your fifty dollar fine."

"Children of Nostradamus don't pay fines with money."

"Shit."

They reached the door into the back alley and Conthan flung it open. He stuck his head out. "All clear." They jumped narrow road behind the gallery and slammed the door behind them. He looked down the way to the street with cars passing by. They started walking at a brisk pace, nearing their freedom.

Both men froze as a figure landed in front of them, falling into a crouch. The shadow looked up and they recognized the glow from the eyes. "Shit."

"Jed Zappens, you have been found in breach of your release agreement."

Conthan put his hand up, trying to block the Child. "He had nothing to do with this. He's an innocent bystander. We're leaving peacefully."

The figure raised his hand and Conthan could see he had a gun. "Whoa, calm down, he said. "We had nothing to do with what is going on back there."

"Stand down, human," the figure's voice said.

Conthan realized he was standing in front of his fellow artist. It had been unintentional, but he couldn't let something like a rowdy crowd cost a man his life. He put up both of his hands. "Let us go."

"Any further discussion will be seen as an act of aggression. Jed Zappens will be terminated."

"No."

Conthan felt his arm being pulled just as he saw the red light begin to protrude from the end of the gun. Jed yanked him backward, stepping between him and their assailant. In that moment he felt panic, anger and the disgust at what was happening. The entire alley lit up red as the light pierced Jed.

Time began to slow down and a surge of pain emigrated from the pit of his stomach. It crawled at a pace that felt surreal. He watched the light emerge from Jed's back. With only inches between him and sudden death, the pain in Conthan's chest built as if it would rip through him. Conthan's vision blurred and he could see a single dark spot form in front of him. The laser hit the dark spot and vanished into nothingness.

He fell to his knees as time sped back up. He reached for his chest and realized that he was still whole.

"Class I identified," said the Corps soldier. "Immediate termination."

Conthan looked up, confused, and realized that the gun was pointing directly at his face. He watched as the soldier pulled the trigger and the pain surged through his brain.

"Not today." It was his voice, but he wasn't speaking.

He realized he wasn't in control of his actions as he held up his hand and pushed the pain through his body to his palms. The black spot returned and he watched as the laser emerged from the gun and vanished into another dark hole. He could see a similar spot appear just to the side of the soldier. The laser projected outward from the darkness, searing through the soldier's head.

Conthan felt the pain release his body. He fell to the ground. He lay next to a gasping Jed Zappens. Conthan turned his head to see the man. "I'm sorry," he muttered.

Jed sucked in a ragged breath and blinked several times, tears beginning to stream down his face. He reached into his breast pocket and dragged out an old folded envelope. "For you," he said through clenched teeth.

Conthan's voice had left him. He wanted to scream for a medic but he couldn't find air enough to fill his lungs. He started to reach for the envelope but hesitated before snatching it from the dead man's hands. He crushed it in his grasp as he watched the light vanish from the artist's eyes.

"Run," said a voice.

Conthan rolled his head to see that there was nobody left standing in the alley. He sucked in air and tried to sit upright. "Hello?"

"Run!"

He didn't dare question the voice. In front of him was a dead Corps soldier and a dead artist. He moved through the alley and finally out into the street. His feet picked up speed, his stumbling turning to a fast run. There was no stopping him as fear set in.

He had killed a Corps soldier. He was now marked for death. As he ran, he could hear the echo of the soldier's words. "Class I," he had said. Conthan couldn't shake the feeling that life as he knew it was over.

***

"That's our cue," said a portly man. He stopped leaning against the wall and started turning up the cuffs on his dress shirt. He reached up and loosened the tie tightly wrapped around his neck.

"And here I was beginning to think you looked handsome," said a young female holding a flute of white wine.

"Alyssa," he said, "you flatterer."

"I take back all the comments about you needing sit-ups," she said, giving his belly a rub.

He chuckled. The room was descending into

chaos as patrons tried to push their way past one another. Outside, the fight between the anti-powers coalition and the Children sympathizers became physical. Cops in riot gear were beginning to step over the broken glass and come into the gallery itself. As law enforcement blocked the exits, the crowd of fringe artists screamed, trying to get away from the confrontation.

"What's the plan, Dwayne?"

The man tossed the tie onto the floor, stepping into the crowd. He turned to the exit Conthan charged toward. He watched the two artists escape through the door. He rubbed his thumb across the tips of his fingers. As he sped up the motion, small sparks began to form.

"We keep them away from those doors."

She nodded. Without missing a beat she tapped the flute against the wall, the glass shattering to the ground, leaving the sharp stem. She walked closer to the policeman reaching for his weapon. A protester charged the policeman, using the wood of his sign as a spear.

Dwayne began shaking his fists, the small sparks now leaping off his hands. He paused as Alyssa stepped between the officer and the protestor. She dropped quickly to one knee, jamming the flute stem into an officer's leg. She used his momentum to flip him over her head and into another officer. The second cop grabbed for his weapon and looked down when he couldn't find the grip.

Alyssa dropped out the magazine and removed the barrel of the gun. She used the butt of the gun and slammed it into the man's helmet. He reached up to grab her hand but found she moved faster than expected. The young girl, barely old enough to be drinking, dropped to the floor, sweeping her leg outward, hooking it on his feet and sending him to the ground. As she spun around, she swung her hand downward, smacking him in the windpipe.

Dwayne smiled at the elegance with which she moved. She pulled the officer's baton from his utility belt and stood up, meeting his eyes. "Are you going to start pulling your weight?"

He pointed behind her. She turned as protestors lunged at her. She spun the baton around, cracking the jaw of one man. He fell backward as she punched with the heel of her hand into the woman's chest. The woman collapsed to the ground, hissing at the pain radiating through her body.

Dwayne stepped beside his comrade. He gave a slight shrug. "You seem to have things under control."

"No thanks to you," she said.

He threw out his hand, knocking her to the side as a man behind her raised a gun level with her head. Dwayne grabbed the firearm by the muzzle. Sparks jumped from his hand, passing through the gun, leaping across the skin of the man. Dwayne watched the familiar spasm as the electricity wrangled his heart, throwing it out of rhythm and sending him into cardiac arrest.

Alyssa hit the ground in a roll and bounced back to her feet. The hair on her neck stood on end as the air began to smell like burning hairspray. A soldier with a gun strapped across his chest stepped inside the broken window. The people were fleeing the scene, screaming as they recognized the black and red patch on the man's sleeves.

"Corps," she whispered.

"Not Genesis Division," Dwayne shouted back to her.

Dwayne knocked the spasming man to the side just in time for the soldier to replace him. Dwayne held up his hands, sparks arcing between his fingers. The soldier reached out, the pain of the lightning burning his skin.

"You've—" Dwayne said as the man's grip tightened. The mechanics in the soldier's arm began to take over, "—got me now."

A flash of light illuminated the room as a bolt of lightning jumped from Dwayne's chest into the cyborg. The soldier's weapon fell and the skin on his exposed chest melted away, along with the flesh of his arms.

The soldier picked up Dwayne and threw him back along the floor as if he weighed nothing. Dwayne watched the man wince, the pain starting to register. Even with neural inhibitors working in the soldier's head, he was beginning to feel a stinging sensation along the charred skin. The soldier turned his attention to Dwayne's companion.

Alyssa closed the distance between them and swung the club at the man's head. The wood splintered as it connected with his jaw. Dwayne could hear her gasp. The amount of metal he must have inside to resist the blow was alarming. He had seen the cyborgs before, men in the military trading their flesh for synthetic parts, but this was even more than usual. He assumed the man was a casualty replacement, a wounded veteran turned into a robot to keep the military's investment from dying.

The man reached out for her, his reflexes faster than the police officer's. She knocked the hand to the side and shoved the splintered club into its upper arm. The man didn't scream. She'd be pissed, she didn't like when they refused scream. With the speed of his movements, Dwayne had to assume there wasn't much human left.

She was fast. She was skilled. She wasn't Dwayne. As the man grabbed her by the throat, she felt his strength threatening to crush her windpipe. She pulled the club from his forearm and drove it into his eye socket.

She braced her feet against the man's chest and pushed off, launching herself backward along the floor. The soldier reached up to pull the spike from his eye as he started to wail. Alyssa averted her eyes from the screaming man falling to his knees. She stood up while Dwayne clambered next to her. The soldier stopped moving on the ground. Alyssa eyed Dwayne's charred shirt and pink skin peeking through.

"We good?"

He looked back to the door, still firmly shut. "That should have given him plenty of time to get out of here."

"Now for us," she said.

As Dwayne stepped forward, a group from the party rushed past him to the door, looking back in fear. He stepped over the glass of the bay window leading outside and helped Alyssa step over the remaining shards. The street had mostly cleared; some spectators hovered to see what was going on. He could only assume the mob had vanished as the Corps soldiers arrived. Even the most passionate protestor wouldn't risk the wrath of the machine men.

"Dav5d has a car ready for you," said a woman's voice.

Across the street, a car's engine turned over and the driver's side door opened. Dwayne checked both directions as he crossed the road. Dav5d had chosen a high-end speedster. Dwayne looked back at the destroyed art gallery. He didn't fully understand why he was needed, but he sensed pieces were beginning to fall into place.

"We're heading home, Vanessa."

Chapter Six

December 1st, 1992 9:02AM

Mark removed his lanyard, tossing it to the floor in a rush. The nurse pointed to the sink, telling him to scrub up. He threw his blazer next to his lanyard and began washing his hands. He rolled up the sleeves on his dress shirt and continued furiously scrubbing. He washed off the soap and the nurse patted down his arms and pushed open the door into the room.

The scream that ripped through the air startled him, causing him to freeze in his tracks until it subsided. The woman lying on her back, her legs firmly secured in stirrups, made eye contact with him as her back arched. Another scream filled the small room. She had seen him; there was no escaping now, he was in this to the end.

He rushed by her side and gripped her reaching hand. She had taken off her wedding and engagement rings when she began to put on the baby weight. He was thankful as her grip threatened to break his finger. He gripped her bloated hands while brushing away hair blocking her vision.

"You're doing fine, hon," he said, giving her hand a light squeeze.

"You're never having sex with me again." She half-laughed as she gritted her teeth.

A nurse on the other side of the bed took her hand and began making breathing sounds. Mark realized he hadn't started the breathing they learned in Parents 101. He started the hissing noises and his wife let out a deep sigh as the contraction passed.

"You sound ridiculous." She laughed again.

She was the funny one. She was the lighthearted one. She was the better half of their relationship. He was the worrier, the one who pored over bank statements and focused on future goals. She was the reason they were having a baby. On their first date he told her, "Your laugh is the most beautiful sound." She said the baby was going to fill their house with same joyful noises.

"I love you," he said, basking in the start of an amazing journey they were embarking on.

The doctor stepped up to the table and smiled at the young couple. He pulled his mask over his face and sat in front of the stirrups. "So I hear we're going to have a baby today."

"And stop the fun?" She started screaming before she could give him the signature half-laugh she was known for.

The doctor began talking to the nurses. Mark ignored the man as he focused on his wife. His wedding ring was going to leave a mark as she clenched his hand with a vise-like grip. He only froze as the word "complication" left the doctor's mouth. His wife grunted out a sound he could only assume was a question about what was going on.

Mark could see the motion in the room from the corner of his eye. He didn't turn away from his wife. There wasn't much he was sure about in the world. He would doubt every decision in his adult life, but this was the first in which he was certain of a positive outcome. Months ago, a very tender woman had assured him his mother would survive her bout with cancer. With the odds stacked against her, she conquered her own body and the cancer was clear. The same woman had said his child would be healthy. He never questioned her predictions, and now, he understood what it was like to know the future.

His wife's eyes were terrified of what was happening. She wanted answers, assurances her newborn was going to be okay. As the doctor moved in a rush, she did everything she could to distract herself from the pain.

"It will be okay," he whispered. He leaned in close on the bed, propping himself next to her. He rested his hand on her face and forced her to see his eyes. She looked panicked and he couldn't blame her. The baby hadn't been born yet and she was already in love with the little person. She had removed his desk and bookcase for a crib and rocking chair and put together more infuriating contraptions to transport the child than he could imagine.

He rubbed his thumb along her cheek. Her eyes tried to focus on him but he could see through the pain radiating throughout her body. He leaned in close to his wife, his forehead only inches from touching hers. He kept eye contact, showing his confidence in the situation.

"He's going to be okay," he whispered to her.

She only responded by grunting and gritting her teeth. The doctor moved about, talking to the nurse and doing something hidden by the modesty cloth draped over his wife. Tears rolled down her cheek.

"I promise you, he's okay," he whispered to her.

Her body relaxed and the pain seemed to vanish. Elizabeth didn't let go of his hand as he whispered more sweet nothings to her. She wanted to sit up and see the doctor, but her body felt weak and she waited for some sign.

The two nurses in the room moved frantically. She didn't break eye contact with her husband as he continued to stroke her face. She was tired and she wanted to sleep. She waited as an empty feeling began to creep into her chest.

There was a single cry. She held her breath, unsure if what she heard had been real. Seconds were an eternity as she waited. The silence was broken by a series of shrieks. Without any signs of embarrassment, tears rolled down her face at the overwhelming joy that began to flood into her being.

"I promised you," he whispered as he kissed her forehead.

The doctor explained there had been a problem with the umbilical cord that had caused a lack of oxygen to the baby. They would need to keep both mother and child overnight to monitor their health, but he assured her the newest addition to their family would be okay. He helped remove her legs from the stirrups and tried to make her feel more comfortable. Then he handed the infant off to the nurse, who turned to a changing table. The doctor congratulated the parents. The new parents were so tightly entwined with one another they weren't listening to a word he was saying.

The phone began to ring, breaking sounds of mom and child crying. Mark kissed his wife. "Everything is going to be amazing."

Elizabeth leaned back on the bed, glancing at the ringing telephone. She pointed to her face and motioned to the mess by her legs. She smiled. "If you're still with me after seeing this…"

He kissed her again. "You're beautiful."

The phone continued to ring. The nurse swaddled his newborn and placed his boy into the outstretched arms of his wife. He pushed back her hair and kissed her brow. She leaned into Mark's arms and smiled up to him.

"How did you know?"

The emotions were running strong in his heart. His beautiful wife was holding his firstborn child. His mother was outside, waiting to meet her first grandchild. He had no doubts. He thought of the woman handing him letters wrapped in a single white ribbon.

"Eleanor told me," he whispered.

Elizabeth didn't reply. She had been terrified when Eleanor was shot and agents had detained her husband. He had answered their questions as truthfully as he could, but she was convinced his association with the psychic had threatened her family. It wasn't until months ago he confessed to the letter he kept hidden away in his sock drawer. He told his wife about how Eleanor saw the future and knew his mother would survive cancer and that they would have a healthy baby.

She couldn't understand the life of the soothsayer, but she knew her husband's respect and conviction for the woman made her an angel hovering over their family. He squeezed her hand again.

The phone didn't stop ringing.

He let go of her hand and picked up the receiver. He barked, "What?"

"Yes, sir," he replied quickly. He didn't say another word. The phone rolled off his shoulder and dropped to the floor as he walked toward the television. The nurse stepped next to the new mother and offered to take the child and help her clean up before her son's first feeding.

He couldn't hear the conversation anymore as he fumbled with the buttons on the television set suspended from the wall. He didn't try to change the channel. He simply stared at the box, unable to comment or explain to his wife.

"…Seabrook, New Hampshire is gone. If you're just tuning in, the Seabrook Nuclear Power Plant has just exploded. We have no word yet on what caused the explosion, but we do know there was a catastrophe resulting in failure of the systems at the Seabrook Nuclear Power Plant."

"God help them," said the woman at the news desk.

He could hear Elizabeth gasp at the announcement. His mind was moving a million miles an hour. His wife, still covered in sweat and grime from giving birth, his newborn son, his office calling him to alert him to the news, all of it caused his head to swim. He was unsure of what his next move would be.

The television flickered and turned to static. Mark reached up and smacked the side of the box. The static began to take the shape of a person. He stepped back to see the solid outline of a man on the TV.

"United States of America," said a voice through the static, "land of the free and home of the brave. We are calling out your discreet operations. We know all about The Culling. Individuals who for years have been in your employ, using their more-than-human abilities to further your goals, will not die in vain. Killing empaths, slaughtering clairvoyants, and the genocide of telepaths will be responded to in kind."

"Eleanor," he said in a hushed voice as he realized what they were talking about.

"The United States has declared war on the wrong people. We can see you coming. We can hear your plans. We will not be eliminated. You've seen our reach."

The static turned to an aerial shot of a cluster of buildings. A small explosion began in one part of the structure and a chain of bursts followed. He didn't need to see the rest to know it was another nuclear power plant being attacked.

"The Northeast belongs to us now. Cease species

war."

The televisions went black. No static, no sound, just a blank screen. He turned to his wife; her face showed worry. She didn't know what to say to her husband. The joy of her baby boy was being replaced by the horror of domestic terrorism.

"You'll be safe here," he said.

"Just go," she said. "We'll be fine here. Go help save the world."

He pushed the door open and grabbed his blazer and lanyard. As he threw on his White House badge, he realized he didn't even know the name of his son. He started to jog down the hall. Every room, people were staring blankly at the television. Even nurses paused, unsure of how to continue their day.

Mark turned through a door leading to the stairwell that would take him to the garage. He jumped down the steps two at a time and shoved his way through. As he quickly walked to his car he couldn't help but think of Eleanor.

"Is this what you couldn't predict?" He was terrified that the darkness had begun to take root.

Chapter Seven

May 16th, 2032 11:52PM

"Why bother speaking?"

Vanessa pondered the question for a moment. It had been years since she found a human to be so candid with her. The young woman at her side was forthright and direct. "It tends to put humans at ease when they can hear my voice."

"Is that why you hide your face?"

Vanessa smirked at the woman's bold assertion. "Sometimes I forget if I'm speaking with my mouth or my mind. It helps hide my mistakes."

Twenty-Seven nodded at the answer. The sun broke the horizon and the light washed over their faces. She pulled off the hoodie and tucked it away in her bag. She eyed the woman walking next to her. While they had been together, the angel had never appeared to be wet. Twenty-Seven knew there was something more than met the eye about the person guiding her down the road. Vanessa listened to the woman's thoughts as they sped through her mind.

"Are you real?"

Vanessa continued as the woman stopped. The sun cast a brilliant light on the world in front of her, providing a sense of beauty to the upcoming day. She turned to see the woman holding her ground. She didn't need to ask why. The woman's thoughts were loud, broadcasting as if she was saying them aloud.

She doesn't get wet when it rains? Where are her wings? If she can speak to me without actually speaking, can she make me see things that aren't there? What if she's not real? What if I died? How do I...

"You have no way of knowing."

"Angel of the Outlands," the woman said flatly, "what are you hiding?"

"Asks the woman tried and convicted for murder."

Twenty-Seven didn't flinch. "If you can read my thoughts…"

I do not judge.

Did I ask for validation? "Lead on," Twenty-Seven said.

"You trust me?"

Twenty-Seven walked past Vanessa, her eyes fixed on her feet. "I have no choice."

The buildings had begun to crumble from disrepair. There weren't many skyscrapers in Springfield, but as they approached the bridge leading them into the city, plenty rose into the sky. Cars were scattered across the streets, windshields smashed in, many still containing the remains of the occupants who were trying to flee the city. Twenty-Seven paused as she looked into a Subaru on the side of the road; the backseat contained a small skeleton still in the baby seat.

She tried to focus on the grass breaking through the cracks in the concrete. She assumed the angel was capable of seeing her thoughts. She didn't try to hide them. She had expected something more Godly about her, something that earned her the title of Angel. She appreciated the woman's intervention, perhaps saving her life, but she was left with more questions than she was willing to answer.

Posters lined the city's buildings. The government had reached out to the survivors, offering them protection if they could make it out of Massachusetts. She couldn't imagine how many people had survived. Was it possible people in the depths of parking garages or even basements could have survived the initial blast? Would the radiation kill them?

She tripped over her own foot as she looked at the graffiti covering dozens of posters glued to the side of a building. In black spray paint and nearly up to the second floor was a symbol. She studied it for a moment before she recognized the outstretched wings. She looked at the woman to her side again. The people who remained paid homage to the angel.

They walked in silence as they reached the edge of the city. The buildings became smaller in the southern portion of the metropolis. The large structures were behind them and the city turned into smaller residential homes. She stopped as she saw movement behind one of the cars. She didn't hesitate, dropping behind a parked SUV.

Vanessa caught Twenty-Seven peering around the corner, staring at her stretched wings. Vanessa did everything in her power to be visible to anybody who might be watching. Vanessa motioned for Twenty-Seven to stay tucked behind the vehicle. Vanessa could sense the woman's thoughts, pondering if she could detect anybody nearby, as well as several nearby thoughts alerting her to the trap she might be stepping into.

"Angel," came a voice, "you bring company."

"She is with me, Victor."

A man appeared from the doorway of what had once been a cafe. Twenty-Seven noted the gun on his hip before she noticed the burns across his face. Perhaps in his late fifties, he looked like any other man, but a dark red patch covered at least half of his face and neck. She didn't have to be a doctor to know the signs of radiation burn.

"Who is she?" asked Victor.

"She's a convict, sent to the Outlands by the government."

"Angel, you know we don't take degenerates the government sends here to die. We're a peaceful people."

"Says the man who wears a gun," she said from her hiding spot. She wasn't the weak woman she was a year ago. There was no way she was going to let a man decide her fate. The woman who had taken punch after punch was dead. She was Twenty-Seven.

"Child, do you think we're the only ones here?

I'm sure you've seen the looting already."

"Victor, she was sentenced to death for protecting herself."

Another voice yelled, "How do you know she ain't lying?"

"You dare question me? I see into the hearts of men, just as I have seen into Victor's, or yours, Timothy. I have seen her heart and I have deemed her worthy." The angel's voice boomed. Reverberating in each of their chests, the words hovered in the air as if they had been spoken by God himself.

Twenty-Seven noted the angel was speaking with her mouth. The loud words were heard by her ears, not her head. The angel had more tricks than she could imagine, but she couldn't figure out the game being played. She had been frank in their discussions, secretive, but up-front with most questions. However, she attempted to put the fear of God into these people.

They do not know I can read their thoughts.

Why do you hide it?

The angel turned her head, looking over her shoulder past the magnificent raised wing. Her eyes connected with Twenty-Seven, who could read them as if she was capable of reading her thoughts. She could see the sorrow written across her brow and the cost of her deceit etched in her crow's feet. *You know I am not an angel.*

"A telepath," Twenty-Seven whispered in her hiding spot.

Chapter Eight

May 17th, 2032 12:32AM

Mr. Cowan,

As you ponder the situation laid out in front of you, it is clear that things will never be the same. Before you are many decisions, but alas, beyond this point I cannot see nor predict your future. You are an element that seems to defy the strands of probability. I fear that before you lies a path that will test the fortitude of your soul. I wish I could give you more than a simple direction. I have done everything in my power to see you safe to this point. I wish I could tell you that somewhere on the other side of the darkness will be you, standing triumphant. However, I cannot. For that, I am sorry. What I can do is start you on your hero's journey.

Go to Sarah.
With Regards,
Eleanor P. Valentine

***

For the fourth time, Conthan read the letter line for line. The woman who wrote it was older. He could tell by the elegant strokes of her pen she had written it slowly, carefully, deliberately picking each word. He marveled at the beautiful calligraphy.

As he finished the letter, he stared at the name at the end. It wasn't a common name, but something about it stuck in his head. He couldn't put his finger on it.

"How do you know me?" he whispered.

He reached into his pocket and pulled out his phone. The small clear plastic object turned opaque as he pressed his thumb against it. He whispered the woman's name and gasped as her image appeared on his screen. Every high school student was required to take modern history. One of the most notorious individuals in the last century was Valentine, a psychic driven crazy by her ability to predict the future.

Browsing further through the document, he could hear his former teacher barking about the importance of history in shaping the future of mankind. Eleanor had been an aide to the first female president. Near the end of her term, Valentine had started to have crazy dreams predicting outlandish future possibilities. The insanity led her attempt to kill the president. Eleanor had been shot, but historians claimed that it was the defining point in history that would lead to "The Culling" of all mentalists. Telepaths had the ability to read minds and telekinetics could move things with their mind. Eleanor was a precog, a person capable of seeing the future. Anybody identified with mental abilities was "put down" for national security.

The military had kept a detailed list of anybody with these gifts, using their abilities for decades before the Nostradamus Effect took place. During the culling, they began to tear people from their homes and exterminate them in the streets. The article showed a video of a man screaming at a soldier, whose hand violently shook as he turned the gun around and shot himself in the face before his fellow soldiers shot the telekinetic. The military developed a zero tolerance policy for people with the ability to manipulate the world with their mind.

Only months after the assassination attempt, a terrorist group detonated a bomb in two nuclear power plants in retaliation to an extremist government. The bomb left a good chunk of New England uninhabitable. Vacated, Boston would become known as the Danger Zone. The radiation rendered it unlivable, making it the new dumping ground for the unwanted people of the United States. America turned into a militant state.

"Bus is heading out, kid," said a guy behind a dirty glass window.

Conthan examined the empty bus station. It had been fairly busy when he arrived, but the patrons had moved on to other destinations while he was doing research. He looked at the man behind the glass protective shield. "Thanks," he said, standing up. He walked down the aisle and out the door to where a bus was idling. He looked at the side of the vehicle and could see a yellow biohazard sign next to the words 'Danger Zone.'

He began to step onto the bus and the man at the wheel stopped him. "I need to see your ID and signed disclaimer."

Conthan hovered his hand over the palm reader. A series of screens flashed, warning him about the perils of entering into the Danger Zone. He pressed his thumb to the glass, signing the document.

"You understand that you will be inside the Danger Zone and when not in a proper facility, you will be exposed to mild amounts of radiation. This could lead to radiation poisoning or worse, death." The man had apparently memorized the document and was spitting it back verbatim.

"I've been before," Conthan said.

"We don't see many civvies make the trip more than once."

"Going to see a friend of mine."

The driver's eyebrow rose at the statement. There was only one location to be reached on this bus route. The look on his face went from curious to saddened. "I hope it's worth the trip, son."

"Me too."

Conthan moved back to an empty seat. He was surprised by how many people were on the bus. It was a mix of civilians and what he assumed were guards for the facility. He tried to maintain his composure as he scanned the number of armed. He knew they were like the Corps, augmented with various enhancements to their bodies. All of them would be modified to help screen them against the radiation. He had to wonder, what other enhancements did they have?

He sat against the window and looked at the letter again. It was forty years since Eleanor had been killed in the Oval Office. What were the chances forty years later, a letter would find its way into his hand, courtesy of a dead artist? He attempted to think of the journey the letter had to take to reach him at exactly the same time he discovered he wasn't human anymore.

She must have predicted it all, he thought to himself.

Eleanor was the most notorious precog to have ever lived. She had been recruited by the military to train developing mentalists. He had to wonder if she had been aware of just how important this series of events would be. The world knew the United States enlisted fortune tellers, but nobody understood quite how far they could see or what the reach was for their powers.

Conthan paused at the thought. Nearly twenty years later, the nuclear bomb and the President's assassination attempt would be overshadowed by a planetary effect commonly called the Nostradamus Effect. To this day, the exact causes of the event are still subject to speculation, but the most commonly accepted explanation is that a variety of stellar anomalies resulted in some sort of cosmic radiation affecting all of mankind.

Cults began to emerge, claiming Nostradamus had predicted the end of the world and mankind would cease to exist in 2012. Nostradamus himself, believed to be one of the earliest psychics, had foreseen the future of mankind. However, lost in interpretation was that mankind would not end, it would find a way to evolve. Those affected would begin to show signs in the next few years.

The mentalists that once could be measured in the hundreds were no longer the godliest of the human race. The mutagenesis produced a vast array of results, each of the Children showing unique traits. The Children of Nostradamus became more common and the military was forced to respond as their powers became a danger to the general populace. That is when they began to round up anybody with potential.

Conthan sighed deeply as he thought of his childhood friend. He wished he was visiting under better circumstances, but he was happy to be seeing her. She wasn't going to believe what had happened since their last visit.

He leaned his head against the window and looked out to the storm clouds in the distance. A sign read 'Danger Zone, 150 miles.' He closed his eyes and tried to ignore the fact that he was a mouse walking into the lion's den.

The bus began to move forward, vacating the lot. Outside the tinted windows, he watched the city pass him by. In the middle of the night, the Twin Towers remained lit like giant glowing obelisks reaching the gods. Gears began to crank and turn as the lead shielding closed on the windows, rendering the bus immune to the impending radiation from the Danger Zone.

He didn't dare call Gretchen or Sculptee. He always assumed his mouth would land him in a detention center, but being a superpowered human had never crossed his mind. Gretchen was probably pissed; he imagined her going berserk as the Corps put the art show to an end. He hoped everybody made it out without injury.

He turned back to his phone and began searching the web for any coverage of the event. It had happened almost four hours ago and not one live feed from New York showed any interest. He went to the websites of both groups of protestors and saw that there was not only no mention of the attack, but no mention of protesting the show. It didn't surprise him; the government was masterful at manipulating the media. Even The Culling, a mass genocide, was spun as an effort to protect domestic interests.

He paused at the thought. He went back in his browser to the article about Eleanor. "What if she wasn't mad?"

***

The Sheraton had once been glorious. The building was a mere eight stories tall, but standing in the center of the hotel one could look straight up to the skylights above. The red rugs had been vibrant before the cleaning staff had been burned away. Now, the conference rooms were turned into makeshift hospitals and the rooms above were crowded with people attempting to survive on the fringes of society.

Twenty-Seven rubbed the muscle in her left arm. Victor had ordered her to be given a shot for the radiation sickness. He warned her it would keep her alive, even if she wished she could die. After barking that simple command, he had walked off with a group of men to discuss matters of importance with the angel.

What would happen if they knew the angel's secret? She wondered just how much the angel was manipulating them. Twenty-Seven had been young when The Culling took place. She had read the horrific accounts of the military sweeping through homes, killing anybody suspected of being a mentalist. It didn't matter if it was for national security, or for the protection of the human race, it still showed the worst humanity had to offer.

She had only known the angel for a day and already she could tell the woman preferred to be cloaked in mystery and intrigue. She was no different than her, a human, only she was cursed, a Child of Nostradamus.

I am not.

How can you not be one?

Twenty-Seven found a bench overlooking a dingy grand staircase. She could imagine women in beautiful gowns being escorted down the stairs by gentlemen in tuxedos. At one time this would have been the ideal place for a prom or perhaps a wedding. Now, the dirt was married to the carpet, and dings in the brass railing had left it dilapidated and near falling apart.

My gifts emerged before the Nostradamus Effect.

We were not many, but we existed, more hidden than we are now. I survived The Culling because of a wise woman who foresaw a shadow darkening our existence.

Twenty-Seven mulled over the woman's words. She replayed the last sentence and hung on the phrase, "a shadow darkening our existence." She remembered a letter that had once been delivered to her home in Brooklyn.

The hotel melted away in a streak of mixing colors. Twenty-Seven gasped as the world around her began to collapse in on itself. From the colors emerged new scenery, a place she had once lived. She looked down to the mail slot, and the letter floating toward the ground.

Twenty-Seven took a step closer to the door and became aware she was not alone. She turned her head to a mirror mounted in the entryway. Where her reflection should have been, the angel stood, gazing at her, watching her every movement.

What happened next?

Twenty-Seven reached down for the letter, surprised at her lack of fear. Her fingers touched the something and she recalled the sensation of fine linen paper. She admired the address on the front of the envelope. She knew the author was a female by the swirling letters and precision penmanship. She carefully tore at the corner until she could remove the slip within.

She unfolded it and paused at the fanciful script. She turned the envelope over, but there was no return address. She began to read the words.

Dear Samantha,

I have no time to waste in this letter, a shadow darkens our existence. My heart breaks for the abuse you have suffered at the hands of men. There is a chance to break the cycle and make a new life for yourself. I do not offer you simplicity, or even a pleasant journey in the days to come. I do offer you a chance to reclaim a woman you have come to mourn.

72-13-26.

I cannot tell your fate far beyond the wall. In your journeys you will meet an angel. She will need you as a symbol of what she has to gain as she wages a war within. Guide her. If your messenger is slow, go to meet him.

Sincerely,

Eleanor P. Valentine

Before the angel could inquire, Twenty-Seven spoke. "My grandmother used to say that. Do not wait for world to come to you, meet it. She had been a strong woman. She divorced my grandfather during an age where it wasn't acceptable. She became a pariah in her community. But she never looked back."

Twenty-Seven turned to the stairs and began the ascent upward, toward the study. The numbers made no sense, but she knew where she would find the answer. As she approached the door, she hesitated. On the other side was a room she had been scolded for entering even to clean. Her husband treated it as his escape from the world. Here he would drink brandy until he was intoxicated enough to tolerate holding her down and raping her.

She opened the door. She trembled with the first step. As her foot touched the carpet she continued to think of her grandmother. The woman would have fought back. She would have cursed as he smacked her. She would have swung back in defiance. She would have killed him.

Twenty-Seven paused at the thought as if it was the first time it crossed her mind. She was sitting at the desk now. She had the combination to the safe sitting in the bottom right drawer of his desk. With a shaking hand, she spun the numbers until it opened and revealed the firearm inside. With the weight of it in her hand, her heart began to race.

It is a memory, Twenty-Seven. This is not happening now.

The downstairs door slammed shut. Her muscles tensed. She had been here before. He would stand at the threshold to the office. He would bait her. He would tell her she was nothing without him. He would ask her how she would live without his money. He would end the insults with asking what man would want her now that she was used goods.

She pulled the trigger once.

Her husband reached for his chest. He didn't utter a word as he grabbed onto the doorway and fell to his knees. As she approached, he reached forward, grabbing her blouse, exposing her bare breasts. She watched as he died. She stared at the body, numb to emotions telling her she must save him. His body stopped moving and she continued to stare at the demon lying on the ground.

The nightmare had ended.

She reached across the desk and took the phone. She dialed and raised the phone to her ear.

"9-1-1, what's your emergency?"

"I just killed my husband."

As she looked up from the rust-colored desk, standing between her and the man she murdered was a woman in a robe. She blinked several times before she remembered the woman rescuing her in the Outlands. Her memories poured into her mind as she recounted the trial, the prison, the execution at the wall.

This will not be pleasant.

The angel stepped forward, her form floating through the desk. She reached out and touched the trembling woman's shoulders. Between blinks she went from the chaos in her husband's office to standing on the mezzanine of an old hotel. Her hands trembled as she gripped the railing.

I am sorry, Samantha.

She shook her head. The memories started to settle back into place. She let the sensation of cold metal under her hand ground her. "Samantha died."

Or perhaps Twenty-Seven was born.

She leaned over the railing while she pondered the philosophical point of view. It had been just over a day since she was placed in the Outlands. She had befriended an angel and joined a rogue group of humans and now she was waiting to see what came next. In a conference room on the floor below, she could see the angel talking with Victor and several of the other Outlanders.

She walked down the grand staircase, marveling at the splendor. Even years past its prime she could imagine the many people who walked down the stairs and pictured themselves as princesses. She stood at the doorway to the conference room and listened.

"You want us to attack the facility?" Victor asked.

The angel nodded. "They are coming for you. It houses the largest collection of Children on the globe. Inside are people of power, people whose only crime is an astronomical anomaly. Those Children of Nostradamus are allies waiting to be acquired."

A man next to Victor shook his head, obviously displeased with the idea. "You want us to die to save them?"

"When did your heart become so closed off you began to think of your fellow man as 'them,' Rodrick?"

"We have had our run-ins with the government. You know we have no love for them. But what about my people? They're going to die."

"You're dying now," the angel said.

Twenty-Seven knew what she meant. The moment they entered the Danger Zone their exposure to radiation began to increase. They were living close enough to hot zones now that it would slowly cause burns similar to Victor's and eventually it would kill them. Her freedom came with a doomsday clock, and each minute it ticked down.

"What are you offering, angel?"

"Your home is killing you. We will take you north, into Canada. We can make you new identities. We can give you a chance to survive."

"We will not give up what's ours."

Victor held up his hand, silencing the man. "What do you want from us?"

"We will need your vehicles, weapons, and anybody who can fight."

Rodrick pushed away Victor's hand. "What are you going to do to help us fight your fight?"

Twenty-Seven eyed a man and two girls walking into the meeting. She stayed hidden just out of sight of the room. She didn't dare interrupt their meeting. While the angel had assured her they would take her in, so far they had treated her like an outsider.

The man looked as if he was from a science fiction movie, his torso covered in leather straps that ended in shoulder pads. The leather didn't leave much to the imagination, showing his build, that of a football player who had seen a few too many beers. His hair was closely shaved to his head, leaving just enough of a shadow to show he had any. The rest of his body showed no body hair at all, leaving him almost glistening in the neon lights. His face was hardened, not mean looking, but showing that he had a story to tell and not much of it would be happy.

One of the girls must have been his sister. Twenty-Seven could tell by the chiseled jaw they were siblings. Half her head was shaved while the rest of her magenta hair fell onto the side, covering one eye. Similar to her brother, she wore little clothing. A simple band of cloth hid her breasts and her short spandex shorts seemed to elongate legs leading into black chunky boots. Of the three, she looked the most ready to kick ass.

The last girl seemed reserved compared to the others. She wore a skirt that reached past her knees, slit up to the waist on each side giving her full range of motion. Her sleeveless blouse hugged her body, giving her a modest appearance. A hijab covering her head, mixed with her dark complexion made Twenty-Seven think she must be Middle Eastern.

"Who are they?" asked Victor.

The angel turned to her companions. "God has provided us with emissaries."

Twenty-Seven gasped as a bright light filled the room. The man caused lightning to jump from his body to his arms. One of the girl's arms started to glow a bold blue.

"Children," Twenty-Seven whispered in awe.

***

"You're just another freak," said a large black man. "Your stint with the Paladins is over."

A group of young military men began whooping and hollering at the statement. Jasmine stood in the middle of the group and turned to stare at her provoker. "Got the balls to back that up, Vlad?"

He stood, pulled off his utility vest, and peeled his black t-shirt over his head. "More balls than you can handle," he said, walking closer to her.

The common room, not large, was mostly empty except for a couch on one end and several crates they used as seating. They didn't spend much time in their bunk area. Her team was known for going to the field every opportunity they could; what little downtime they had, they spent at the bar. They were the best and they drank like they were the best.

Jasmine stood in the middle of her six-man squad. She had been addressing rookie when Vlad had interrupted her. The man was dangerously thick, his muscles flexing without effort. "Stand down, soldier."

"Ain't even fucking human," Vlad spit back at her. He had been her second in command for nearly six months. She didn't like him. He was less a soldier and more of a bloodthirsty killer. His reason for being in the field had no honor; he simply wanted to add to his body count.

The crowd got quiet at the statement. "Only reason you outrank us is because we need you in front to take bullets for us," he said. It always came back to this. She'd had arguments with him before about being a Child of Nostradamus. He saw her as weak. She saw him as jealous.

Before he could open his mouth again she brought her fist up and clocked him across the jaw. His head barely moved from the impact. He reached up and wiped blood from his lip. He spit on the floor and clenched his fists tightly. "Oh, this is going to be fun."

He brought up his knee. She jumped back before it made contact. His muscles were beginning to bulge more than normal. She had no doubt he was activating his enhancements. There was no way he could match her physically without the technology making him more than human.

She snarled at him. "I'm not human? I've got more original parts than you."

He lunged, trying to strike her in the nose. She knocked his fist out wide, amazed at how quickly his enhancements were increasing his strength. She could feel the tension in his arm, the muscles beginning to speed up. She reached behind his neck and brought him down onto her knee as hard as she could. It was only a matter of seconds before his response time outmatched hers.

He staggered backward. "What? No powers? Think you can take me any other way?" She had respected him despite his bloodthirsty tendencies. He had listened to orders like a good soldier, but she knew this day was inevitable. She had no sympathies and certainly no respect for a soldier creating dissent amongst the ranks.

She didn't need to activate her powers for a typical fight. Thankfully being a Child of Nostradamus came with natural boosts to her abilities. Her speed, her reflexes, and her stamina were twice that of any man, and her resiliency to pain and damage far exceeded that of any human.

She focused as her assailant lunged with another fist. She grabbed it and sidestepped him until they were back to back. She reached over her shoulder, clasping her hands around his head. Leaning forward, she launched him onto the ground. She thrust her fist down at the man's skull. He rolled out of the way, and her knuckles smashed the pavement, leaving small cracks. She hissed from the impact of the blow as the bone in her hand resisted turning to powder.

He spun around, using his legs to kick her feet out from under her. The crowd had begun to roar. It wasn't abnormal for sparring matches to take place in the common area. There were more dried puddles of blood on the floor than could be counted. The crowd didn't understand the unsaid tension being hashed out between the two powerhouses.

He was on top of her, reaching around her neck, squeezing down on her windpipe. "No powers, huh? Want to die a martyr?"

She punched him in the throat, causing him to lean backward while straddling her torso. She reached up with her legs and hooking them around his neck, pulling him back to the ground. She punched hard at his groin and felt his entire body tense up from the blow.

Jasmine untangled herself from Vlad and stood up. She didn't flinch, staring down the rest of her squad. It was bad enough she wasn't human in their eyes, but occasionally that was overshadowed by the fact she had breasts. She had grown accustomed to being one of the guys and reminding them she was in charge. "Anybody else want to give it a try?"

The man on the floor swung at her, connecting with her stomach. The air rushed out of her lungs. She pushed him back onto the ground and stood behind him with her hands on his neck. She locked eyes with the new kid as she tightened her grip on Vlad. "The punishment for insubordination?"

Sims stood up, realizing this was more than a friendly sparring match. He held out his hand, trying to talk her down. "Don't do it, sir."

She didn't blink as the fear began to register on the fresh meat's face. "I will not have it on my team." She spun Vlad's neck. The crack echoed throughout the room as his body jerked one last time. She panted as it fell to the ground. It was him or her, and with each battle against her captors, she felt her humanity slip away.

Sims pulled out a gun from his hip and pointed it at Jasmine. She held Vlad's dog tags in her hand as she stared down the barrel. The metal felt inviting, calling to her abilities. As the soldier pulled the trigger she focused on the steel of the dog tags.

Pain rippled through her body, almost forcing her to scream aloud. She felt the bullet touch her skin and impale on itself, never penetrating her hide.

She didn't hesitate as she walked over to Sims and put her hand around his neck. "Insubordination is puni—"

An electric current coursed through her skull, searing her insides. It felt as if a red-hot poker was burning behind her eyes. Her stomach began to turn at the agony. She puked on the ground while curling up in a ball.

"Jasmine," came another man's voice. "What is the reason for a dead soldier in my facility?"

Sims looked at the man in a business suit. "Vlad challenged her. She took him down."

"I see," said the man. "And you felt the need to fire upon a superior officer?"

"She killed him," he said. "Of course I'm going to defend one of my own. She snapped his neck like it was nothing."

The man in the suit cleared his throat. "She is one of you. This is not humans versus powers, this is us versus the world. Do you read me, Sims?"

"Yes, sir."

"Report to lockup. We'll see how thirty days in solitary treats you."

Sims nodded without question, more fearful of the man in the suit than anything he could encounter in lockup. The businessman eyed the next soldier in line. "See to it that the rest of your platoon is ready for departure. Some of you are in dire need of skin grafts. Make sure everybody has been cleared by the Body Shop."

"Yes, sir," they replied in unison with a salute.

Jasmine grit her teeth at the mention of the monster-maker's lab. Once upon a time, it had been a resource to save wounded soldiers and repair damage from the field. Over time they had taken a more aggressive approach, removing limbs and replacing them with "enhancements." The soldiers in her squad were some of the most heavily modified people on the planet. Muscles were laced with nanotechnology increasing strength and speed. Parts of their brains were modified with circuitry and chipboards, allowing them to react quicker, access the military networks, and process data at uncanny speeds. She couldn't help but look at most of them and see there were barely souls contained in the electronic husks.

The suit walked closer. He kneeled next to her

on the floor, smiling at her grimace. "Jasmine," he said with a flat tone, "you're coming with me. Something has come to our attention."

She coughed as she got onto her hands and knees. She took a deep breath and tried to focus her thoughts. The pain radiating from the base of her skull made it impossible for her to turn off her abilities. For the moment she was trapped inside her metallic skin.

"Yes, sir," she hacked, spitting onto the ground.

The man waited for her to pull herself to her feet. She was several inches shorter than him, but he understood he did nothing to intimidate her. He reached out and touched her cheek, pressing hard enough it should have hurt. He ran his hand along her neck, giving her throat a push as well. She tried to hide her disgust at him treating her like an oddity, but she understood he was a scientist and consumed with the Children of Nostradamus.

"You are quite remarkable."

She didn't reply to his musings. She was busy trying to control her breathing and forget the searing pain that had rendered her a pile of mush on the ground. She didn't blink as he poked at her.

"I would have so much fun with you in my lab, Jasmine."

"I'm sure you would," she hissed, making sure her annoyance was obvious.

He reached into his breast pocket and took out his pocket square. He held it out for her. "Perhaps another time. Right now, the general would like to meet with you. We have something that we need to review. It could be a rogue Class I."

Her eyebrow rose while she wiped her face clean. A pyro and now a Class I? She couldn't hide her surprise. She turned back to the man lying on the floor in a heap. She examined the rest of her squad, still standing at attention, to see if anybody was giving her wayward glances. She respected them as much as she could. She didn't like this arrangement, but if she was going to do it, she was going to do it right.

She followed the man down the hall. Despite his business suit, she knew him as the head researcher in the Body Shop, a subsidiary of the Genesis Division. The Genesis Division oversaw all aspects of super humans. From researching them, to detaining them, to finding ways to fight them, it was the marriage of the military and a civilian company trying to right the wrongs of the world.

He stopped walking but didn't turn to address her face to face. "Still feeling pain while you transform?"

She knew it wasn't concern; it was scientific curiosity. "Yes."

"I'm sure we could find a way to enhance your abilities. Perhaps dampen your pain receptors. I'm sure we could also find a way to speed up your transformation."

"No," she said flatly. "I won't be a cyborg."

He turned. The smile across his face disturbed her more than if he was angry. "What humanity do you have to lose, Jasmine?" he asked, walking down the hall. "You're not even human."

She bit her tongue as she followed the man. She hated him, loathed his very being, but she knew not to piss him off. He had no problem flipping the switch and frying her brain. To him, she was nothing more than a genetic abnormality to study.

She stopped for a moment to see through a set of glass doors leading into the Body Shop. She shivered as she saw the technicians poking at one of the soldiers. She valued her humanity too much to undergo modifications. She watched as a shirtless man held up his mechanical hand and flexed his fingers. She could see the look of power flash across his face.

Years ago the Body Shop had been part of a relief fund giving wounded veterans access to artificial limbs. When the charity was taken over by a private company and partnered with the Genesis Division, the program jumped leaps and bounds. Limbs became computerized, leading to nanotechnology being infused into parts of the body. The rich and powerful began to treat them like minor body modifications.

When the military involved themselves, the focus turned from helping wounded veterans to preventing them from being wounded. Now it was common for eyes and eardrums to be augmented to make a better soldier. Military who rose through the ranks became frequent visitors of the Body Shop, enhancing their muscles and replacing entire limbs.

Jasmine shivered at the thought.

Through several more corridors, they reached the war room. There were a dozen techs sitting at computers surrounding a massive table in the middle of the room. Every tech paused at her entrance. She may be in charge of the squadron, but nobody let her forget she wasn't one of them.

"Jasmine," came the general's booming voice, "we have a job for you." She watched the large man's face as she walked closer to the massive table. In the entire complex, only the portly man was capable of intimidating her. His sheer size was impressive. Coming in just shy of seven feet, he must have weighed somewhere near four hundred pounds. He was not somebody who blended into a crowd. She had watched him school veteran soldiers on the mats before. He might be large, but he was muscular and in control of his body. If she hadn't known better, she might mistake him for a Child of Nostradamus.

"Reporting, sir," she said, clicking her heels together and saluting.

"Jasmine," he said with a tone that instantly told her the severity of the situation. "Your squad has a job."

"Details, sir?"

He waved his hand over the table and half a dozen screens appeared, hovering in midair. She reached out and pulled one closer to her. "What am I seeing?"

"A Corps Soldier was killed last night, shot by his own gun."

"Suicide?"

"Somebody else shot him."

"Sir, our guns are genetically programmed…"

"I know," he said, gritting his teeth. "If this case wasn't peculiar, you wouldn't be standing here."

She closed her mouth, worried she was already on the verge of aggravating the massive man.

She stayed quiet, waiting for the general to give her a better clue of what they were dealing with. He flipped his wrist and a screen began playing back a low-quality video. From the angle of the film, she knew it was taken with the soldier's ocular implants. "His implant recorded this."

She watched as the soldier's gun pointed at a man wearing an inhibitor collar. The gun projected a narrow laser and dropped the Child. Before she could make out anything more, the implant seemed to go on the fritz and the video feed became static.

"That was a powered," she stated.

"Registered," he said. "Jed Zappens, barely a Class III. His powers involved auditory mimicking. There is no way he could have stopped a Corps soldier."

"The other man?"

The general looked at her with a serious expression. "We believe he is a Class I threat. Unfortunately we can't give you many more details than that. His powers could involve telekinesis or spatial relocation," he said.

Jasmine examined the static image. She had been a member of the Corps for years and she could count on one hand how many Class I's they had encountered. She saw a glimpse of panic on the perp's face and wondered if it had been an accident.

She stiffened her muscles and eyed the general. "What do we know of him?"

"I'm downloading all available information to you now. You'll be heading out to the Danger Zone to intercept him."

"The Danger Zone?"

The general gave a stifled laugh. "He kills a Corps soldier and then he takes the only bus from New York to the Danger Zone. Either something is about to go down, or we have one seriously stupid shit on our hands."

Jasmine checked the image of the kid again. He could only be in his twenties, and barely so. He looked like any other young man, nothing special sticking out other than the hint of a tattoo creeping up his neck. "We're on it, sir."

"Jasmine." She raised her eyebrow at him. "We will be providing two synthetics to accompany you into the Danger Zone along with your squad. Your squad undertook a beating earlier. I will be making sure the Body Shop outfits them with some new enhancements."

She wondered why the extra firepower. While she was considered to be in charge of the squad, she oftentimes felt they were there to watch her as well. At any moment, if the general ordered it, they would turn on her. She knew that even at the top of the food chain, she was still less than them.

"Jasmine." He stopped her. "One more thing. We put you in charge of this squad because you're ruthless and effective at your command. But have no doubts, you're a powered, and killing humans is not condoned."

"Yes, sir," she said.

"Do you have the situation under control?"

"It's five by five, sir," she said. "Had to take care of some obedience issues."

"Good," he said. "You're a valuable asset, but do not question that I will terminate you if you become a liability."

She grit her teeth and nodded.

She put her hand over the table and watched the meter of his wristband fill as it began downloading all the information. Time for the final question. "Apprehend or terminate, sir?"

The general paused at the question and looked at the scientist. She knew without a doubt the head of the labs would love to get his hands on a Class I. It was rumored he conducted experiments on the powered far beyond simple exploration. She had begun to suspect the military allowed him access to powered people she acquired, but it was the private company in charge of the Genesis Division that allowed him to delve into his darker sciences.

The general's face was vacant, showing no emotion as he spoke. "If he is deemed containable, apprehend."

Otherwise terminate, she thought.

She turned and walked up the steps, aware every person in the room was staring at her. She exited, trying not to grumble out loud. She may respect the general, but she didn't have to like him.

"Another one sent to his grave," she whispered as she headed toward her squad.

***

The complex was visible from more than a mile away. It was a fortress, a giant cube within forty-foot-tall walls. Every so often along the wall, a tower rose in the air, housing massive guns following the bus as it neared its destination. The land around the facility was flat and barren, making it impossible to surprise the guards.

A monitor hanging over Conthan's seat displayed the feed from the cameras mounted on the roof of the bus. He had been here once before, long before the wall and towers had been erected. The facility seemed ominous before, even a bit frightening, but now it was a military infested fortress. Soldiers walked along the wall, guns strapped around their shoulders. In front of the gate, two large humanoid mechs scanned the area while holding their weapons directly at the bus.

"Holy shit," he muttered under his breath.

The bus pulled to a stop and the driver flipped on the intercom. "Exit one at a time. You will be searched and scanned. Please be aware that the Corps will terminate any threat from this moment until your departure."

Conthan gulped. He looked down at his hands and prayed there wasn't some sort of technology capable of explaining what he was. He stood and filed out of the bus with the others. Several guards carrying assault rifles greeted them. He knew he wasn't in the civilized world anymore. They were on the edge of the Danger Zone, a desolate area void of human inhabitants. Any further toward Boston they would begin to experience symptoms of radiation poisoning. Off in the distance, he could almost see the fence separating them from the Danger Zone. The fence seemed puny in comparison to the defenses surrounding the facility.

One of the guards held up a small orb and it began to hover in midair. A red laser emerged, working its way up a newly arrived employee. Conthan watched as the guards looked to the computers mounted on their wrists. The readouts were flashing so fast he was shocked they could keep up with the information.

He watched the guard with the orb closely and could see his eyes were more silver than brown in color. It gave away the bionic implants, and the small exposed circuit behind his ear was most likely a radio receiver, which meant he had some sort of auditory augmentation. Conthan could only guess he had some sort of muscle enhancement, and by the look of his hands, they were also robotic.

He was surprised that for all their alterations, they were hunting powered people for being different. Powered people were altered against their will. These humans had gone out of their way to sell their humanity for upgrades. He had the same thought of the guards at the art gallery, but those Corps members paled in comparison to these soldiers. He wondered if it was because of their detail or because of their rank that they were provided with so much time at the Body Shop.

The small metal ball hovered in front of him. He held his breath as the red beam crossed his body. He had nothing to hide—almost nothing to hide. The guards stared at their computer screens and paused for a moment. Conthan tensed as the seconds dragged on. The scan finished and the ball moved on to the next person in line, however, one of the guards began to approach him.

"Conthan Cowan," the guard said.

Conthan's body tensed at the name. "Yes, sir?"

he said squeamishly.

"We rarely have returning visitors."

Conthan choked on his words. "I, uhm…" He paused. "I'm here to see Sarah Mathis. She was a close friend."

The man started to reply but paused. Conthan could tell he was receiving orders from somewhere. His eyes came back into focus. "She'll be brought to one of the conference rooms to speak with you."

Conthan was a bit shocked he was able to get access to her with no advanced warning. He expected to have to pitch a fit and scream about crimes against humanity. The ease almost made him more suspicious of what was going on. "Thank you."

The letter was neatly tucked into the inner pocket of his leather jacket. He tried to understand how Eleanor could have orchestrated this entire event. Had she known this would happen? Was there a man working on the inside? Did somebody else receive a letter allowing him passage? He was thankful for the help beyond the grave, but his stomach tightened. There was a plot unfolding around him and he didn't like that Eleanor hadn't revealed the whole story.

The soldier nodded and moved on to the remaining people in line. The man reached the last individual in the line and the red beam began to scan him. Conthan watched as it reached his waistline and paused for a second, then continued.

It got quiet, so quiet it was awkward. Nature seemed to hold its breath. A wheezing sound could be heard and then a *thunk*. The man at the end of the line buckled and fell to the ground.

The soldiers turned back to the crowd. "He was armed."

Conthan took a moment to process that the sound had been a bullet flying through the air. The *thunk* had been it penetrating the man's skull. Nobody flinched, as if it was a common occurrence. Nobody had any questions about what they had witnessed, or at least none they would voice aloud. Even the couple of civilians were so terrified they kept their eyes forward and avoided eye contact with the guards.

A soldier kneeled and ripped open the man's pants. He lifted up a small gun-like object. "Ceramic pistol with three rounds. He thought our scanners only detected metal." The guards chuckled for a moment.

What the hell have I gotten myself into? Conthan thought.

Chapter Nine

May 17th, 2032 3:01PM

...will be a time when you begin to doubt yourself. This doubt is not rooted in your own insecurities, but in the role you play in a grander scheme. To this point, you have played by the rules set forth by your position. Today is the day you begin to feel the doubt consume you. There will be a single moment in which you find yourself questioning the beliefs that have allowed you to survive.

I cannot challenge your beliefs, as I cannot see into the soul of an individual. I can, however, give you a path that will allow you to begin atoning for your past. The moment you ask yourself if what you're doing is right, simply pause. In that moment's

hesitation you will find yourself set free.
  Be at peace.
With Regards,
Eleanor P. Valentine

***

The silence in the small ten-by-ten room was absolute. Conthan was amazed by the perfection of the walls; it appeared as if there were no seams. There were only two plastic chairs mounted to the floor, and a small surveillance orb hovering in the corner.

He reached out to the small orb. As his hand approached the sphere, it moved higher, just beyond his fingertips. He pressed his hands against the wall, searching for a point where the angles changed, but found they messed with his sense of touch as much as his eyesight. He jumped as a hiss filled the room. Hydraulic locks retracted within the walls as a door slid open, a seam appearing in the wall. Standing in the opening was a portly man wearing a designer business suit.

"Mr. Cowan," he said calmly, "I find it curious that you have returned to the Danger Zone."

"I'm curious like that."

The man tapped the ID badge pinned to his chest, similar to the one they pinned on Conthan at the gate. "The radiation here can be somewhat alarming for those not granted certain precautions."

Conthan was already tired of listening to him. He could tell the man liked the sound of his own voice and was going to do everything in his power to lord over him. Against his nature, Conthan bit his tongue and let him have his moment.

"You do not like me?"

Conthan's eyebrow lifted at the accuracy of the statement. "I have a general distaste for everybody."

"Such a cynic, for someone so young. I am the Warden of the Danger Zone facility," he said, stepping into the room. "You are only being granted this audience because I find your friend an astounding research subject. Perhaps she will cooperate more with a friendly face supporting her."

"Bullshit," Conthan mumbled.

"Speak your mind, Mr. Cowan," the man said. "Your words are written across your face."

Conthan paused at the statement. The man was being horribly cryptic, trying to bait Conthan into some sort of argument. He couldn't figure out the game being played. He was beginning to suspect he was an unwilling participant in a bigger scheme.

Instead of participating, Conthan shrugged his shoulders in disinterest. "I'm just here to see Sarah."

The man's eyebrow rose. Conthan smirked at the reaction; he had spent years in these games of wit with his foster mother. The man could be a mind reader and Conthan would find a way to dodge the game.

Both men waited for the other to react. Conthan wondered how much of the Warden's bulk was muscle. Conthan imagined leaping into the air, driving his knuckles into the man's jaw. He wondered if the man would react or accept the blow to prove he was stronger. Conthan watched his eyes study him, predicting his next move.

"So be it Mr. Cowan," the Warden said, "I will be back to debrief you."

"I'm sure you will," Conthan replied.

The Warden turned about and exited. Several moments later, two guards walked into the room half escorting, half dragging Sarah with them. Conthan watched as they sat her down in the chair. She offered no resistance as they put cuffs on each of her wrists, leading to a circular object they set down on the floor. With the flick of a button, the cuffs magnetized and secured themselves to the floor, keeping her hands stationary at her side.

"You will have ten minutes," said one of the guards. "Your interaction will be monitored, and should any action be considered aggressive, you will be terminated."

A guard pressed a button on the back of his glove. The orb in the air buzzed to life. A red beam scanned the room and then vanished. The ball hovered just above their heads as the guards stepped outside. It remained stationary, resting on the edge of the room, watching them. The door hissed again, closing into place, and the seams vanished as if they were never there.

"Sarah," Conthan said, "how are you?"

Her body looked like an insect with its exoskeleton on top of muscle. He could see the inset of her eye sockets, and within, beautiful blue eyes. She didn't look like the woman he had once known, but he was delighted to see she was still alive. He resisted reaching out and taking her hand, but he was sure he wasn't hiding the shock written across his face.

"Sarah?"

She didn't respond to his voice. He got to his knees in front of her and looked at the hovering ball of metal. He reached out and touched her hand, the sphere not moving as his fingers creeped along hers. The bone felt sharp under his fingertips, reminding him of a bird's talons. "Sarah, what have they done to you?"

He rested his hand on hers and squeezed the boney appendage gently. "Are you in there?"

Her eyes shifted slightly, making contact with his. He felt a bit of hope until he realized she was looking through him like he wasn't there. He reached up and touched a spot on her cheek that gave way to exposed skin. "Can you hear me, Sarah?"

Conthan closed his eyes. Tears rolled down his cheek. He had waited so long to see her, and even sitting in front of her now, he felt she was miles away. He smiled at her. "I had my first gallery show," he said, not knowing what else to talk about. "You'd be embarrassed."

He could feel the words catch in his throat. "They were paintings of you. Remember that drawing I did sophomore year? That was the idea for the whole thing. It was amazing to see a room full of people admiring you. It was going great until all hell broke loose. It was great though."

He saw her lips shift into a fleeting smile. He wasn't sure what was wrong, but somewhere inside the husk of calcification was his friend. "Someday

I'll come back and I'll show you the oil painting I did. It was almost as beautiful as you."

He was staring at her face when he realized the room was getting darker. He looked up to where the metal ball was hovering. After a few seconds it was swallowed by the shadows. The room grew dark enough that he couldn't see the walls. He stood and turned about. Other than Sarah, the room was gone. He couldn't explain why, but he was certain they were no longer standing in the cell.

"Be calm," said a gentle voice.

The hair on the back of his neck stood on end. He recognized the voice from the other night. "Who are you?"

He spun around to see a middle-aged woman wearing a flowing gown. He was struck by how bright she appeared in the void of darkness. "Be calm, Conthan," she said. "I am here to help you again."

"How did you…" He paused before he finished the statement. He didn't know much about powered people, but he was fully aware this was some sort of mentalist. They were hunted and killed on sight. "A telepath?"

She nodded. "Conthan, you have to listen to me," she said. "You are not safe here."

"No shit," he said. "I'm some sort of freak and for some reason I came to the most secure facility in the world because a note told me to."

The woman's brow furrowed as she processed the information. Her eyes were deep pools; he found himself fixed, caught in her gaze. "You received a letter from Eleanor."

"How do you know that?"

"You are not the only one she is guiding," she said. "My letter told me that you would be here. It told me that I must reach out to you and do whatever I must to protect you."

"Why me?"

She shrugged. "Eleanor couldn't see the future beyond our interaction. Something about you is extremely important."

"What does Sarah have to do with this?"

The woman held her hands out to her side and he could see her take several breaths. Her face scrunched up in concentration. "Say what you must, I can only do this for a moment."

"Conthan?"

He turned around to see Sarah. Where she had been covered in bone before, she was now the flesh and blood girl he had first met. "What happened?" he asked, wrapping her in a hug.

"Conthan, you need to get out of here."

"Why? What's wrong?"

"This place isn't what you think it is," she said, looking over her shoulder. "It's a research facility, but I don't think it has anything to do with the government. The Warden..." She paused. "He's not human."

As quickly as she had appeared, she faded into the darkness. Conthan panicked and looked back to the woman in robes. "What happened to her?"

"This is far more taxing than I anticipated," she said calmly. "I couldn't keep her here as well. He knows we are here." The woman's face looked strained. Her soft features were beginning to give way, revealing a multitude of wrinkles. Her skin melted into a sickly green.

The woman grit her teeth. "Conthan," she hissed, "we're going to help you. But…" For a moment the woman in front of him transformed, her skin a dark green and her hair the darkest black he had even seen. "We are going to need your help."

He began to freak out. "What can I do?"

"I will help you," she said, "but do not fight me."

"I'm not fighting you," he said, perplexed.

"Beware the Warden," cried the woman as arms reached out of the shadows and pulled her backward into the nothingness.

Conthan felt the darkness close in on him. As he opened his eyes, he realized he was still in the room, kneeling in front of his friend. Sarah's affect hadn't changed. None of it had been real, he thought. He pulled his hand away from her cheek and saw that she had shed a tear. He wiped it away from her cheek and heard the familiar hiss of the hydraulic locks.

"Mr. Cowan," came the Warden's voice. "Come with me."

Conthan looked to his friend and then to the large man. He could hear Sarah's words echoing in his head. What about the man was there to trust at this point? Everything about him seemed creepy, and Conthan was not looking forward to another exchange with the arrogant prick.

He followed the man down the hallway, amazed to see there were very few guards. He assumed the entire building was automated, the locks and cameras feeding into some central hub. He reached another locked door and watched as the Warden leaned in and let a small sensor scan his eyes. The door opened and they entered a part of the building that looked more like the interior of a mansion than a prison facility.

"I thought we could talk in my office."

Conthan passed two guards as they entered. Unlike the guards who escorted Sarah into the cell, these two had blank looks on their faces. Their smiles seemed to be permanent fixtures. Instead of military attire, they wore beaten leather jackets. They were out of place in the facility, but it was their creepy smiles that disturbed him the most.

The Warden's office was covered in decadent wood paneling and a lavish carpet. The massive desk was flanked by a leather couch and several monitors mounted to the wall. Despite the plush décor, Conthan was very aware he was still a hostage inside the facility. There were dozens of guards ready to gun him down the moment he presented any sort of opposition to the Warden.

He thought back to the letter, why had it suggested he come to such a dangerous place. He was in one of the most secure facilities in North America, shy of a military barracks. And even worse, he was a powered individual in a place where powered people were housed, studied, and killed.

"What brings you here, Conthan?"

The Warden spoke as if he knew Conthan's secret but wanted him to confess. "I came to see a childhood friend."

"I see."

"Your smug tone is kind of irritating," Conthan replied flatly.

"My smug tone comes from years of studying people. What I find odd right now…" He paused. "You are an anomaly. Nobody returns to the Danger Zone, especially none that aren't invited."

"I'm special," Conthan said, "so sue me."

"I suspect that," the Warden said, settling into the chair behind his desk. "The question is, what is special about you?"

"I've been told I have a mouth that won't quit," he said.

The Warden avoided the bait and stared at the young man. He was studying him and Conthan had no idea what he was looking for. "What is it you want from me?" asked Conthan.

"I want answers."

The Warden leaned in, resting his elbows on the desk. Conthan felt the man's eyes boring a hole into him, and for a moment a stinging sensation began behind his eyes. He grit his teeth and let out a slight hiss. "If you're just going to stare at me like a piece of meat, I think I can be on my way."

The Warden's eyes went wide as he leaned back in his chair. "There is indeed something special about you, Conthan Cowan."

Conthan knew something had just happened to alert the Warden and he wasn't sure what it was. Since last night there had been far too many weird situations for him to figure out on the go. He needed somebody to explain the secret world of superpowers to him. He thought of the woman in the robes and he wished she was there to help him.

So far, she had been the only one appearing to support the stupid decision to come here.

"Why did Sarah say not to trust you?"

The Warden's face showed genuine surprise. Conthan had lost time and time again to his mother's mental battles. He found the fastest way to unsettle your prey was to be honest.

"She spoke to you?"

"Yes," Conthan said honestly. "She said that I shouldn't trust you. And I am beginning to believe she has good reason. What could that be?"

The Warden regained his composure and eyed one of the monitors to the side of his desk. He stood up and walked over to the screen. "Play back conference room A, visitation of Sarah Mathis."

The monitor sped through the encounter and the Warden looked to Conthan. "It appears she never said anything and yet you speak with conviction. How did she relay her lack of trust to you? I think you may have overplayed your hand, Mr. Cowan."

"I think you think I'm playing a game."

"We are all pawns in a much larger game," he said, walking over to Conthan.

The Warden reached out, faster than his large frame should allow, grabbing at Conthan's leather jacket. "What secrets are you hiding, boy?" He placed his palm on Conthan's forehead. His hand was large enough to encompass Conthan's head, squeezing it, holding him in place.

The room faded away into nothingness. Focused on the Warden's sneering face in front of him, Conthan backed away, stumbling over his own shoe and falling. The large man began to turn fuzzy, blurring before his eyes. "What the fuck?"

The Warden took a step forward and his image faded away until a shadow replaced him. Whips of black tendrils rose off the shadow as if he was a man made of smoke. Conthan's heart raced as he saw the frightening transformation. "You're not human."

"No more than you are, Mr. Cowan," said the shadow.

"Sarah could see you," Conthan said. "She knew what you are."

"The question is, how did she tell you without speaking those words?"

A wisp of smoke shot out and pushed against Conthan's head. The Warden's avatar began to growl. Conthan swatted at the smoke, trying to keep it from touching his face. "Even the Children of Nostradamus have a breaking point. How do you continue to evade me?"

For a moment, the shadowy figure didn't move. Conthan was reminded of the soldiers at the art gallery and the way they paused as they received instructions from afar. He had to assume something was going on in the room they were standing in. He wrestled against the Warden's grip, pulling his jacket free just as the woman emerged from the shadows.

She had been docile, even delicate. Now she was enraged. With each step her robes transformed into armor surrounding her small form. Behind, emerging from folds, large angelic wings spanned twice her height. She reached by her side and pulled out a long sword.

Her eyes were filled with fire. "Run!"

The last image he had of the two was the shadow turning toward the angel, reaching out to block the impending blow of the sword. Conthan gasped for air as the light rushed in on him. The Warden stood in front of him, his body appearing lifeless, taking breaths but not reacting to the world around him. Conthan imagined himself reaching around the man's neck and squeezing the life from his body. He could end it right then. He shook the image from his mind. Only yesterday he was the wise-ass artist and now he was contemplating killing his second person.

"What the fuck is going on?" mumbled Conthan.

He looked to the monitors to see guards outside the facility running with weapons held high. There were a dozen ragged vehicles riding outside the perimeter. People inside the cars fired weapons at the guards. He stared at the monitors when one flickered to the image of a black man wearing sunglasses. The man tapped the glass. "Conthan," he said, "we're springing you out. I'll open the doors."

"Who are you?"

The man's face showed no emotion. "We're the cavalry."

Conthan wasn't assured by that. His options were to walk into a firefight or to stay here and deal with the Warden when he returned to his body. He felt it was only a matter of moments before guards busted through the doors and began firing on him.

He turned to see the two figures in leather coats. They were lifeless, unmoving, and appearing vacant. It was the same look that Sarah had earlier. He wondered if somehow the Warden gave them commands. Telepaths were known to take control of people and force them to do things they didn't want; perhaps this was the same ordeal.

Conthan jumped as the door to the office opened. To his surprise, there were no guards on the other side. He hesitated, looking about to see if somebody was approaching the Warden's office.

"Run, Conthan," he said to himself.

He began to run.

Chapter Ten

May 17th, 2032 3:30PM

Conthan skidded down the hallway, running into the wall as he rounded the corner. He reached an intersection that led to all locked doors. He stared up at the camera with panic etched on his face. It was bad enough he was powered and at the facility, but he was pretty sure he had assaulted the Warden, evaded capture, and was now part of a conspiracy.

"This day is just sucking."

The light above one of the doors turned green. As it opened, he could see one of the small metal balls flying down the hallway, attempting to catch up to him. The lens on the sphere glowed an angry red as it closed the distance. Conthan jumped inside the door and slammed it shut, cutting off the drone. The space beyond was like the others, a long corridor passing around the outer perimeter of the building.

He looked up to the security camera. "You have me running in circles. Find me a door that goes outside."

Somebody yelled on the other side. The light above the door turned green but before it could be opened, it turned red again. He hoped the guy helping him was smarter than the guards. He waited and saw none of the other doors were lighting up. He began to panic. "Get me out of here."

He started walking down the hallway until a loud hissing sound erupted from one of the walls. He paused and listened as the sound grew louder. It sounded like something was cutting through the metal. "What the fuck?"

He looked up to the camera and ran to the next door. He punched at the keypad and realized there was no way he could get through. He put his back to the wall as the hissing got louder.

"Going down swinging," he said as he balled his fists.

He walked closer to the sound and prepared to fight back. "Superpowers I don't know how to use," he said, "don't fail me now."

He watched as the metal wall turned red. "What the hell?" The red started to expand as the tip of a torch breached the wall. He backed up as flame continued to melt through the exterior. He realized it wasn't a torch cutting through the metal. On the other side was a young girl, her outstretched hands pulsing a light that turned from red to white, vaporizing the walls around her. "Almost got you."

"Who the hell are you?"

"The rest of the cavalry."

"How many of you are there?"

"Not enough," she said with a devious smile.

The computer guy lacked facial expression, but this girl, she seemed to have a wild gleam in her eyes.

"We're going to die."

"Sooner or later," the girl retorted.

She pushed her hands down and the last of the wall melted away. She shook her arms and the pulsing blue light vanished. Nothing was left but lines of heat radiating off her petite hands. "Neat trick, huh?"

"Where are we going?"

She reached up to her ear and pushed a button. "Do we have a ticket out of here?"

She frowned for a moment when nobody replied. "Apparently our headsets are being hacked. So we're going to do a lot of running, maybe some dodging, and if we live, we'll call it a good day."

"You're fucking crazy," he said.

"I was once," she said, reaching out to him.

He instinctively reached out and grabbed her hand. He was surprised that it wasn't any hotter than his own. She pulled him quickly, scalding metal searing through his pants as his leg brushed the side of the melted wall. She dropped down to a knee and looked at his leg. "You'll be fine until we get out of here."

Conthan didn't dare look at the singed fabric and the burn that most certainly occurred. Instead he tried to take in his surroundings. They were in the massive courtyard he entered an hour earlier. The bus was still idling, waiting to take home the off-duty guards. The walls surrounded the giant cube housing the facility were bustling with activity as guards scattered around them, their rifles ready to fire.

He estimated it was two hundred feet between where they were squatting and the wall cutting them off from their freedom. The yelling grew more furious and the guards were less interested in what was going on in the courtyard than what was happening outside the gates.

"Who are you?"

"Skits."

"Skits who?"

She shrugged. "I was told to rescue you. Here we are."

"Who's we?"

"My brother," she said as if it explained everything. "Alyssa, too. Vanessa and Dav5d, I take it you've already met."

"The angel and guy on the computer?"

"Sure," she said. "We're trying to keep your ass alive."

"How do we get out of here?"

She pointed to the radio in her ear. "Until somebody tells me the plan, the goal is to stay alive."

"I saw cars outside?"

She nodded. "Outlanders. They have a grudge against the people in this facility. Unfortunately they're not as gifted as we are. We'll be lucky if they survive," she said. "We're a loose collaboration, you can say."

"So you came here without a plan?"

She smiled. "I'm not the superior strategist I look like."

Conthan ducked as a bullet grazed by him.

"We're sitting ducks out here." In the facility courtyard there was nothing other than the small building they were hiding behind. He assumed it was strategic not to have obstacles in the area between the building and the wall. *The bus*, he thought, *it's the closest defense we have.*

He felt the heat begin to radiate from his savior. Conthan fell backward; it wasn't fire, it was almost as if there was molten liquid hanging in the air around her arms. She moved her hands quickly in small circles until the blue created a small shield covering them. "Plasma," she said as if it explained everything. "I can keep this up for a while."

"Until they start charging us?"

"Dwayne," she screamed, "assistance!"

Conthan watched in disbelief as a stout man stepped from behind the bus, growling loud enough to be heard from a distance. A bolt of lightning shot upward and smashed into one of the towers, knocking a turret to the side. Another bolt slammed into the tower, causing parts of it to fall away to the ground below.

"Thanks," she yelled.

"Your brother?"

"Yeah," she said. "Don't piss him off."

"Cause the first thing I thought when I saw lightning shoot out of a small man…"

"You've got a mouth on you," she said. "I like that."

"Incoming," he said, pointing across the yard at two incoming guards.

"Alyssa's got this."

"Who…?"

A door flew open from the facility. A small girl lunged at one of the guards, knocking him to the ground. She twisted her body, turned around mid-flip, and tumbled away from him before he could react. A small device was strapped to the guard's wrist. It began to glow red as he pointed it at her. She knocked the man's hand high and raised her knee to his stomach. The man went to punch, but she pivoted to the side of his body. Using his momentum against him, she kicked his legs out from under him. As he fell to the ground she grabbed his hand and pressed it to his temple. She pushed his wrist, flashing a red light through his head and illuminating his skull.

As the other guard crawled to his feet, she kicked with all her might against his face. He turned over onto his back and started to sit up. She crouched behind him, grabbing his head and spinning as hard as she could.

"Do we have a plan yet?" Alyssa yelled from the two corpses.

"Did she just kill them?"

"It's not a game, kid." He knew she wasn't kidding.

"How are three of you going to get us out of here?"

"You make four," she said, "and from what I'm told, you have your own gifts."

"Used exactly once."

"Oh." Skits said surprised. "I was not told that."

Alyssa ran over to the two of them. The girl couldn't be much older than Skits. She wore a hijab wrapped around her head, hiding part of her face, shoulders and chest. Conthan didn't need to see her skin, her eyes gave away Middle Eastern heritage. For a moment he pondered if it had been racist assuming she was another white girl.

"Suggestions?" she asked.

"Mechs," Skits said, standing. She shook her hands and the blue fire vanished. "You watch the kid."

"You're like five years younger than me."

"Ignore her, she's a pain in the ass," Alyssa stated.

Skits began to take strides toward the two-legged humanoid machine. The fire radiating from her hands started to spread up her arms. The blue light began to radiate outwards as the plasma started to consume the top of her body. She ducked under the arm reaching for her. She slammed herself into the man-sized mech. "Bring it, bastards," she hissed.

Her hands pushed through the machine, leaving molten metal in their wake. She repeated the action through one of the legs and the mech tumbled to the ground. She turned to see another mech with two guns pointed directly at her. The guns began to rotate, spitting out bullets as she held up her hands in a defensive posture. The bullets reached the plasma and rained down to the ground in a shower of liquid metal.

She stepped toward the mech, focusing on her palms, willing the fire to reach further. The blue reached out and touched the edges of the guns. "Thanks for playing," she said as they melted to the mech's shoulders.

She clapped her hands together and the blue

sliced through the mech, leaving it incapacitated. She turned just in time to see a much larger version stomping toward her. She dug her heels in. "Dwayne," she yelled, "watch this show!"

The heat in her hands was distant, like feeling the warmth from the sun on a sunny day. As she growled, it began to spread further up her arms, enveloping her chest and then her face. The heat licking against her skin started to sting.

Conthan gasped at the sight of the fiery teenager. Her body was engulfed in the blue light and he had to shield his eyes when looking directly at her. He glanced at the girl next to him. "She's going to get herself killed."

"Probably," she said, "but not today."

They both watched as Skits turned her attention to the guns firing at her. She dug in her heels and pushed the plasma in front of her body. A small projectile hissed through the air, hit the plasma, and exploded, launching her backward along the ground. "Okay, maybe today," Alyssa said, running toward the fray.

Conthan stood up and started running after her, not knowing what he was supposed to do.

Alyssa began to wave her arms at the mech. "Shoot me," she screamed. "Look at me being all sort of threatening!"

The mech paused and turned toward Alyssa. "Oh shit," she said, sliding along the gravel.

Red dots appeared on the ground around Alyssa. Bullets started to rain down. She rolled backward and sprung up into a flip. Conthan held his breath as several laser sights focused on her body. Alyssa spun her body as bullets whooshed by. She landed on the ground, her muscles twitching from the effort.

"Down you go," yelled Skits as she slammed her flaming upper body into the leg of the mech. She let her hand slide into the mech as the metal gave way to a wave of liquid steel. She began to scream, forcing her hand deeper into the leg of the machine.

The mech kicked, knocking her onto the ground. Its leg was nearly severed, but intact enough to hold it upright. As the red dots centered on her chest, she froze. She tried to force the plasma to engulf her body again but found that she was running low on steam.

The lights narrowed on her body. A bolt of lightning cut into the mech's leg, knocking the killing machine to the ground. Another bolt slammed into it and the life seemed to leave its body.

"We need to evacuate," the lightning man said. "If they keep sending in reinforcements, we're going to run on empty."

"What about the people outside the gate?" asked Conthan.

"They were never part of our escape plan."

The man scanned the space between the building and the wall. "This rescue sucks," Conthan mumbled under his breath.

Skits shrugged her shoulders as the blue light about her body faded. "Call in, Vanessa."

"I thought your radios were out?"

The man looked to Alyssa. "You reach Vanessa, we're going to need to run interference," he said, pointing toward the wall.

Dwayne rubbed his hands together and threw them out wide. In an arc he brought them back together in a loud clap. As his hands connected, a charge of lightning projected from his body, speeding toward the wall. Lightning smashed against the structure, causing it to explode, sending soldiers tumbling into the courtyard.

He watched soldiers raise their guns. He jumped behind the large fallen mech as bullets began to pelt the machine. Placing his hands on the metal, he started to grumble, reaching for the life-spark in the robot. He found the power core and the energy radiating outward through the wires. He began to draw on the electricity it contained, at first a little, and then he could feel it open up and his body greedily siphoning from the machine.

"Vanessa," Alyssa said out loud, "we need an escape route. We're under heavy fire and there's no way out."

"Who are you?"

Alyssa held up her finger to silence him. "Oh shit," she said as a large plane hovered over the yard.

"Dwayne," she screamed. "Paladins!"

The man didn't hesitate. He stood, electricity arcing between him and the robot. His eyes sparkled. Loud crackling could be heard as the electricity jumped from his torso to his hand. Where before the lighting had poured out of his hands, this time it emerged from his chest, projecting outward, hurled at the small craft hovering above the yard.

Skits turned to Alyssa. "Anything?"

146

"She seems occupied," Alyssa said in a shrug.

It dawned on Conthan who they were talking about. "She was with the Warden, but not really, she was kind of in a place." He panicked. "I can't explain it."

"Telepath stuff," Alyssa said. "None of it makes sense."

Alyssa turned to the siblings. "We're on our own," she yelled.

Dwayne stopped the arc of lightning and pulled the last of the electricity out of the machine. "I don't have much left."

The three of them stood shoulder to shoulder as the hovercraft struggled to maintain its position. Doors under the craft opened and lines began to roll out. Several soldiers began sliding down the ropes.

"What now?" Conthan asked, standing next to his rescuers.

"You have roughly twenty seconds to master your powers and become useful," Dwayne said. "Until then, you're a liability."

"Can't argue that," Conthan retorted.

Dwayne gave a slight nod to the two girls. "We've trained for this."

Conthan didn't hide the surprise on his face. For some reason, he hadn't thought the super powered people had to do anything other than be super. It hadn't crossed his mind survival was an everyday event for them.

Conthan ducked behind Skits as the blue light shielded them again. Bullets reached the plasma and dripped onto the ground. He could hear her steady breathing as she tried to focus. Dwayne unleashed another bolt of lightning at the wall, knocking guards off the other side. He stepped from behind the shield and started taking shots at the oncoming Paladins.

Two fell before he ducked behind the shield again. "Four on three." He smiled. "We've got this."

"Got it," Skits said as she leaned forward and started into a charge. The shield began to fade until she whipped her hands out to the side, the blue touching the edge of two Paladin rifles. The guns warped at the touch of heat and the owners threw them down.

Conthan watched as the girl's hands became living weapons, throwing one punch out and then another. The Paladin dodged, ducked, and stepped outside each of her movements as if he were baiting her. He stepped inside her grip, grabbing her arms and throwing them out wide. He kicked her hard in the torso, sending her flying onto her back.

"On it," Alyssa said, running into the fray.

Dwayne looked up to the craft and could see another figure beginning to slide down the rope. He held up his hands again and several bolts of lightning intertwined and separated until they finally struck the craft, sending plumes of smoke into the air. He continued to pour it on, redirecting his efforts to the final descending figure. As the bolt tore into the soldier, he watched them plummet to the ground.

"Vanessa," he said out loud. "I don't care what you're doing, we're outmatched."

Conthan looked at him. "She was with another

telepath."

"A what?"

Conthan stayed crouched down near the ground. "I don't know, she was fighting somebody in a place that wasn't here."

Conthan had no idea what he was talking about, but by the ghost-like expression on Dwayne's face, he knew it made sense to the man. Dwayne froze for a moment. "If there's another telepath, we need to get out now. Teleport us."

Conthan could see he was talking to him. "I don't know how."

"You've done it before, right?"

"Once."

"Do it again!" he yelled.

"Damn performance anxiety up in here."

Dwayne started running after the two girls. It dawned on Conthan the people fighting right now were trying to save him. He watched as guards began to line the walls and shots were fired all around him. He could only assume the Outlanders had vanished and now attention was being brought to the crowd inside the prison. He looked down to his hands and flicked his wrists. "How the hell does this work?"

He tensed his muscles and felt none of the sensation from the night before. He paused as the soldier that had been hit by lightning stood up from the ground. Her clothes were in tatters, barely hanging onto her body. He was amazed she'd survived, let alone was able to walk. Her determination showed as she stormed toward the fray.

Conthan gasped in the eerie hush as gunfire ceased. He could hear the aircraft landing outside the gate, but inside, all the soldiers held their positions and waited for orders.

"Dwayne," Conthan yelled, pointing to the woman.

Everybody turned to see her approaching. Dwayne began making hand gestures to the other two women. "Conthan," he shouted, "how's it coming over there?"

Alyssa watched as the woman came closer. "Who the hell?"

"Captain of the Paladin," she said. "Surrender or be exterminated."

Alyssa took a fighting stance, ready to drop the woman to the ground. The woman didn't attempt to engage other than a lightning-fast fist to Alyssa's stomach. Alyssa attempted to bend with the blow but she buckled over like a lead weight had slammed into her gut. She fell to the ground, gasping for air.

"Last chance," Jasmine said.

Dwayne thrust his hands out, the last of the electricity surging through his arms and slamming into the chest of the woman. Her approach halted. She leaned forward, and took another step, ignoring the blasts. He stopped the ineffective barrage. "Not human," he said.

Skits jumped in just as the last of the electricity dissipated. She let the plasma engulf her hand. Putting her body into the punch, she landed it on the woman's shoulder. The woman hissed at the contact. "Terminated."

150

Conthan watched as the scorched woman brought her fist back to hit Skits. He wanted to do something to help. Everybody was going to die for his sake. He felt the tingling start at the base of his skull and his eyes lit up as he recognized the sensation from the night before. The tingling turned into a mild pain at the front of his brain. He focused his sight on the fist lunging toward Skits.

Skits gasped as she watched the woman's fist vanish from in front of her. She jumped back as the same fist appeared next to the woman's head, hitting herself against the side of the face. Skits and Dwayne turned to Conthan. He could see their eyes were both wide.

"Teleporter," Dwayne yelled, "get us out of here."

"I don't know what I'm doing," he said. He focused on the tingling sensation in his skull. He saw the woman stand up and he pointed his hand, trying to concentrate on where she was kneeling. A bolt of pain ripped through his skull as a void opened beneath her. The darkness wove through the space between the gravel and the woman and he swore he could feel every point of contact between her and the ground.

She yelled as she fell into the blackness. He felt a tug on his body as another black hole opened nearly forty feet in the air. She emerged from the space. Instead of flailing, she tucked her body into a ball and slammed into the ground, sending dirt and dust into the air.

Dwayne was holding Alyssa. "We need you to make one more. We need the other end of it to be far, far away from here."

Conthan looked at him blankly. The boy's eyes were dark, nearly ebony. Conthan felt the tingle in his body beginning to fade. "I don't think I can."

Yes.

Dwayne smiled at the voice. "Close call."

Skits put her hand against Conthan's forehead. "Don't fight it."

A numbing sensation washed over his body and he realized he was seeing out of his eyes, but as if down a long hallway. His body moved without him. He went to speak but realized no sound was coming from his mouth.

Relax, came the voice. *I'm going to help.*

Who are you?

The same person who saved you earlier, said the voice calmly.

His hands were in front of his body and a black void opened in thin air. He could hear the gunfire begin anew and he pushed Dwayne into the void. He jumped in after and suddenly a harsh cold washed over his body.

Where are we?

He could feel her hesitation. Then the sensation of falling, but more as if it was a memory. He couldn't see anything. All around him, blackness radiated outward, stealing the warmth from his body.

A white light appeared on the other end and as quickly as the darkness consumed him, his body was bathed in sunlight. He rolled along the grass and stared up at the sky. He could see Dwayne holding Alyssa above him. He went to speak and he didn't have the energy to open his mouth. He closed his eyes and let the sun warm him while he lost consciousness.

Chapter Eleven

June 8th, 1992 4:31PM

Mr. Davis sat in a small room watching a television suspended from the corner of the wall. On the screen, a man busted into a small home. The red door exploded in a fury of splinters as the metal ram slammed into wood. The camera caught several men as they ran into the room, all holding assault rifles.

They made hand gestures, signaling each other to move into tactical positions. The man in the front passed through the living room, his rifle held up to his face as he charged up the stairs. Another door was busted open, and inside, trying to hide on the far side of the bed, were a mother and her daughter. The woman clung to the tween tightly, shielding her eyes from the scene unfolding.

The soldier in front didn't stop to talk; he didn't hesitate. Three shots, one in the mother and two in the daughter's head. Both bodies slumped against the wall, lifeless.

154

The scene changed to two reporters behind a desk. "This footage was leaked online earlier today. The soldiers were sent to the home of Penelope Rogers and her daughter Chloe. It is another casualty in the effort to suppress mentalists. Chloe was a registered, exhibiting telepathic abilities. At this point there is no information if Chloe or her mother were part of the terrorist group responsible for the reactor meltdowns in the Northeast."

The camera zoomed in on the female reporter. "In other news, protestors continue to rally against The Culling. Protest leaders state that the government has overstepped its boundaries, creating a genetic civil war and demonstrating tactics similar to the Holocaust. Protestors continue to gather outside the White House rallying against the president's decision to eliminate all registered mentalists."

"Mr. Davis," said a small man in a freshly pressed suit, "I have your files for you."

When Mark didn't turn away from the television, his assistant waved the files in front of the screen. Mark looked up, shaking his head. "Sorry. What were you saying?"

"I brought your files."

Mark rubbed his eyes, trying to keep himself from falling asleep. He took the manila folder filled with papers. Leaning back, he stretched his neck and twisted his torso, loosening up stiff muscles.

"How long have you been waiting?"

"Hours."

The small waiting room was inside a military complex just outside of Washington, DC. The decor reminded him of the later 70s, wood paneling and old chairs with orange cushions. The walls were bare other than the single television in the corner. He had been inside numerous military installations and they all had a certain feel to them, a mix between outdated and barren. This one was no different.

"Do you want me to bring anything else?"

"That's everything, Carl. If anything, can you check on Mrs. Davis? I have no idea how long this will go on and I don't like the idea of her sitting at home alone with Valerie."

"Absolutely." Carl gave him a handshake and he was out the door. Mark remembered being a wide-eyed intern at the White House. It was only a few months ago he was interning with the Office of the Chief of Staff for a special project labeled "Second Prospect." The office answered directly to the president and helped develop the training facilities utilized by the mentalists. It had been a long six months and Mark felt the weight of the world on his shoulders increase daily.

Each night the news ran a similar story. Innocents were being gunned down in their homes in an effort to eradicate people with the ability to see the future, read minds, or even move objects by thinking. Several times he recognized the lifeless bodies. They had been applicants, people looking for help learning to cope with the immensity of these gifts. They had come willingly and he had been the one to sign the paperwork asking they be admitted to a research facility.

One of the doors pushed open. Two men in black

suits with earpieces attached to the side of their heads stood in the doorway. "This way, Mr. Davis." He followed one of the suits through the door while the other stayed close behind him. Whenever he had been in the presence of the president, the Secret Service agents had always dwarfed him, making him feel insignificant and dangerous all at the same time.

The corridor snaked through the building until he reached a glassed-in conference room. He had been expecting the room to contain only the president, but it appeared as if she had several Joint Chiefs of Staff in attendance. Mark walked into the room and stood at the end of the table opposite the president.

"Mr. Davis," said the president, "please have a seat."

"Do you see what's going on out there, Madame President? There is a war brewing."

The woman didn't bat an eyelash as she leaned forward, resting her elbows on the table. "Mr. Davis, if you've come to state the obvious, we are drastically overpaying you."

"I'm sorry, Madame President. Some of the people on the news were my charges. Every time I watch the news, I see bodies. They're children."

"Mr. Davis." The president signaled to the two agents. "I suggest you get your emotions under control and come back when you can present yourself appropriately."

Mark threw the manila folder onto the table. The papers slid out in front of president. "I've detailed the conversion of one of our research facilities."

One of the men in uniform pushed the manila

folder away from him. "Mr. Davis, I agree, we've already had to deal with the ramifications of Second Prospect. You're saying we sanction these people?"

Mark ignored the man. "Madame President, we can convert the research facility in Massachusetts. It's inside the radiation zone of the attack. It's a wasteland. It will allow us to not only keep the people away from the general population, but to continue studying them. Do you think the Russians or the Chinese have given up their programs? Absolutely not."

The president took one of the pages from the folder and looked it over. She raised her eyebrow, set down the paper, and picked up another sheet. She glanced from it to Mr. Davis, then folded her arms as she leaned back in her chair.

"Why are you suggesting this, Mr. Davis?"

"Does it matter?"

"Entertain me."

"People are being killed. At least here we will have the opportunity to save them. Study them in seclusion. It would be better to create a maximum security prison for them than watch them be slaughtered on the evening news."

"This is preposterous," said one of the men in military garb.

"Says the man with his finger on the trigger," Mark spat out.

"Know your place, Mr. Davis," the president said. She turned to the man sitting at her side. "You as well. At least Mr. Davis can blame his insolence on youth."

"Madame President," the man said, "this will

cost us millions of dollars and will put American lives in jeopardy."

She lifted her hand to silence him. "We have domestic terrorism running rampant. I want you to take care of that. Mr. Davis"—she shuffled the papers back into the folder—"I will arrange a meeting with you and a private benefactor who supported my campaign. They would be interested in this concept of yours."

"You're putting me in charge?" He couldn't hide the shock on his face. She stood up and walked over to him. She was the most powerful woman in the world, and she was striding toward him, offering him an opportunity far beyond his years of experience.

"Can you think of another man for the job?"

He avoided her eyes as he took the files. She rested a hand on his shoulder, staring him straight in the eye. "I am taking my chances with you, Mr. Davis. Do not disappoint me."

"No, Madame President."

She shook his hand. He turned to walk toward the door. One of the military men at the table cleared his throat. "What's the name of this prison you're suggesting?"

Mark tried to hide his chuckle. The military was obsessed with giving code names to any initiative they partook in. There were code names for code names. They loved to play their games of deceit, something he was obviously not very well versed in.

"The place I am building," he corrected, "will only be known as The Facility." He clutched the folder in his hand and pushed the door leading out into the hallway. He looked through the glass to see the president smiling. She was pleased with him, but the smile spread across her lips looked wrong, as if there was more going on behind the scenes.

The Secret Service agents escorted him out of the building. He wiped his hand off on his pants. He had met with the last person to see Eleanor alive. The woman hadn't steered him wrong; she had been right at every turn. He knew he played a dangerous game getting close to the woman who signed the executive order killing the mentalists. He wished he had guidance at this point, something to show him he was making the right move.

"I hope this was part of your plan, Eleanor," he muttered under his breath.

Chapter Twelve

May 17th, 2032 10:30PM

Pain pushed through her brain as teeth clamped down, grinding back and forth in an effort to stifle a scream. The jolt of electricity forced her to her knees, while the bile built in her throat until she threw up on the grates beneath her. She continued to cry out as pain burned into the base of her skull. She tried to look up but her muscles seized, betraying her.

"Why?"

She opened her mouth to answer but found herself vomiting again. As fast as the searing jolts had started, they vanished. She gasped, waiting for them to return a second time. Her skin was on fire as she tried to lift her head, the echo of pain reminding her just how bad it could get.

The man in the suit threatened to push the spot on the back of his hand, a button linked to her implant. She winced at the impending convulsion but he stopped short and sneered at her. "I'll ask you again, Jasmine…" He paused for a moment, his hand dancing around the spot on his hand. "Why did you let them get away?"

"I didn't," she growled.

"Who gave the order for the guards on the wall to stop firing?"

She looked at the smug smile on his face. "Why would I ask them to stop?"

"Because…"

"I'm invincible," she interrupted. "Why would I tell them to stop firing?"

"The glory?" he mused.

His entire body froze. His brain was being fed information. She guessed it was a video feed of the events as they had played out. He didn't want her to answer the question, he wanted to continue to play with her. What she called torture he referred to as scientific curiosity.

"So you're right."

"Didn't think about that before you decided to cook me?"

He almost cracked a smile. "And miss a chance to perform another round of tests on you, Jasmine? Never."

She spat onto the floor as she pushed her way to her feet. "Why the hell would the guards stand down?"

He closed his eyes, focusing on the information being fed into his brain. He sorted through personnel files and looked over the radio logs and video feeds of several cameras. "The moment you hit the ground, it seems all radio chatter ceased. There was no motion or discussion across the radios. All the guards simply stopped."

"I get worried when the brains of the operation doesn't have an answer," she said.

"Curious…"

***

Conthan opened his eyes. He was in a room he didn't remember entering. It was dark. He spun around, looking for the door. He spun around again to a single chair in the middle of the room. He reached out in the darkness, fearful that his eyes were playing tricks on him "Hello," he whispered.

The chair stood out against the darkness as if an unseen light source was shining down on it. Between his blinks, Sarah appeared, staring blankly off into space. He shook his head, recalling how similar this was to when Vanessa had first appeared in his head. He knelt in front of Sarah and realized she was unaware of him. "Sarah, can you hear me?"

She was as unresponsive as she had been in the research facility. He reached up to touch the spot of smooth skin on her cheek when he saw the dark figure behind her. He slowly stood. Wisps of smoke rolled from the shadows, wrapping around Sarah as if they were elongated fingers. "What do you want?"

The figure laughed. The sound was deep and boomed like they were in a small room. The figure faded into the background, but the sound grew louder and louder. Conthan finally had to cover his ears to stop the pain, but the sound wasn't from outside, it was emanating from inside his head.

"Who are you?"

"I am all," said the voice. The shadows encompassed Conthan, wrapping around his feet, threatening to crawl up his body. The chill rushed along his skin, causing him to shiver. The darkness continued creeping inch by inch, threatening to consume him. He fought to push it down, but his limbs began to freeze, his muscles unwilling to cooperate.

Conthan shot up in his bed, jolted awake from the scene in his dream. His heart raced. His face dripped with sweat while his limbs continued to feel the chill. He gripped the sheets around him, relieved as the warm cloth beneath his hand grounded him. He was thankful there was a light on in the room. "Now where am I?"

Last thing he remembered was the firefight in the facility yard. He remembered hearing the woman speak to him and seeing the black discs. He looked down to his hands, startled to think he was capable of doing those things.

He recalled the sensations vibrating through his body before the disc opened. A tingle emerged at the base of his skull, a reminder of what it took to summon his abilities. He stared at his hands in disbelief. "I'm a teleporter?"

Yes.

He jumped at the voice. "What the hell? No more speaking in my head."

"So be it," came a much harsher voice.

The figure stood in the door. "Who are you?" he asked.

He watched as the woman from his mind came

forward. Dark robes wrapped around her body, which almost glided into the room, appearing otherworldly. He tightened his fist on the sheets to remind himself he was still in reality.

"My name is Vanessa."

"A telepath?"

"Until earlier today…" She paused, "I would have said the one and only."

She must have been in her mid-forties. Her hair was a bright blonde and flowed down behind her shoulders. The robes wrapped tightly around her body and bunched into a collar, hiding the bottom of her face. It was surreal to see a woman he had only seen in his dreams up to this point.

"You look a little different without the wings," he mused, "or the sword."

"I keep the sword locked away," she said, her eyes giving away her grin.

He got up out of bed and grabbed his leather jacket from the floor next to the mattress. He was easily a few inches taller than her, but he was surprised at how intimidating the woman before him appeared. "I don't know what to say."

"Thank you would be a start."

He blushed at her direct nature. "So, thanks for not letting the Warden kill me, and then those guards, and I take it you had something to do with the rescue squad."

She turned to look out the window. "We try to protect our own."

He thought about the statement. A day ago he was a human like ninety-nine percent of the world and today he was one of the minority. He was one of those people on the television, hunted down and put into places like the Facility. He was like Sarah.

"The Children of Nostradamus."

He froze. "You can read my thoughts?"

She nodded. "I can't shut it off." She looked him in the eye. "At best, I can only sift through the chaos in each of your minds."

"Nothing I think is ever safe around you?"

She smiled. "Nothing."

Dammit, he thought.

Indeed.

"Okay, enough of that."

"You have never been curious? Never questioned why you didn't get sick as a child? Or perhaps why your foster mother would take you out of school for days at a time for no reason?"

He began to reply and stopped. "How'd you know that?"

"Your story isn't unique," she said. She turned back to the window. "As the Children of Nostradamus began to emerge, those with suspecting and loving parents hid them away. Like any good parent, she sought to protect you."

"Are you brain scanning me or something?"

She shook her head slowly. "Dwayne's father did the same for him. As his abilities manifested, he was pulled from school. Skits, on the other hand, exhibited no abilities until a neighbor caught her burning through a car door."

"You mean my mother knew I could teleport?"

She let out a condescending laugh. "They keep you in the dark, don't they?"

He waited for her to explain.

"Do you know where we are, Conthan?"

He looked out the window to the skyline. It reminded him of New York City, but without all the modernization. The buildings, some spanning over thirty stories, were in disrepair. The street was filled with cars and grass grew through the middle of the street. He tried to imagine where on the globe they could be.

"The Danger Zone."

He instinctively looked down to the small badge still pinned to his shirt. The color indicator was now black, a sign he was going to die from radiation poisoning. She wasn't nearly as panicked as he pulled the badge off his shirt. She took the badge and tossed it from the window.

"Where the Children of Nostradamus have hundreds of recorded abilities, there are certain things we all have in common. We have a natural immunity to all illnesses. We have higher endurance, we heal quicker, and because of this…"

"We can survive radiation."

She nodded. "Our bodies have adapted so that our abilities do not kill us. Otherwise"—she pointed out the window to a bar across the street—"Dwayne and Skits's abilities would incinerate their bodies."

He had never stopped to think about the physiology behind the abilities of powered people. He simply thought, *they can because, well, that's what they do*.

She chuckled again. "If only we were so lucky."

"How do you know all this?"

"We are not all common folk," she admitted. "For some time we had several doctors here. Most of what I know I've learned from reading their notes. Unlike the research facility, they truthfully studied our abilities."

"What does the research facility do?"

"I would have guessed they were studying powered people to weaponize them as a new form of biological warfare." She paused. She closed her eyes for a long period and opened them again. "Now, I have no idea."

Conthan looked down at his hands. "Is it safe to use it?"

She nodded. "There are very few people here anymore. The danger of your power to any living object is negligible."

"What about the doctors?"

"Dead."

He wanted to ask, but he could tell the wound was still fresh. His observation answered his own question. "Sorry."

"You are an astute young man."

He looked out the window to see a light shining from the bar across the street. He was amazed there were streetlights still functioning in the city. The sight of a deserted Boston saddened his heart.

"Dwayne keeps them running. We were a community for some time. We had doctors, engineers, even a member of the government. We rescued who we could. We were stronger for them. We have lost many during rescues, others, we lost to their own despair."

He glanced at her from the corner of his eye. She was beautiful and at the same time a sadness caused by burden hung on her shoulders. He could swear for a moment the blonde hair was gone and her face emerged a sickly green. As he turned his head, she appeared normal again; had it been a figment of his imagination?

She held her finger up to her hidden mouth. "Shhh, it's our secret."

Without warning, she jumped from the window. He leaned out to see the red robes plummeting toward the ground. He wasn't sure how she had hidden them in the room, but white wings spread wide and she sailed through the street. Her body glided to where streetlights faded into nothingness.

"Okay, it officially got crazier."

Conthan pulled on his jacket and ran out of the room and down the hallway to the stairs. He charged through the exit door and jumped down stair after stair until he reached the bottom. Despite the exterior of the building looking as if it hadn't been touched in decades, the interior was fairly well taken care of. The hotel was always meant to look old, classic, and represent a period of decadence. Now, with the outsides decaying, it appeared as if it were frozen in a time the world had forgotten. Emerging from the building, he could see that it was indeed a dead city. Lights flickered, but there was only him to appreciate their fight against the darkness.

He walked toward the building. Inside, Dwayne, Alyssa and Skits were gathered around the bar. He was amused by the sight of Alyssa behind the counter mixing drinks. The scene before him looked like a twisted interpretation of his favorite Hopper painting.

"Nighthawks," he mumbled to himself.

Skits waved to him. He thought about the painting hanging in Chicago. Standing in front of the masterpiece had been the first time he had cried before art. He had always wanted to go back after art school and see if his appreciation for that painting had changed. Now, it seemed his future was taking a much darker turn and the only way he'd see it was if he could figure out how to teleport inside.

He crossed the street and opened the door.

"Conthan!"

He sat down on a stool. "How'd you sleep?" asked Alyssa.

"Other than some evil creature trying to devour my soul"—he shrugged—"not too bad."

"Vanessa told us about her encounter with the Warden," said Dwayne.

"Meet her yet?" asked Alyssa.

Conthan thought about the angel jumping from his window. Other than Sarah and Jed, she was the first person with abilities he had met. She was different. He wondered if it was because of her physical abilities or being a telepath. He couldn't imagine what it would be like to see inside the thoughts of every person around him.

Skits laughed at his deep thoughts. "Yup, he's met her."

Alyssa poured a shot of whiskey into a tumbler and pushed it across the counter to Conthan. "It seems drinking makes the crazy easier to hear."

Conthan took the glass and looked at the amber liquid. He took a sip, letting the alcohol burn his throat.

Dwayne rested his elbows on the bar. "I remember doing this, being one of the new guys. You have a thousand questions, what's the first thing you want to ask?"

Conthan did indeed have a thousand things going through his mind. If he had to focus on one in particular, he wasn't sure what stood out most. He looked at his hands and then at the others. "Why?"

"Going to need to elaborate, mate," Dwayne said.

Alyssa took a seat on the bar next to Skits, both watching his face closely. He made a fist with his hands. "Why save me?"

"We like the rush," Skits said. "Something about almost dying that makes you feel alive."

Dwayne waved for her to stop talking. "Vanessa told us you would be at the facility. We try to protect our own and it was obvious you needed help."

"How'd you know I was…?" He paused. "One of you?"

Dwayne fished into his hoodie and pulled out a sheet of paper. "I was given this letter years ago. Not exactly sure who she is"—he handed the letter to Conthan—"but she was interested in you."

Conthan recognized the letter the moment it touched his hand. "The woman who wrote it is Eleanor Valentine."

"How'd you know that?"

"I got one too," he admitted. "She was a psychic for the president in the early nineties. She attempted to kill the president and was shot. She gave a letter to somebody I knew, who passed it on to me as he was dying."

Alyssa scooted closer to them. "Do you think she knew about this? Us? I mean, our little posse of powers?"

Conthan nodded. "I think she knew exactly what she was doing."

Dwayne unfolded a crumpled letter and flattened it out on the bar. He started to read it aloud. Conthan paused as he realized she had included the dates for Dwayne. Conthan gawked at the last line.

"As the Nighthawks gather, continue to protect. Your futures will be a struggle to illuminate a darkness that will fall on future days." He set the letter down on the counter.

"Nighthawks?" asked Skits.

Conthan smiled. "It's a painting by my favorite artist. It shows the solitude of individuals sitting in an ice cream bar. Two men and a woman sit together, but all alone, as they deal with whatever demons they must. Behind the counter is a man preparing drinks, concerned by his patrons but accepting the situation because it's the same every night."

"Deep," said Alyssa.

Dwayne smacked his hands down on the counter, startling Conthan. "Nighthawks it is."

"Dude," Skits interrupted, "next thing you're going to suggest is we start giving ourselves code names."

"I'm not wearing spandex," Alyssa said.

"I have a lot of questions," Conthan confessed. He looked down to his hands and flexed them, thinking about the black void he had created.

"First…"

***

Jasmine rested her hand on the glass staring into the operating room. Her teammate's body writhed in agony as he screamed out. His voice was muffled by the transparent doors, but she couldn't stop seeing what was transpiring. Her skin crawled. She continued staring at him, determined to overcome the challenge her stomach was proposing.

She watched as the scientist in the room tore away at the Corpsman's pants, pulling them back from the horribly broken limb. There were bits of splintered bone sticking out from his knee and blood pooled on the floor beneath him. The scientist yelled to his two assistants, who began attaching plugs and diodes to the man.

The white coats moved about the operating room, grabbing instruments and beginning to diagnose his situation. She knew the outcome. His humanity began to slip away the moment he reached the Body Shop. They would ignore his modifications plan, forgetting to check the "No Enhancement" barcode on his neck.

At least you'll be alive to complain, she thought.

She almost believed the people inside the room were doctors. They moved like a trauma unit she had seen as a child. Glass computer screens replaced the cloth curtains that had existed once upon a time in emergency rooms. Surgeons were a dying breed as more financially advanced hospitals left behind doctors and nurses for coders and software developers.

His humanity vanished as the scientist plunged a needle into the thigh of the man's broken leg. As the plunger pushed down, he began to scream, his spine bowing, threatening to hurl himself from the table.

The nanites, mini programmers, scoured his veins, beginning to rob him of his soul.

One of the assistants held out a clear plastic panel, high enough that all could see. The panel snapped to life as an image appeared. Clearer and clearer, Jasmine could see the musculature and circulatory system of her comrade. With only a few taps on the screen, the blood flow came to an end. The man in the white jacket held a small tool to the man's leg and the laser began to cut away at the soldier's flesh.

Jasmine stared at the scene, trying not to blink. Her eyes watered at the smell of burning flesh. His body was being consumed by the machines of godless men. As the assistant handed the doctor a metal leg, she knew he would begin the slippery slope to becoming a machine. At first he would comment on how amazing it was to walk again. He would be impressed with the hydraulics and how much sturdier it was than his other leg. Then he would replace the weaker leg.

He would be persuaded to give up his soft baby blue eyes in place for synthetic eye-shaped cameras. He would opt for the cognitive process enhancers that would allow him to react faster in the field, saying, "It'll keep me alive."

Jasmine turned away from the door. She tried to justify wrapping her arms around herself and hugging tightly. She tried convince herself she was trying to settle her stomach. She willed herself not to cry. Her teammate would survive, but she mourned him giving away the one thing she craved.

She took a steadying breath and leaned her head back against the sheet metal coating the walls as she slid down to the ground. She let her hand rest on the base of her skull where a small scar revealed a violation on her body. On the other side of her skin, a piece of technology kept her subjected to the authority of her owners. Her epidermis tightened, absorbing the properties of the metal against her back, and she welcomed the pain rushing through her body. She breathed through clenched teeth as the transformation happened. She slammed her fist into the ground, leaving a dent where her knuckles connected.

"More human than you," she whispered, trying to convince herself.

***

The streetlights had stopped shining where Vanessa landed. The building was dark except for several candles in windows. Her foot touched down on the balcony, her wings flapping to slow her approach. She let her wings stretch out and brought them close into her body, nestling them against the fabric of her red robes.

The bar was five stories down and a block away. If she concentrated, their thoughts were loud enough for her to hear. She pulled back, focusing on the chill of the night air. As the voices faded, she took a deep breath, enjoying the silence. From here, words were nothing more than emotions. She smiled as Conthan cheered at the first use of his powers by his own will. She closed her eyes, letting her thoughts drift to the encounter earlier that day. She had been blessed as a telepath, emerging at an early age. Her physical mutations had been a curse, but she spent the better part of her entire life learning her potential. Today had been the first time she had encountered another telepath. The experience was thrilling. The ability to meet a person on the playing field of the mind and wrestle using determination, discipline, and guile was intoxicating. There was fear—the potential within her mind was dangerous. She always knew if she decided to choose a darker path, she would be a force to be reckoned with.

She wrapped her arms around her body and squeezed tightly. She knew this encounter had been a test of skill and a show of talent. Without a doubt she would have to face him again. Ever since she touched the shadows of his thoughts, she could smell him, lingering like a day-old cigar. Worse, she could feel his mind reaching out, spreading its influence like a virus.

"Eavesdropping," she said out loud.

"Says the woman who can hear my every thought."

She turned to a man staring at her. His skin was so dark it appeared as if he was emerging from the shadows. He stepped forward and took a bow. "How are you, fearless leader?"

176

"Do you really need to ask?" she questioned.

His eyes darted over her body and she could hear his thoughts racing at a tempo she couldn't follow. Unlike the others, whose thoughts were like drips of water, his coursed like a river and she could only hear the deafening roar. His mind was like a hurricane and she was trying to pick out the sound of a single blade of grass moving.

"You're worried about your encounter today," he said. "You're fearful he is capable of following us here."

"It bothers me that you know me so well, Dav5d," she said.

"You provide far too many contextual clues for me not to know," he said. "Besides, I'm the closest thing you have to a fellow telepath."

"You are," she said. But after meeting the real telepath earlier, she was astonished by how different it was. Like the rest, Dav5d was a Child of Nostradamus. Where the others had outward-facing abilities, his brain was his gift. "You can predict the outcome of a million equations, but there is an embrace of two telepaths that even your powers can not mimic."

His brain worked like a computer. He analyzed her timbre, the way her hips shifted or the pace at which she blinked. His senses collected data while his abilities made sense of each component. She could hear him attempting to process the information, but found his abilities stumbling when attempting to analyze emotions or unexplainable feelings. "I will have to take your word on this."

He reached out and touched her shoulder. Both

their powers flared with the contact. She began to see his mind more clearly while it processed data her senses were acquiring. He was aware of the rough texture of her hand as she squeezed his. He intentionally ignored the sensation and looked out to the city before them.

She smiled. "Thank you."

"Someday," he said, squeezing her calloused hand, "you will have to explain."

"Someday," she repeated.

They were standing on the balcony of a church that overlooked several converging streets. Lights flickered, illuminating the solitude below.

There was a twinge of sadness as he looked at the emptiness surrounding them. This was their home and he would be forever grateful, but he couldn't help but know it was a wasteland abandoned by the masses. He was glad his people had a place to survive, but what had once been a magnificent city had been reduced to a hundred and now to only a dozen individuals.

"We're a dying breed," she said.

"They've become efficient at killing us," he replied. "Or worse, capturing us for research."

He was a tall man. Despite the lack of light, she could see his dark complexion, partly with her eyes, partly with her mind. He had a worried look on his face, something she wasn't used to seeing. She wished she could pry into his thoughts as easily as the thoughts of everybody else. "You know what is coming?"

"Since my powers developed I've been able to quantify and calculate life. I see the world as a complex math problem. Each action causes another, and at my best, I can foresee the consequences and alternatives before they happen. Through probability I can predict the future. I wonder if this is what psychics experience when they foresee the future. I wonder if my power is an evolution of psychics. What if I simply follow the lines of probability to a determined outcome, what psychics call the future?"

The wind brushed his cheek. Based on its direction and the humidity in the air, rain was going to hit them in roughly twenty-seven minutes. He spoke softly. "Eleanor Valentine has proven a challenge. Analyzing the intent of a woman almost forty years dead is more difficult than it may sound. What could she have seen to cause her to interfere in our lives? With each pen stroke, she was confident her messages would reach us and bring us to this apex in time. Her involvement has required more meditation than I have ever had to apply to a problem. I haven't felt stymied intellectually since I was a child."

"I can't begin to imagine the complexities involved," she admitted.

"Her predictions are converging," he said. "The letter to rescue Conthan and your letter to find Dwayne's sister prove Eleanor wanted our lives to intertwine. Some of us, I believe, happened upon this operation as fate intended, but what if Skits was never meant to be found but for her interference? And without that letter, Dwayne would have never stayed, which would have resulted in Alyssa moving on. Conthan would be dead and it would only be you and I."

"You assume that the future is malleable."

"If it isn't," he said, "then Eleanor simply played a role she was destined to play. Her decisions would have never altered the future."

"Then our lives are not our own." They both paused at the immensity of the philosophic discussion before them. "For a man who believes he quantifies the entire world, I'm glad to see that you have faith."

"What do we do with this knowledge?"

She raised an eyebrow. It wasn't often he asked questions unless he was collecting more data. "What does your data tell us?"

He let out a loud sigh. "Going forward, my predictions are limited."

"The darkness Eleanor spoke of."

He nodded. "We're converging on something and it bothers me that my powers aren't helping decipher what lies before us."

A shout came from behind them. Where there had only been empty space, Dwayne tumbled to the ground. He shook his head, sitting up on the stone balcony. "Conthan's powers suck." He shivered despite the thick hoodie he wore. "It's like going through a meat locker and then landing on my head."

Both Vanessa and Dav5d stepped back as they saw the small charges of electricity jump from his hands to the ground. Dav5d knelt next to Dwayne. "You're going to need to discharge in the next two hundred and nineteen seconds before your powers surge."

Dwayne rolled his eyes. "Precogs," he mumbled.

The electrified man held up his hands and let his muscles relax. The small sparks began to pick up and as his hands began to glow brighter. Electricity began to pour out of him. The bolt of lightning dissipated over the buildings, but not before the loud crack and smell of burned ozone filled the air.

He let out a deep breath and looked to the other two. "So, Conthan is able to access his powers. He obviously sucks at them, but he's able to use them."

"Good," she said. "We're going to need him."

"A teleporter would make extractions easier," Dwayne admitted. "We could have been in and out of the prison with no problem."

"Agreed," she said.

They could hear a voice shouting from the street below. "You win the dare!"

Dav5d chuckled. "He'll fit in."

"So what's next?" asked Dwayne as he patted the smoldering edges of his hoodie.

Vanessa turned to him. "I need to meet with the Outlander council again. We need to make sure we're still on amicable terms. I have a feeling that they will be less than cooperative after today's events."

"I'll go with you," Dav5d interjected.

"No," she said flatly. "Part of our alliance has been discretion. They're at ease around the angel of the Outlands. After meeting Dwayne, Alyssa, and Skits, I am painfully aware they view us as potential threats. And with the death of Outlanders, they'll be looking for somebody to blame."

"And us?" asked Dwayne.

"Train Conthan," she said. "We have all discussed this darkness looming over our futures. I have faith his heart is pure." She looked down to the three standing outside the bar. "If he is somehow connected to it all, I want him as an ally."

"When do you leave?"

She gazed off into the distance. "In the morning," she said. "I have a feeling time is not our friend."

They all grew quiet as they watched Conthan open another void in the air. Vanessa smiled at the confidence she could see building in the man. She knew for him, this was a form of playing hero. She worried about when reality caught up to him and he saw none of them were the heroes of comic books. For now, she was happy to see he felt as if he belonged.

Chapter Thirteen

May 18th, 2032 10:07AM

Are you all right, Twenty-Seven?
I am.
"I am," she said.

There was a pause. Twenty-Seven watched as people rushed back and forth, yelling for medical supplies. Since they had returned from the raid, there had been little rest. She had played medic until a small child had been brought in. Unlike the wounded soldiers who participated in the raid, the kid had died from radiation poisoning. His small body had admitted defeat and given up, shutting down organ after organ.

I can feel the guilt washing over you.
I saw a child die today.
"I saw a child die today," she said aloud.

She rested her face in her hands, trying to remove the image of the kid's scarred face from her mind. Two more people ran into the makeshift trauma ward with supplies and began barking orders. A man was going to lose his leg. There was a surgeon who lived with them. He was capable, a volunteer who came to the Outlands like it was a third world country in need of saving.

I am sorry.

Twenty-Seven didn't know how to respond. She was a housewife torn from her home for standing up to an abusive husband. She didn't expect to be thrust into the middle of a fight between opposite sides of the fence. Worse, she didn't expect to watch a child die. She covered her face while she cried.

I am coming.

What can you do?

Twenty-Seven dropped her hands, and instead of seeing the red carpet of the hotel, she saw pavement speeding by. She gasped. She could feel the wind blowing in her hair and the sharp turns as a person dodged and weaved through abandoned cars.

What's happening?

I am coming to you. Right now you're seeing what I see.

How are you doing this?

I assume all telepaths have the ability to enter another person's mind. I'm unsure if they have the ability to call someone into their own.

The hotel was visible, but as if it were a distant memory. Instead, in that moment she was flying down the interstate at breakneck speeds. There was a calm about her despite the potential disaster. The hair on her arms stood on end as it responded to the phantom sensation of wind crossing her skin.

Vanessa's robes flapped in the wind as she

leaned the bike to the side, darting around a tractor trailer. She quickly reversed the lean to dodge a car. She gripped the accelerator and turned it further, watching the gauge on the bike push ninety-five miles per hour.

You're riding a motorcycle?

My wings make riding in a car difficult. I have never been a fan of confined spaces.

Twenty-Seven was amazed with how fast the woman reacted to oncoming cars. There was something freeing about the potential for danger at every turn. *There is no danger,* she thought. At the first sign of losing control, her wings would carry her to safety. She wondered if the angel had always been so in control of her world, riding the fine line between reckless and secure.

All good observations.

Twenty-Seven could feel the woman's smile on her own lips.

There was a long pause before she asked, *We're going to die. I mean, me, I'm going to die here, aren't I?*

Vanessa considered the question. She had always avoided thinking about the longevity of the Outlanders. Their ranks rarely increased unless she brought individuals banished by law enforcement. If the bandits that ran rampant in the Outlands didn't kill them, the radiation would ultimately end their lives prematurely.

See? said Twenty-Seven from her perch on a hallway couch.

This is the first time somebody has been able to hear my thoughts. I apologize, child. I am on my way. I believe I have a solution for all in the Outlands. I will be there shortly.

Twenty-Seven blinked and was again in the hotel. She took a deep breath as her body adjusted to the lack of wind cooling her skin. A man holding blankets dropped several in front of her. She reached down and grabbed them. "What can I do to help?"

***

They entered through the large mahogany doors. A grand staircase, made from a stone he could not identify, led them to the second floor of the museum. His synapses were firing, recalling lectures from art history. Each vase they passed up the stairs reminded him of long-forgotten cultures and how they used the vessels.

The others walked in front of him, oblivious to the masterpieces in their presence. He reached the rotunda at the top of the stairs, greeted by large marble sculptures of men holding spears. The titans lorded over him, threatening at any moment to break the silence with war cries or rallying Greek armies.

"You've never been here before?"

Conthan stared up to the stained glass dome covering the rotunda. The world outside was falling apart, decaying around them. In these walls, decay was a mark of triumph, an object's determination to survive past its time. It wouldn't be long before the building was reclaimed by nature.

"No," he muttered.

Conthan caught Dwayne staring at him. Conthan noticed a hardness about the man. Physically he was a big softy, but something about his eyes and the clenched jaw made him seem tough. The scars on his neck and shoulders looked like a road map to a lethal destination. He was the leader in the field, barking orders to keep them all alive.

Dav5d rested his hand on Conthan's shoulder, startling him. "You studied art history? College?"

Conthan was unnerved by the man. Dwayne assured him Dav5d wasn't psychic, but his ability to read a person was frightening. Conthan nodded. "I studied at Parsons. I recognize the statues from textbooks."

"Your eyes were darting back and forth slowly enough so I knew your frontal lobe was processing the information. The amount of time that lapsed suggested it must be a memory."

Conthan walked around the rotunda. Dav5d's abilities and social skills lacked Vanessa's finesse. Where Vanessa could reach into his mind and pull at specific thoughts, with Dav5d it was his actions betraying him. He had close friends growing up, but every person kept secrets. It was becoming more and more apparent there would be no secrets between him and his newfound friends.

"You get used to him," Dwayne said. "For a human computer, he's slowly learning to respect people's personal boundaries. You're just a new equation to him. Once he has you figured out he'll leave you alone."

"So many parts of that sentence are wrong," Conthan said, walking through a set of doors into a room filled from floor to ceiling with European masters.

"You should see him with my sister. He's still yet to figure her out."

"She's a little…"—Conthan paused, seeing the change on Dwayne's face—"…random?"

"Smart man," Dwayne said, patting him on the back.

"Her predisposition for acts out of the ordinary could be attributed to a restructuring of her neural pathways during electroshock therapy."

"Shut it, Dave."

Conthan raised his eyebrows. The human computer reminded him of a kid in high school who suffered from an extreme case of Asperger's. The kid had been a genius in math class, able to do things even the teacher had difficulty doing without a calculator. However, he had trouble expressing himself and more often than not would wind up yelling during conversations to make sure he was heard. He lacked the ability to read social situations. Dav5d was that kid on mental steroids. He put a mental pin in the conversation; he'd ask Dwayne about his sister at a later time when it was just the two of them.

"We should get started."

"What exactly are we doing?" asked Conthan.

"We're going to slap some doohickeys on you and let Dav5d figure out how you work. I'm here for moral support while you learn to control your powers."

"I've used them once on my own."

Dav5d reached into his pocket and pulled out

small transparent circles. "These will read biological signs as you access your powers. I will be able to figure out the stressors necessary for you to create these voids."

Conthan caught the expression on Dwayne's lips. "Why are you smiling?"

"I'm the stressor," Dwayne said, flicking his palms open. Small sparks rained down to the floor below.

"Oh shit," Conthan groaned. "You're all psychotic."

"Back up," Dwayne said. "You'll need a little breathing room."

Conthan took several steps backward as Dwayne did the same. The room was well over two hundred feet long. Conthan continued putting space between them. He knew they were going to test his powers. He didn't think the senior member of this operation was going to hurl bolts of lightning at him for a warmup.

"I want to go on record that you're both assholes."

"I see why Skits likes him," Dav5d said with an awkward grin.

"She's always been a fan of loudmouth men."

"Much like her brother." Dav5d smiled at Dwayne, forcing the awkward expression until it seemed almost painful.

"We need to work on your puns."

Dwayne pulled off his t-shirt, tossing it to the ground. Sparks continued to jump from his hands to his torso. He had done this with a dozen newly awakened Children before. This was the first time the person on the other end of the room had an ability more impressive than his own. He had spent the better part of a decade tackling the wild nature of his lightning. He hoped with some guidance, it wouldn't take Conthan as many errors to get a grip.

Dav5d pulled out a small silver ball. He let it go in the air and it began scanning Conthan, projecting a plethora of vitals in front of Dav5d. "I'm ready."

"Ready?" Dwayne asked Conthan.

"To have lightning hurled at me? Yeah, I woke up thinking this would be…"

Bolts erupted from Dwayne's fists, flying in the general direction of the newest recruit. Lightning struck the floor and punched a wall near Conthan, leaving burn marks as it sought out its target. He jumped out of the way, rolling along the floor.

"Not liking this!"

"Heart rate elevated. His neurotransmitter epinephrine levels are rising. Temperature rising and lung activity rising."

"He's scared, I get it."

Conthan clenched his fists, trying to find that sensation at the back of his skull. The smell of burning ozone brought him back to reality, distracting him. Dwayne had both fists up. The snap of the lightning sounded its release from his hands. Conthan ducked, his hands covering his head.

"You're not going to be able to duck forever."

"His vitals are remaining far calmer than I would have expected."

Dwayne held his hands to his sides. The snap sounded again as electricity flooded from his skin's surface all along his hands and torso. The lightning arced all about the room, more wildly than when he started. Dwayne squinted, looking away from the electricity.

Conthan raised his head long enough to see there was no way to duck the oncoming barrage from his trainer. He fell backward, landing on his butt. The lightning slowed. The pain ruptured through the base of his skull. The floodgates opened.

Conthan made no gesture. Survival was the only thought he could focus on. *Do not die.* The black disc appeared hovering in the middle of the air. There was no resistance as he opened the portal into nothingness. His mind raced, moving more quickly than the lightning approaching him.

His eyes were open, the scene before him didn't vanish, and yet he wasn't looking through his eyes anymore. One end of the portal was open and his power screamed to create an exit. It took effort to not let his abilities chose the destination of the second void. As the wave of lightning entered the portal, a surge in his brain forced him to open a second to the side of Dwayne.

Dwayne didn't have time to react as lighting poured out of the second portal, hurling him against the wall. He hit the floor with an oomph and sucked in a deep breath. He inspected his body for burns but was lucky enough the electricity only knocked him to the floor.

"It's fascinating," Dav5d said, passing his hand through the portal. He watched it appear from the void on the far end of the room. The small sphere in the air produced a red beam, scanning the black circle hanging above the ground.

"You have produced a miniature black hole, or the closest thing to it I can relate. You've managed to bend space." Dav5d turned to Dwayne, who was picking himself up from the ground. "Most of the Children of Nostradamus have benign powers that are repeated elsewhere in nature. Alyssa and myself and even Dwayne only have control over our own bodies. Yours, Conthan, has a release valve that is a bit more of a spectacle. Vanessa, Skits, and now Conthan are able to control things beyond their physical selves. Vanessa's abilities defy a scientific explanation for the time being."

Conthan stepped closer to them. His eyes were black orbs, void of any color.

"Conthan, however, is altering a fundamental constant of physics."

"I have no idea what you're saying," Dwayne said, trying to even his breathing.

"We would have said he was a Class I." Dav5d examined the readouts. "He is something we haven't seen before."

"Could there be more?" Dwayne asked.

Dav5d shrugged. "I have no idea."

"When the human computer is at a loss for words, we have a problem."

Conthan watched as the sphere entered the void. As it hovered, half in the portal, he let the tension in his body relax. The portal shut fast. As it closed around the small orb, he could feel the resistance, the pain surging outward from his brain as it sliced through the metal. He yelped.

"Damn," Dwayne said as half of the sphere fell to the ground. He turned to see the other half where the other portal had been. "Nifty trick."

Conthan's body felt different. He was thrilled he had opened a portal through space, but with each new discovery, it was as if he were starting to take up residence in a stranger's body. He took a deep breath and turned to the others. "Ready to go again?"

Chapter Fourteen

May 19th, 2032 7:12AM

"She sent our men to die," cried Roderick.

"She has no respect," cried another.

Vanessa shifted on the stool, making herself comfortable for what was going to be a long discussion. Sitting in a makeshift war room, half a dozen men and women stared at her. She attempted to keep her chin lifted, showing an air of grace about her. Her wings were tightly drawn to her back, but visible for all to see. Every so often she would relax them, calling attention to them, a reminder of who they were talking to. She had been associated with Victor and Roderick for years; she knew how to exploit their belief in her origins.

There must have been several dozen people housed in the hotel. If she focused on her breathing, the individual thoughts became white noise she couldn't make out. Every time her attention returned to them, they became louder. A woman cried because her husband was shot today. Another person cried out in pain as the surgeon stitched the last of the cuts on his arm from a stray bullet. A child innocently played with building blocks as he tried to recreate their home.

Can you hear me?

Twenty-Seven was scrubbing at the blood on her hands. She was exhausted from helping in the makeshift hospital. She was an expert at changing bandages and cleaning stitches. She had found herself sleeping on the floor late this morning. A stranger had placed a blanket over her. The smile on her face faded as she saw the blood.

I can, replied Vanessa.

I had a dream last night. I woke from this. I was home again. I was in my house, wearing my clothes, and preparing dinner.

Vanessa listened with her ears to the Outlanders in the room. They had begun to discuss things completely unrelated to her. They were angry and their anger was causing the flaws in their society to surface. There was rage in their words. In their minds was something far more dangerous…fear.

You do not sound sad to be here.

He was there. He was dead, but there. It was like every other night. He walked in the door angry. He began to berate her/me. He began to insult me—I mean her. Whenever that poor woman resisted, he would tell her nobody would love her like he did. He chiseled away at her self-esteem until there was nothing left.

You killed him in your dream?

No. Twenty-Seven did.

The hair on the back of Vanessa's neck began to

stand from the sensations washing over her. Vanessa had felt bad for the woman at first. The angel had rescued her. Vanessa resisted smiling at the feelings of confidence she was receiving.

She will be a magnificent woman.

Vanessa turned her head slightly to look through the windows into the hallway. Twenty-Seven was standing there, giving her a slight wave. Twenty-Seven reached the doors, pushing through and sitting in the corner of the room. The newest addition to their ranks listened intently to the discussion escalate and return to the subject of dead friends and family.

"I am truly sorry," she said very quietly.

The people froze as she spoke. She had become almost statuesque in the room. Roderick, his arm in a sling across his chest, snarled at her interruption. "What is that, angel?"

His words were dripping with venom as he emphasized both syllables. She hated being equated to religious iconography, but she had no problem allowing them to find solace in her presence. She looked to each of the Outlanders occupying the room. "I am sorry for your losses…each and every one of them."

"Your apologies don't bring them back," a woman cried out.

Vanessa looked at the woman, who was wearing an old military jacket, her face covered in grime. On one hand, she pitied the Outlanders, their lifespan ticking away more quickly than it should. She had come to respect them, their bold nature and desire to be free. There was pride evident in each of them, layers below their desire to do good. Even Roderick, his anger visible through clenched teeth and drawn fists, was a decent man who wanted the best for the people he adopted as a family.

While Outlanders were survivalists, they were reduced to relying on their limited resources. Radiation allowed pathetic crops to grow. Scavenging was essential to their existence. Each of the people in the room showed side effects of the radiation, red patches and skin discoloration. They had either fled the police states of the civilized world once the bomb hit or were sent here by the same police others renounced.

"My heart is heavy," she said. "People I rescued from banishment paid the ultimate price. I brought them here, to a sanctuary created to be a bastion of humanity in a cold land."

She bit her lip. She could feel the emotions wrapping themselves about her. She would return to the church and mourn the fallen. Her tears would wet the floor as she prayed for forgiveness. She let out a breath she didn't realize she was holding and made eye contact with Twenty-Seven. Sitting across the room, her latest rescue was watching her, eyes fixed on the winged woman. Vanessa took solace knowing one person still had faith in her.

She listened to their thoughts as they mulled over her words. The Outlanders were a self-governed tribe, but they listened to her wisdom. None believed she was an angel sent by God—they knew she was a Child of Nostradamus—but it didn't stop them from putting the burden of their lives on her shoulders. She watched them all turn to Victor, their leader.

He pondered his words before speaking. He had been elected by the group years ago to take charge of the Outlanders. On a typical day, he oversaw minor disputes amongst his clan and helped make sure everybody was capable of surviving another day. He hated it. He would sever a limb to help another person, but carrying the burden of the people around him was killing him as fast as the radiation.

"They will send death squads. They will send mechs. They may even send Children. Angel, our only option is to move further into the Danger Zone. The radiation will be the least of our worries if they send soldiers after us."

"My offer stands, Victor."

"How do you know your plan will work?"

"I have faith," she said flatly.

Roderick sauntered toward her. "You drop people here as a penance. You expect us to make good on promises you make to these bandits. Who the hell do you think you are?"

He took another step toward her to poke his finger into her chest. She moved forward and thrust her hand against his chest. He launched into the air with a grunt, then smacked against the ground. Nobody in the room moved to help him.

"You witnessed those in my charge earlier today. They have gifts that will take you to a home that will not kill you. Do not leave your people to die, Victor."

He will not take my offer.

Why? We're going to die here.

He doesn't trust I can keep his people safe. He wants a certainty I can't provide.

The white noise diminished. Vanessa pried further into Twenty-Seven's mind and felt a cool sensation press against her own. She reached out with her thoughts, pouring her emotions and thoughts into Twenty-Seven. Something reached through Twenty-Seven's mind, trying to grab at her. Vanessa panicked.

"The Outlanders aren't here anymore, Angel—or perhaps I should call you Vanessa?"

She froze at the statement. Victor spoke, but the voice had changed to a deep, booming bass. The man in front of her changed; his back straightened while his fists clenched. Vanessa could smell the difference in the air.

She smiled at the man. "What are you doing here, Warden?"

"I don't think you understand the capability of my powers, Vanessa," he said, dragging out the sound of her name. "The capabilities of *your* powers."

She didn't move a muscle in reaction to his taunting. "What I can do is far different than what I choose to do," she said. "As you discovered earlier."

"You caught me off guard," he said with a hint of anger. "It has been so long since I've been in the company of another telepath."

"You mean, a mind you cannot dominate."

"Hush," the man said. "I could easily infiltrate that mind and wreak havoc. But peons do the job better."

She tried to not let the surprise show on her face as each of the other humans stood up and turned toward her. She heard the whispers being broadcast to each of them. Their hands all moved toward weapons tucked into waistbands and holsters. An echo of safety switches being flipped off filled the room.

"Ours is a power of the mind," he said. "But where God made us strong, he forgot about the vessels holding this incredible gift."

"Gift?" she asked.

"Don't be coy," he said. "You revel in your powers almost as much as I do my own."

"There is a difference between us," she said as she stood up, brushing off the back of her robes.

"What is that, my lovely?"

She stretched out her wings. "My body is anything but frail."

She spun and her feathered appendages slammed into Victor's side, knocking him to the ground. She jumped upwards, using her wings to suspend herself in the air, and kicked the nearest man in the jaw, sending him smacking against a wall. She dropped down, her elbow making contact with the collarbone of a small woman.

"Be gone," she cried, letting the sound echo in her mind and directing it outwards.

She could see the facial expressions flicker on several of the people as they came back to their senses. "You need to flee," she said to the confused humans.

"What is going...?" muttered one of the Outlanders.

They froze and turned back to her and spoke in unison. "Vanessa, we do not approve of this violence."

One of the fallen humans grabbed onto her robes. She kicked at him, sending him backward. The darkness of the Warden's presence enveloped the people around her. She knew what he was doing. She couldn't match him. Her ability to take over the body of another person was minimal, but she could see she had little choice.

She drove her thoughts into Twenty-Seven, gripping on to her with all the willpower she could muster. Vanessa could see the darkness as if it was in the room clinging to the woman. She directed her rage, using it as fuel to force the man from his host. The moment it loosened its hold she grabbed onto Twenty-Seven. She was now seeing through both her eyes and the eyes of Twenty-Seven.

Two bodies moved in concert, dancing around one another, punching, kicking, and shoving the opposition away. The angel used her wings to keep the attackers at bay while Twenty-Seven punched and threw others away from them.

Both individuals halted when Vanessa heard a bang and felt a stinging in her chest. She looked down and could see her robes and the military jacket Twenty-Seven wore at the same time. A dark red stain began to emerge from the jacket and her connection to the woman began to grow dark. She pulled her mind back and started to scream aloud.

"I'd like to think I am above using a gun," said the voice, "but it does have its uses."

Vanessa froze and called out to the person most

likely able to hear her, the last person whose mind she had inhabited. Conthan. The man lay in his bed, asleep, exhausted. She felt the ache of his muscles from rehearsing his abilities. She felt the natural resistance inherited by the Children of Nostradamus as she pushed at his defenses. She pooled the rage and anguish, used it as ammunition, and she felt his resistance shatter and his muscles tense as he woke from his slumber.

Vanessa's body went limp as a man punched her hard across the face. With his minions surrounding her, he was capable of seeing her from a dozen different angles. He stared at the angel before him. She could hear his thoughts as he realized she was far more impressive than he imagined. Her image melted away like an illusion, her alabaster skin transitioning to dark green. He was even more fascinated as the feathers of her wings began to fall away, and he realized that he had plenty of secrets to pry from her mind.

***

Conthan reached out, knocking a light from the nightstand. He tore at the sheets, trying to push them away from his body. He jumped out of bed and fell to the floor. The plush rug under his knees reminded him he wasn't in his own apartment. Reality washed over him. He was in Boston, in a hotel, deep within the Danger Zone.

"Vanessa," he called out.

His heart raced. He steadied himself, trying to control his breathing. The sun was still shining through the windows. His muscles hurt from working with Dav5d earlier, and they fought him as he raised himself to his feet. What was supposed to be a brief nap had lasted hours. He sat on the edge of the bed, surprised Vanessa wasn't in the room with him. There was the fleeting sensation that she was watching him.

The door burst open. Dwayne's hand was already starting to radiate light. He turned to the corners of the room, looking for danger. "You all right?"

Conthan shook his head. "Vanessa is in danger. I think. I mean, I'm not entirely sure."

"How?" Dwayne paused for a moment and shook his head. "Never mind. I'll get the others. Meet downstairs."

Conthan closed his eyes and had an image of Vanessa being dragged into the shadows by smoky tendrils. She was in a hotel not too different from the one they lived in now. Around her there were people littering the ground, barely moving. He didn't know how much was real and how much his mind created, but he knew the fear on her face was legit.

He reached for his jacket and walked toward the door. He had no idea what they were going to do to get her back. He had no idea how he was going to be of use, but after a morning of training and a power nap, he figured there was no better time to become a member of the team.

"I'm so going to get killed."

***

Her boots jingled as she walked into the school. She reached for the handle to the door leading toward the lobby and found it was locked. Jasmine appreciated their need for security to keep the school safe. She pulled harder, snapping the lock and forcing the door open.

It had been years since she had been in any sort of school. It brought back more than her fair share of unpleasant memories. School must be hellish for every teenager, but when you were a Child of Nostradamus, it required extra effort to blend in. She had never been good at fading into the background. The readout on her wrist showed the blueprints of the school and which room she was currently in. She looked at the secretaries through their glass window. They both stood up to speak with her.

"Can we help you, miss?"

Jasmine pointed to the patch on her jacket. Their eyes opened wider, but she was certain it was because of the brand on her neck marking her as a Child of Nostradamus.

"I'm here for an extraction."

"You can't just barge in here," one woman said boldly.

Jasmine was wearing a dark red body suit with a black tactical vest. Her belt hugged her hips tightly and she reached down to one of the guns it held. Tapping the weapon, she eyed the woman. "I am sanctioned to fire upon anybody who interferes with my orders."

Both women froze. "Uhm," one stammered, "go right in."

Jasmine continued walking into the hallway. Only one student was in the hall. The teen girl gave her a disgusted look, rolled her eyes, and walked into the bathroom.

"I see not much has changed."

Jasmine followed the layout on her wrist as she navigated the halls. Unlike every extraction before, she was going against protocol. Instead of bringing in backup, she left them stationed outside the main doors. She was here to apprehend a Class III, and she didn't see any reason to interrupt an entire school to bring a sixteen-year-old girl in for questioning.

"Resistance?" asked a voice in her earpiece.

It wasn't the first time she had thought about walking into a school carrying two loaded guns. In her weaker moments during puberty, she thought about massacring a locker room full of girls who ridiculed her. Her father's guns were kept in a desk drawer in his office. It wouldn't have taken any effort. She had played the scenario out a thousand times. Before she fell victim to revenge, she had been extracted in a process not much different than this.

A trio of students backed up to their lockers as she walked by. It was juvenile, but she smiled at them as she passed. They weren't Becky Saunders, but at least for a moment she felt vindicated. She stopped in front of K007, a sign on the door reading 'Mrs. Haley.'

The teacher was projecting a map on the board. She pointed to an area just east of the Mediterranean. Jasmine wondered if the class was geography or a history class. Sitting two seats back, closest to the door, her target scribbled notes furiously.

Jasmine took a breath and reached for the door. She never liked collaring Class III Children. Their powers were harmless. It got even worse when it was a teenager who was doing everything to simply fit in. She opened the door and the entire class froze, staring at her less-than-modest uniform.

The teacher walked up to the soldier, keeping her voice down. "Have mercy on the poor girl."

"You reported her," Jasmine whispered.

The woman nodded. She leaned in close and said, "The administration made me. She's a sweet girl and has enough problems at home. You must remember what it was like at that age."

The students began to mumble about the exchange, very aware of the woman and the guns she wore on her hips. The instructor turned to the class and in a flawless teacher voice said, "Rebecca, this lovely lady needs to talk to you."

The girl's eyes darted back and forth. She stood up and walked toward the door. She looked at Jasmine and then to her teacher. "I'm sorry." She began to cry.

Jasmine remembered it happening much the same way. Instead of a single woman entering the classroom, it had been half a dozen soldiers with guns drawn. There was no way to hush the whispers as Rebecca's classmates began to talk about the insignia on her vest.

Rebecca's face was wet from the tears. She tried wiping them away but couldn't stifle her sniffling.

Her voice was shaky as she spoke. "I promise not to do it again."

"You've been identified as a Child of Nostradamus." Jasmine began her speech. "You will be taken to an intake facility and your powers evaluated. If your powers pose no threat to humanity, you will be released and allowed to live amongst humans."

"I am human," cried the young girl.

Jasmine gripped her gun at the outcry. Most soldiers would have sedated the subject and taken her out in restraints. Jasmine nearly stumbled as the girl reached out, grasping her in an embrace. Jasmine watched as the girl's skin turned as red as her jumper. Her powers were developing, and still controlled by her emotions. She didn't need to be tested, she needed a mentor.

"Why are you doing this to me?"

Jasmine pulled the girl off her and kneeled next to her. "You'll be back in school within the month," she said. "Behave and work with the people at the facility."

The girl wiped her face with the sleeves of her shirt. "How do you know that?"

Jasmine pushed the girl back. She remembered how terrified she had been on the car ride to the facility. It wasn't the men holding guns or the fact they had stolen her in the middle of the day. She had been worried about disappointing her father.

"I'm a Child of Nostradamus."

The girl's eyes opened wide. "Then why are you doing this to me?"

Was it duty? Was it because she believed in the

mission? Jasmine asked herself the same question. Her reasoning didn't extend far beyond survival. She had once felt that it was the right thing to do, taking powered people that were causing chaos off the streets. Now it had become a witch hunt for people with anomalies. She thought of the man who was able to fling lighting; he was dangerous. This girl, her biggest concern was her first kiss.

Jasmine listened as the radio in her ear began to talk about activity in the Danger Zone. The government wouldn't send humans on this mission. She would be sent alone, perhaps with mechs. It was only a matter of minutes before new orders were barked into her ear.

Jasmine took the girl's shoulders in her hands. "I'm being called away on another mission."

"What about me?"

Jasmine pulled out her earpiece and covered it. "I can't tell you what to do. But they will continue to come for you as long as they know where you are. My suggestion is, find a way to vanish. Your life as you know it is over."

"My parents?"

"If they won't support you, it's up to you to survive any way you can."

The girl's tears began pouring down her cheeks again. "My life is over."

Jasmine nodded. She wanted to tell her it wasn't going to be a bad existence. She wanted to say she would return in time for her prom. Jasmine couldn't lie to the girl. "Head north to Canada or into the Danger Zone. You won't be safe, but it'll stop the government from coming after you."

Jasmine pushed the earpiece into her ear and heard the gruff voice of the general. "Jasmine, what is your position?"

"Was about to apprehend a Class III. I'm heading back to the transport. We will be able to reach the Danger Zone within the hour."

"We lost radio contact."

She had no doubt he was aware of the entire situation. "I will need backup."

"No soldiers," the man said flatly.

"Mechs?"

"We're sending in prototypes as support. Jasmine," he said with a calm voice. "If this does not pan out, you will be terminated. It is either them or you."

If there weren't a kill chip in the base of her skull, she would have chosen another path. She felt the weight of the decision, the girl in front of her and the battle on the horizon. She was a puppet for people who would just as soon see her dead. Her humanity continued to slip away as she became nothing more than a tool.

"Yes, sir."

***

"What's the plan?" asked Dwayne.

Dav5d examined the other four people standing in the deserted street with him. His brain processed the information at hand. He knew their strengths and weaknesses and had no trouble saying they could easily wrangle the Outlanders.

"There is something bigger at play," he

confessed.

"How so?"

Dav5d didn't believe the Outlanders would risk a fight between the two groups. Their weapons were limited and their reliance on Vanessa for guidance had been the focal point of their relationship. Without her, they wouldn't be able to screen new members or explore deeper into the radiated stretches of the Danger Zone. He continued to compute the data on the Outlanders, their activities, their roster of members, their stronghold in western Massachusetts.

"It does not add up."

"You don't know?" Dwayne hated when Dav5d said he didn't know something. For him to be stumped, there was something wrong with the situation before it began.

"I did not say that. The Outlanders would not do this."

"Then what?"

"It's the Warden," Conthan said.

The glazed over look on Dav5d's face gave away the intensity of his abilities at work. His brain processed information at a speed computers had yet to reach. "I'm finding logical leaps, but it does hold a high probability considering our recent interactions."

"It is," Conthan said firmly. "I saw him, or something like him, in my dream. There's no way Vanessa would have showed me that unless she wanted me to see it."

"Agreed," Dav5d said.

"We go in," Dwayne said.

"The four of you will go. I am going to prepare the rest to leave." Dav5d said.

"You're leaving?" asked Conthan.

"We were many once. The onslaughts have become fewer, but the government is not done attempting to eradicate us. The rest of this tribe does not have abilities as aggressive as yours. If for some reason you were to be held up, they would be defenseless."

Dav5d didn't try to hide the discomfort he was feeling. He was speaking logically, but he couldn't explain the feeling in his gut. He had tried to explain his emotional state by the chemicals being processed in his brain. Dwayne had frequently told him the discomfort in the pit of his stomach was love, but it was difficult to understand. He was a master of information, but the moment his heart came into play, he became confused.

"She'll be okay."

"I'll head west in the trucks with the others. If you succeed, I'll make sure Vanessa's promise is honored and I'll take the Outlanders north. We will meet with Dominique and Trevor. Vanessa would want us to make good on her promises. It is the least we can do."

"Dominique and Trevor?" Conthan asked.

"Did you think we were the only Children? We have allies in Canada. They've taken in refugees who need a life closer to the one they left behind."

Skits cracked her knuckles and rolled her head, stretching the muscles in her neck. She faked a few punches while jumping up and down. "I am so ready to beat the snot out of somebody."

"Dav5d, can you load me up?" asked Alyssa.

Dav5d punched several buttons on the computer attached to his gauntlet. He took the computer off his wrist and handed it to Alyssa. Videos played at an alarming speed. Each showed a woman practicing some variation of martial arts. She then switched to knives, guns, and even a sword. Alyssa watched closely, every now and then mimicking one of the poses in the videos.

"What is she doing?" asked Conthan.

"Muscle memory. She only needs to see it once."

"My mom used to yell at me for trying stuff I saw on TV." Conthan was still surprised at the diversity of their gifts.

"Practice makes perfect. Her body takes the visuals and it's as if she's practiced for years. Watch as she fights. Her body is a living weapon. She can also play the piano better than any I've ever seen."

"Damn."

"She'll retain it for a few days. The more she tries to learn, the faster it fades. It might not be there long, but while it is, she's a master."

Dav5d's abilities forced him to see beyond the random and analyze the significance of each of them being on the team. Dwayne was the leader in the field, fast to action and defensive of the people in his charge. He was the action to Vanessa's voice of reason. His younger sister was always ready to get into a scrape and with her powers, she was arguably the most dangerous. Alyssa had only been with them a year, but she complimented the others with her abilities letting her adapt in the field.

Conthan, the newest member, didn't have the same gung-ho attitude as the others. Dav5d deduced that he would be another powerhouse on the team once he managed his abilities.

Dwayne put his hand on Conthan's shoulder. "Conthan, we're going to be fighting. This isn't a video game. It's life or death." He patted Conthan on the chest. "Do you get what I'm saying?"

"It's kill or be killed," Skits said, her voice void of her usual playfulness.

Dav5d realized Conthan had never contemplated the idea of killing another living person. Dwayne's expression was relaying the dire situation. Dav5d noticed the slight stiffness in Conthan's spine and a minor angle change in his shoulders; regardless of his ethical issues, he was prepared to defend his companions.

Conthan nodded in response but never said he would kill aloud. He didn't like the idea. He was an artist, a person who tried to create beauty. Dav5d knew this lifestyle was foreign to him.

Skits punched him in the arm. "These fuckers deserve no less."

Dav5d didn't care for their more forceful ways, but he was certain there were times when no other options were present. It was a reality each of them faced, and even Conthan, hearing what was expected, was internalizing the discussion, trying to uncover what boundaries he firmly drew in the sand. Dav5d suspected that when it came to his companion locked away at the facility, Conthan would be capable of far more forceful tactics than even he realized.

"It's the world we live in," Dwayne admitted. The man held out his hand, waiting for Conthan to return the gesture. As they gripped hands, Dwayne smiled. "You're family now."

Skits rolled her eyes. "Are we going to have a feeling circle now?"

"Ready, Alyssa?"

The girl looked up from the screen. Her eyes were a milky white. She jumped up and down, shaking her arms, loosening her muscles. As her irises emerged from the pools of white, she nodded.

"I am the shit," she barked, standing up from Dav5d's computer screen. "A little refresher course to keep me on my toes."

"It's up to you now," Dwayne said.

Conthan looked down to his hands. He had been able to make the portals a dozen times this morning. Opening them had almost been easy, but the destination of the other side was erratic at best. As the first and second were mislocated, he grew angry and his abilities began to work against him. Dav5d was impressed with his determination. This group, the Nighthawks, had rescued him and he was determined to not let them down.

"I've got this," he said to himself.

Dav5d watched as Conthan flexed his hands, attempting to call his powers. The kid did as they practiced earlier, focusing on the sensation in his skull and slowly trying to drag it outward. His breathing slowed as he attempted to focus. He shivered from the chill of the portal, a black empty hole nearly six feet tall suspended in air.

"Now to Vanessa," he said.

Dav5d knew Vanessa had been attempting to make Conthan's job easier by giving him contextual clues to her location. At this point, she was more aware of his abilities than he was.

His muscles tensed as his abilities tried to force open the other end of the portal. He wasn't sure what was happening, but it felt as if every inch of his body was on fire.

"He's straining," Alyssa said.

"He's opening a portal further away than he's done before," Dav5d said.

She looked from Dwayne back to Conthan, who was beginning to sweat. "Keep focusing," she encouraged.

He grunted and fell to one knee. Alyssa reached down to help him but paused as he opened his eyes. Dark obsidian orbs shone where they would have been. "Holy shit," she said, stepping back.

"Done," Conthan gasped. "Go quick."

Dwayne grabbed him under the shoulders and they both pushed through the darkness. Skits and Alyssa quickly followed. Dav5d watched the portal blink out of existence as quickly as it had appeared. He looked back to the hotel that housed the handful survivors of their clan. "Godspeed."

Chapter Fifteen

May 19th, 2032 8:46AM

Alyssa ducked below a swinging pipe and slammed her fist into her assailant's neck. She grabbed the pipe from the falling man and used it to block an oncoming fist from a second assailant. With the butt of the pipe, she cracked the man under the jaw, shutting his mouth and sending him to the ground.

With the pipe held out ready to strike, she spun about to a man holding a gun pointed at her. She tried to calculate if she could use the lead pipe to block the bullet. She took a step back as a line of white light flashed and hit the guy in the chest. She turned to see Dwayne emerge hand outstretched as he held Conthan.

"I had him," she said with a sneer.

"Not a solo mission," he said. "We work together."

"Such a wise brother," Skits mocked quietly.

Conthan raised his eyebrows at Alyssa, her chest

heaving as she breathed in and out rapidly. The two men on the ground next to her were breathing but not moving. She pointed to the seared fabric on the third man and the burn marks covering part of his body. "They're not going to be so kind. Do what you must."

"Gun?" Conthan asked, pointing to the weapon.

The other three shrugged their shoulders. Dwayne held up his hands. "I blow up ammo."

Skits held up her hands in a similar manner. "I focus plasma"—she smiled—"and blow up ammo."

Alyssa just rolled her eyes. "I'm a living weapon. No guns."

Conthan picked it up and checked that the safety was off. "So basically I'm the wimp on the team."

Skits patted him on the shoulder. "Somebody has to be."

Dwayne examined the room while the two exchanged quips back and forth. "Be creative with your abilities, Conthan, they're more powerful than you give them credit for."

"If they work."

"Where are we?" Alyssa asked.

"We're in the hotel the Outlanders use as their base of operations. A conference room?" he asked, examining the room. "We need to find where they're keeping Vanessa."

Conthan realized it was the room he had seen in his dream. Based on the number of people scattered across the floor, it appeared Vanessa had put up a fight before being captured.

Conthan touched his forehead. "Vanessa, can you hear me?"

"What are you doing?" Skits asked with a perplexed look.

"Isn't that how telepathy works?"

"You don't need to speak out loud. You're such a newb," she said.

"Sue me."

They ran over to one of the massive doors leading outside. Dwayne held up his fist, signaling them to stop. "If she's here, I can't hear her. That means there must be a dampener where she's being held."

"Dampener?"

"Keeps us from using our powers."

Skits hand began to burn blue. "Nope."

"It has to be the Warden," Conthan said. He tucked the gun into the small of his back as if it were a bad action film.

"Look at him, getting all brave," Skits said.

Dwayne peeked around the side of the door leading toward the mezzanine. There were hundreds of doors, and behind any of them, there could be a wave of Outlanders ready to shoot. The hotel was a giant circle, story after story, and at the center, balconies looked all the way down to the ground floor. He gestured to a man holding a gun several stories above them. Dwayne ducked and pointed across the way. "They're expecting us."

"How would they know we're coming?"

Dwayne raised an eyebrow. "He's got a point. Vanessa never told them she was a telepath. They wouldn't know the cavalry would be here. Something isn't adding up."

"Telepath," Conthan said.

"He's getting annoying," Skits said.

"He's most likely right."

"Then why are we hiding?"

They turned to Conthan. He just pointed out the window. "Wouldn't a telepath be able to tell we're here?"

"Shit," they all said.

"They took her," said a voice in the room.

Conthan's head tilted for a moment as he eyed the girl. "I recognize her from the dream." She was sitting against the far wall, cradling her arm. She appeared to have been shot through it. She didn't make any effort to move.

"Who took her?" asked Alyssa.

Conthan kneeled next to the woman. The blood had soaked through her military jacket and hoodie, coating her limp hand in crimson. He leaned her forward and took the layers off her. He began tearing at the sleeve until he had a long enough band to tie around her arm. Conthan noted the burned numbers on her skin. She was one of the people the government threw out of the States. She was forced here, not so different from his own situation.

"The Outlanders," she said through a hiss.

"Why?"

She shook her head. "They weren't themselves. I can't explain it."

Conthan was learning when something amazing happened and nobody had words to explain it, there was only one answer. "Telepath."

***

Vanessa stared at the two humans in front of her. A Latino man and a white woman stood there, holding guns against their chests, but with the slightest effort her eyes would see what her mind knew: the individuals in front of her were vacant. A specter hung in the air, manipulating their bodies as if they were marionette dolls.

"Why are you doing this?"

"Doing what?" they said together.

"Holding me?"

Both of the humans laughed in unison. She was startled by how they spoke, their voices almost perfectly in sync, as if they were merely extensions of one God-mouth. Her arms were bound to a pole behind her back while ropes reached from the ceiling to her wings, securing them in place. It wasn't enough that the Warden had her restrained, he put more innocent lives guarding her, assuring any escape would result in their death.

The woman walked up to the angel and caressed her face. "I would think somebody as removed from humanity as you would understand why I do it." She stood up straight, smiling at Vanessa's discomfort. "I do it simply because I can."

The pressure started at the base of her skull like two hands were attempting to squeeze her head. The Warden pushed against her mind, forcing her to guard her thoughts. He might have her restrained, but she had spent her entire life protecting herself from the thoughts of others. She couldn't go on the offensive, but she could defend against him indefinitely. "You will never break me."

"You think I need to touch your mind to do

that?"

The two laughed again at the expression flashing across her face. The woman got close to Vanessa, her mouth nearly touching the angel's lips. She quietly whispered, "Who said I was even after you?"

Vanessa realized her hubris would be her undoing. She had assumed she was the one the Warden was after. She could see the look of delight in the woman's eyes. Vanessa let a neutral affect settle on her face. "You're after my people."

The woman nodded. "I currently run the largest prison for powered people in the world. Doesn't it strike as you as odd that a Child of Nostradamus would want to dominate his own kind?"

Her eyes swallowed her emotions as she tried to see the Warden's expressions through his vessel. "You're building an army."

"At my possession are hundreds of the most deadly people on the planet. I am an unknown warlord."

"The government will stop you," she said.

The man laughed, and this time his laughter was cut with a mocking edge. The two Outlanders spoke in unison. "Who do you think put me in this position?"

Her face didn't give away her thoughts, but the silence spoke volumes. The two began again. "I became the Warden because the president trusted my service."

"You manipulated the president?"

The laughter grew to a crescendo. She imagined him sitting in his office, his eyes staring off into space as he manipulated the Outlanders like puppets. Her imagination put a sick smile on his real body's face. "You still don't understand, do you?"

Vanessa didn't need to process the information. Instead, she knew it was time to fight back. She stopped struggling and let a calm flow through her muscles. The unblinking humans stopped laughing at her change in demeanor.

She smirked at the two hosts. "Warden..." Her smirk unfolded into a smile. "You're a monster."

She stared across the room, letting her mind see beyond the wall. "Do it, Dwayne."

***

Electricity surged through his body, ripping from the surface of his skin and projecting outward. From near the top of the hotel, the floors below were in view. He clapped his hands together and they stung with the impact. The electricity continued to hammer a balcony below where gunners were hiding.

His body acted like a battery, and in one act it wanted to dispel the entirety of its charge. It was easy to stop the bolts when the battery was topped off, but as he reached further, scraping every ounce of power, the on switch began to stick. The light shot wildly toward his target, knocking against walls, shattering brick, smashing windows and causing the balcony to collapse. The Outlanders fell to the ground as his powers stopped their hearts on contact. It was lightning in every manner except the source.

His abilities would kill him if he gave into the euphoria he experienced every time he called his powers to the surface of his skin. He closed his fist and willed the lightning to stop.

The crashing sound of exploding windows was silenced. For a moment there was a calm throughout the hotel. Dwayne dropped to his knees as the first bullet flew through the air. He looked down to his hands and saw the heat radiating from them. He felt sick, as if he might throw up. He took a deep breath and pushed the feeling aside. "Here we go again."

***

"How can you…"

Vanessa turned her head as the wall exploded inward. Her captors were hurled against the adjacent wall. The shadow clinging to their bodies dissipated for a moment. For a moment they were themselves again. The darkness returned and clawed its hooks into the humans' backs.

The woman turned toward Vanessa, holding her rifle level with the angel's chest. Before her finger pulled the trigger, Vanessa flexed her wings, ripping the ropes from the ceiling. She dropped into a crouch and spun on the pole, using her wing to send the woman out the hole in the wall.

The man's eyes showed a moment of fear. She hoped it was the expression the Warden was wearing sitting in his office. She smiled as she pulled at the ropes, tearing them apart. She leaned forward, crawling on all fours. The sound of her nails dragging across the floorboards filled the air between the sounds of distant gunfire.

"You tricked me."

"An arrogant man tricks himself," she said, lunging at him.

The man tried to reach for the knife on his belt. She grabbed his hands and slammed her forehead into his, leaving a bloody mess. She leaned in close to his face. "We're coming for you."

"Do your—"

She spun the man's head, cracking his neck. She threw the body across the room and wiped the blood from her face. She let a scream erupt from her mouth. The sound of the guttural cry echoed in the ears and minds of every human in the hotel.

***

"Get me close," Alyssa said to Skits.

Conthan watched as Skits held out her hands as if they were ready to perform a karate chop. In the blink of an eye, the air around them began to show radiant heat, and a second later the air around her hands burst into a dense blue fire. Alyssa stepped back from the intense flare pouring out of her friend's body. Skits moved her hands in a circular pattern, the plasma looking like liquefied glass hanging in mid-air. As the girl moved her arms faster, the plasma took a disc shape.

"On it," she said, kicking the door open and charging down the balcony.

Conthan sat the human woman down on bench. Her arm hung in a poorly constructed sling. "Are you going to be okay?"

"Can you save Vanessa?"

"I'm going to try." He hesitated before leaving her. "How do you know her name?"

"Long story. She can do stuff in your head. She saved me."

"Me too. Why aren't you like them?"

She shrugged.

"Stay here. We have some saving to do."

As he ran out to the balcony he heard a woman screaming from above. Her body was launched from several stories up, hurled down the center of the hotel to the ground level. It thumped against the ground and stopped moving.

"Holy shit," he said. It wasn't a game. People were dying. There were more who were going to die. He thought of the gun at his back. He tried to imagine himself pulling the trigger.

"Warden," he hissed.

Alyssa threw a knife, landing it square into the chest of a gunman. They were near the top of the staircase leading to the banquet rooms below. Scattered about were men and women with rifles. The Nighthawks were very outnumbered.

A horrific primal scream shook the walls of the hotel. The cry sounded like a woman in distress but the echo in his mind told him Vanessa was pissed. He glanced up just in time to see her launch from the balcony. Her wings stretched outward as she plummeted toward them at a brisk pace. She pulled up just before hitting the floor, knocking two gunmen onto the faded carpet.

Conthan balled his left fist and the tingling

started coursing through his body. He charged toward Alyssa and Skits as they fended off two attackers. A third man stepped from behind a pillar, holding a rifle. Conthan pulled out his gun and began to squeeze the trigger. The weapon jerked upward with each trigger pull.

None of his shots hit the attacker. He chucked the gun with all his might and let his balled fist open. A small dark hole appeared in the air, consuming the gun. A split second dragged on for an eternity. The open hole in the air was like an explosion through his body, forcing the second void to appear next to the creeping assailant. The gun emerged, clubbing the guy on the side of his face.

Skits saw the gun strike from nowhere, knocking him to the ground. "Points for creativity."

Conthan squeezed his hand again, but the portals resisted closing. He clenched his fist tighter, letting his nails dig into his palm, and the two holes vanished. He opened his fist, this time directly in front of him. He shoved his hand through the wall of black. The icy sensation coated his arm as if he had plunged it into a bucket of ice water. As the second portal opened, his muscles relaxed.

His hands appeared twenty feet away. He grabbed onto a man's collar and dragged him backward onto the ground. He pulled his hand back and growled at the effort needed to close the portal.

"Don't overextend yourself," Alyssa said through her panting.

They both ducked into the hallway leading to the elevators. "What?"

"Your body can only handle so much at first.

Use it as you need it, but you've seen how fast the fatigue sets in."

"Stop your yammering." Dwayne barked.

Skits dropped to one knee, sweat dripping off her forehead. "They're everywhere."

"They're skilled," Alyssa commented. She grunted as she took a gun from one of the Outlanders. The annoyance showed on her face as she cocked the weapon and took several shots at the Outlanders. She stayed hidden behind the wall while she reached around and pulled the trigger. "Had I known, I would have watched more trick shot videos."

"No need for guns, huh?"

Alyssa glared at Conthan. "Shut the fuck up."

***

Conthan watched Vanessa drop low to the ground, using the wall around the mezzanine for cover. She sprinted with her wings tucked in close to her body. At the last moment she launched herself into the hallway, barreling into the opposite wall. She scurried out of harm's way. "They're possessed by the Warden."

"All of them?"

Vanessa nodded in reply. "All of them."

She looked back to the angel pressed against the wall. "Can you possess a few of them?"

Vanessa shot Skits a dirty look. "No."

All the firing stopped.

"That doesn't usually happen," Skits remarked.

"You cannot stop us," came voices from all

around them. "You won't kill all of us."

Vanessa's mind began to ache. The imaginary hands were pressing against her skull again. "He's trying to get in our heads."

"Why?"

"Superhero army," Skits replied.

Conthan recalled the blank expression on Sarah's face. It suddenly made sense. "How do we stop him?"

"Killing them will only stop him here," she said.

"Then that's where we start," Skits announced.

She stepped around the corner, toward the staircase, while a man holding a knife-tipped rifle lunged at her. The man swung the blade in a wide arc, nearly catching Skits across the chest. She backed up as he lunged again, nearly catching her in the neck.

"Fuck you, dude," she said while her hands generated an intense heat. The blade of the gun pushed into the palm of her hand, cutting to the bone. Skits screamed, the liquid fire intensifying. The plasma thrust forward, encompassing the man's torso. His skin skipped the tender pink a burn would cause. Instead the plasma ate away at it until the smell of burned flesh filled the air.

The man fell to the ground. He didn't react to the hole in his body or his fast-approaching death. His face showed no emotion while he gazed at her. "You cannot defeat me."

"Really? Villain dialogue?"

Before the man could respond, Alyssa kicked him hard in the face, knocking the retort from his lips. She smiled at Skits. "Don't play with the bad guy."

Skits rolled her eyes. "Yes, ma'am."

He didn't try to hide his worry; the telepath's face reflected his own. He could only assume the fear radiating off his body was like screaming "I'm scared." She grunted and her eyes rolled back in her head from the pain. He had to assume it was the Warden. Conthan held the sides of her head in his palms. "We've got this."

As his finger touched her skin, she gasped. Hidden underneath his momentary confidence was a woman in a cell covered in bone shards. Once he realized it was the Warden doing this, he unraveled the truth behind Sarah's drugged state. He gave the telepath a slight nod, knowing she had seen every thought crossing his mind.

"Go," she said.

A calm moved through his body, relaxing his muscles and easing the tension between his shoulder blades. He balled up both of his fists, forcing the tension back into his body. He envisioned a well in his body brimming with a black fluid ready to spill over. He reached into the liquid and began to draw it through his limbs.

A crack of lightning rocketed toward the ground from stories above them. Conthan opened one hand, opening a void, and the lightning vanished into the black disc. He opened his other hand, and another small portal, and the lightning poured out, slamming into the chest of one of the Outlanders. He clenched his fist, drawing both holes to a close, and threw his arms out wide, opening a much larger portal behind the falling Outlander.

Conthan spun around to see an armed man perched on the seventh floor balcony. He opened his hands and the exit portal appeared above the sniper, purging the unconscious Outlander and knocking them both to the floor.

He strained his muscles to force the connecting tunnels to close. An old woman climbed the staircase, running toward their position. He couldn't form a plan. He reacted, opening both hands and letting the energy in him do as it wanted.

The void tried to open. The resistance was greater than for any of his portals before. He grunted with pain and pushed harder. He blinked as his mind attempted to process what it was seeing. Where the woman's upper body should have been was another void, opened from inside of her and expanding outwards, severing her torso. The sensation in his hands turned from tingling to burning. He opened another portal to the side of an Outlander trading blows with Alyssa.

Alyssa stepped back as a bloody torso slammed into her attacker. He was knocked to the ground. Alyssa grabbed the crowbar from the dead woman and clubbed him in the head, leaving his body still.

"That was disgusting," she yelled at Conthan.

The portals resisted his command to close. His muscles ached. In a few short minutes his arms hurt like he spent the day at the gym. He couldn't fathom how Dwayne managed to wreak so much havoc. With a loud grunt, the portals shut. He collapsed to the floor and braced his back against the wall.

Skits jumped onto Conthan and rolled over. She

began pushing the plasma into a shield. The heat bit into his skin. He wondered if it was worse than bullets. He managed to tuck his legs up, making his footprint on the ground smaller. He could see the cut in her hand. Where it should have been a deep bloody puncture through her palm, it was already cauterized into scar tissue. "Vanessa, he's out of commission," Skits said.

Conthan could barely make out his surroundings as she protected him. Bullets turned to liquid as they rained onto the ground. The angel turned skyward to see if there was any sign of Dwayne. There were too many Outlanders for them continue. The Warden treated the Outlanders as pawns, sacrificing them as if their lives meant nothing. He was proving he could outlast them.

Alyssa yelled back at the others, "There are too many of them."

Vanessa turned to see her somersault in the air. She landed on her back and rolled. The bullets were getting closer and closer. Alyssa's body would do what she wanted, but eventually it would fatigue.

Vanessa let her mind view the world and for a moment, each of the Nighthawks saw through her abilities. The moment she stopped looking with her physical eyes she could see the dark shadows wrapping themselves around the Outlanders. As one fell, the shadows would cling tighter to the living. "He's getting stronger as we remove players," Vanessa shouted.

Each of them could hear the buzzing in their heads getting louder. It started as a distant humming and now it was like listening to a raging river.

Vanessa cursed aloud. Conthan knew her wings were magnificent to look at, but her mind was her real weapon. She was useless unless she was able to use her telepathy.

Skits pointed up, drawing everybody's eyes to a dark shadow filling the skylights at the top of the hotel. "Not our calvary, but they're here."

A ship hovered over the window. Its wings held propellers facing upward, allowing it to fix itself in position. The hotel went silent for a moment. The skylight shattered into millions of tiny shards and rained downward. Alyssa and Vanessa ducked under a balcony as the glass scattered across the floor.

The Warden's thoughts were clear. *More toys for me to play with.*

The pressure pressing at Conthan's temples lessened. He turned to Vanessa and could see the relief on her face. The Warden pulled away. It was the first time she could breathe easily. Her expression quickly turned to panic. "He's trying to possess the Paladins."

Chapter Sixteen

May 19th, 2032 11:46AM

The world remained frozen. The inhabitants of the hotel waited for the Paladins to make their next move. A red figure fell from the craft. The line attached to her waist slowed her descent, but not enough to keep her from hitting the floor. Concrete crumbled and debris flew into the air. Vanessa had no doubt, it was the Child of Nostradamus the government relied on.

The angel began to laugh. The Warden's plans were about to come to a halt. "He can't possess powered people."

"Not helping us any," Alyssa said.

Vanessa heard the Warden's thoughts as if he was speaking aloud. "The Warden's going to kill the Outlanders to get the Paladin."

"Not our problem, Vanessa. If we stay, we're going to be shot."

Dwayne burst out of a door leading to the stairs. As Jasmine climbed to her feet, Dwayne pointed at the Paladin's Child of Nostradamus. "Not her! We're so screwed!"

Two more figures jumped out of the ship. Vanessa didn't need to see them to know they weren't human. Their awkward motions and silence gave away their lack of a brain. "She has reinforcements coming."

The two machines smashed into the concrete, leaving cracks along the floor. Their motors hummed to life as they stood. Their bodies were made from metal, covered in a malleable material to make them look human. She knew from Dav5d hacking the government computers they were capable of ripping cars in half. Housed within them were weapons the world had never witnessed before. Before anybody could react, two small black objects emerged from the shoulders of the robots. A burst of red light shot out, piercing and burning through the skull of an Outlander.

Jasmine let the machines do their job while she surveyed the hotel. Of the dozen humans she witnessed on her descent, two survived a laser to the forehead. The machines paused for a moment. The spent weapons on their shoulders ejected and fell to the ground. An identical device appeared on the other shoulder of each robot.

The Paladin didn't like machines for backup. Her team could think quickly and were capable of solving problems. The robots had adequate artificial intelligence, but most of their actions were being controlled by pilots in the government facility. Between the lag time and their inability to assess situations from a distance, she would prefer to be on her own.

Jasmine's years of service hadn't prepared her for what she saw next. She gasped out loud. At the far end of the hotel, a woman in a robe stepped from a hallway. She had never believed in God, but staring at the wings protruding from the woman's body, Jasmine questioned her decisions. The angel let her wings stretch outward, making a spectacle.

Jasmine had heard rumors there was an angel that watched over the banished. The government dispelled the angel's existence as a myth propagated by the desperate residents of the Outlands. Jasmine was to terminate every hostile. She could only imagine the gods would reign down hell for killing their servant.

She understood why the Outlanders worshipped this Child of Nostradamus. Jasmine couldn't help but wonder if the wings she so proudly displayed were capable of lifting her into the air or if they were a cruel joke. Jasmine pointed to the Children. "Contain them."

The machines didn't obey her command. She knew they were receiving orders from headquarters. She tapped her wrist and switched frequencies just in time to hear, "...to bring in their bodies."

"This is my mission, control."

"You're on a secure line, Jasmine."

"Let me do what you sent me here for."

"You've disappointed us twice in the last forty-eight hours."

"Twice?"

She clenched her jaw as the conversation between her and the teenager an hour earlier played over her earpiece. She balled her hands into fists with anger. There was almost no chance they were going to let her live. She had an impeccable track record, but the moment she began to side with the enemy, they would terminate her. She had only given the girl a fighting chance and Jasmine would die for it.

"We'll deal with you when you return."

The machines took a step toward the Children. The angel was blocking her companions, willing to die to provide seconds to their forfeited lives. Jasmine could only think of the girl; the letter she received had prompted her to show her humanity. For the moment, she felt pushing the girl away was the right move. She wouldn't live in a cell being studied like a rat, or worse, have an explosive attached to the base of her brain stem, controlling her every decision.

The robots sprinted toward their prey. The young girl on the ground, hands glowing a bright blue, jumped up from her fallen associate. Jasmine recognized the others from the attack on the Facility. These Children had caused her more grief in a few days than any powered being before them.

One robot lunged over the stairwell, grappling onto the wall, carrying itself closer to its first victim. The moment it had the girl in its sight, the gun moved on its shoulder, targeting her. The girl didn't appear afraid. Jasmine thought she was a fool.

"Run," the older man screamed.

Skits flexed every muscle. The heat radiated through her entire body and liquid flames consumed her upper half. She began to scream at the charging machine. Its shoulder cannon fired. The burst of red light sliced through the liquid fire and seared through her shoulder. The fire licked her wound, cauterizing it instantly. The girl had made a mistake, she should have run.

Her screams got louder as the machine came within arm's reach. Fatigue was setting in. She would be sore for days. She pushed harder and the blue flames leapt toward the machine.

Her screams caught in her throat. The thumping in her ears made it difficult for her to hear. Skits took two steps forward, grabbed the gun, and felt it resist her grip. Her hand ached as she pushed at the weapon and her screams ran out of breath and her throat ran dry. Her hand pushed through the durable metal exterior of the machine. Before she could push any further the machine reached through her plasma and grabbed her neck.

"No!"

Electricity hammered into the side of the robot, knocking it off its feet. Skits fell to the pavement, gasping for air as her powers shut off. The older man attempted to bear hug the machine on the ground. He let it grab him by the shoulders. He sucked in air and the electricity from its computer siphoned through its arms into his body.

Skits coughed as Dwayne drained the robot of power. "Thank God somebody knows what they're doing here." She gasped as he sat up and his eyes leaked energy, causing small sparks. His hands were arcing electricity between fingers as he started to growl.

Jasmine stared in amazement as the man tore electricity out of the machine. Their files on this group were sorely understated. She had assumed even after the assault on the prison they were just rogue Children. No, the way they functioned showed they had worked together before, not quite as skilled as her unit, but definitely cooperative.

"Careful," the girl choked.

He held one hand toward the other robot, which was positioning itself on top of a no longer functioning water fountain. The small black weapon on its shoulder turned toward Dwayne. He let the power pour out of his hand and began to scream. The electricity erupted throughout the hotel. His attention was focused on the machine, directing the lightning as much as he could. The machine fell back several feet. Its claw-like toes dug into the fountain, preventing it from sliding further.

He held up his other hand and let his body purge the energy. Jasmine held up her hands, trying to push away the biting hits of electricity. Her skin might be impervious, but this much energy had the potential to tear through her innards. Between outstretched fingers, she could see the Euphoria creep across the man's face. The bliss of allowing his power to consume him was too much to resist, she knew he'd die if he didn't wrangle in his gifts.

"Stop it, Dwayne," Skits cried out.

The hiss and roar was deafening. The crackling and popping sounded like gunfire. In the depths of his gut, his internal battery was fading. Every cell of his body pumped electricity into the air. It was nearly depleting his body. Even with his death looming above him, he found it difficult to care. With the least amount of effort, he attempted to shut off his powers.

Skits remained behind the man, avoiding the onslaught of vaporizing bolts of power. He turned his head, and the expression on his face spoke volumes. Regret filled his eyes as they returned to their normal deep brown.

"Sleep," Vanessa screamed as loud as she could. Jasmine tried to see past the barrage of lightning from the man. The angel was screaming at the man, commanding him to stop his assault. She had witnessed Children succumb to their abilities before, killed by the havoc their talents could inflict on themselves.

Jasmine stumbled forward as the lightning ceased, landing on all fours, and her skin sparking from the beating she received. Her strongest opponent fell to the ground. She dug her feet into the carpet-covered cement and began charging. She reached to her wrist and touched a metal band. Sharp pain attacked her entire body as her skin changed density, growing stiffer.

Stop.

She looked at each of the three conscious people and only the angel stared back at her. Jasmine had been working for the government for years. No Child had ever exhibited secondary mutations. With the single word hovering in her mind, she knew the angel was more than a woman with feathered wings.

"Telepath," she said out loud.

We are not your enemy, Paladin.

Jasmine pitied the angel. The Middle Eastern girl stood between them. Jasmine expected to feel the woman's body thud into her own. She charged with her shoulder leaning forward, determined to toss the girl aside. Instead she felt her feet knocked out from below, the agile girl sweeping her legs out from underneath her. She slammed into the ground hard enough to crack the pavement.

"Killing your own is a no no," said the girl, lying low with her leg stretched outward.

Jasmine rolled back to her feet and squared off against her. She was one of the most highly trained individuals on the planet and she was being bested by a Middle Eastern girl with no visible powers.

"I'll let you give up now," said Alyssa.

Jasmine laughed at the bravado of the young female. "You can't hurt me," she said in truth.

Alyssa knew the woman's taunt would become action. The direction of her big toe would lead to a right hook. Alyssa caught the fist, pushed it out wide, spinning her attacker about. The steely woman's leg buckled as Alyssa drove her foot behind her knee. Alyssa used her shoulder to force her back to the ground. Then she rolled backward out of her grasp.

"Awww," Alyssa said. "You took a few basic fighting classes, how quaint."

Jasmine eyed the cyborg. Its chassis was melted in several spots, but his humanoid head moved to follow their fight. The eyes of her supervisors watched. She was in a fight for her life against bureaucrats and researchers. If she failed, without a doubt she'd be terminated with the flip of a switch.

Jasmine clambered back to her feet, feigned a punch with her right fist, and instead brought her knee up to connect with the girl. The girl spun out of harm's way, dodging the attack. Her arms wrapped around Jasmine's neck, taking her off her feet. Jasmine struggled but couldn't get leverage to break free.

"Submit," the girl said.

"Never."

Jasmine tapped another of the bands on her uniform and sharp pain rushed across her skin. Her body lurched as it adapted to the new material. Neither metal was more dense than the other, but she knew that the girl would let go as her skin rolled like liquid to its new state.

Alyssa let go just as she predicted. She let her grip break and spun around just in time to catch an elbow thrust. She tried to stop the blow but felt the power behind the assault seemed disproportionate to the woman. Alyssa stumbled backward and the woman was on her quickly.

"Submit."

"Bitch."

Jasmine hovered over the girl, annoyed with the Child's fighting ability. She stared at the fallen girl's eyes, watching as they flicked back and forth rapidly as if they were reading a book at lightning speed. The girl could avoid her attacks, but she didn't seem capable of gaining the advantage.

Alyssa yelped as a red beam struck the Paladin's back. The laser scattered, striking the carpet near Alyssa's head and burning a hole through the material. Jasmine fell to her knee, reaching for the burn behind her. Jasmine hissed, "I felt that."

Even with its lack of eyes, Jasmine could feel the machine staring at her. She knew the general was getting his wish. She was cancelled. The machine continued its mission of terminating all Children. Jasmine turned to see the angel standing between it and her. There was nothing the woman could do with her telepathy. The robots were part of a resurrected program used to hunt mentalists in the nineties. Their artificial intelligence was combined with a team of operators in a building far away tucked away from the influences of their abilities.

"You cannot have her."

The cyborg reached out, grabbing the angel, and hurled her to the side. Her body hit the wall and stopped moving. Jasmine turned her head toward Alyssa while trying to get to her feet quickly. The robot fired another laser, landing squarely against Jasmine's cheek. She cried out as the heat burned her skin.

She tried to get up, but the machine kicked her in the chest, sending her to the ground. She spun over in time to see the heel of the robot's foot descend onto her neck.

"We entertained the idea that a Child of Nostradamus could serve the human race. We see the error of our ways." The general's voice lacked any sincerity.

"Kill me," she hissed.

The motor whirled as the laser charged. Before it could fire, a black hole erupted from the center of the machine, dissecting its body lengthwise. Sparks began to rain down on her.

A man in a leather jacket was propped against a wall, his arms held out wide. His chest heaved as he panted from the exertion. Jasmine returned his gaze.

"Thanks," she gasped.

"Truce?" Conthan asked.

She nodded. "Truce."

Chapter Seventeen

May 19th, 2032 9:02PM

The yellow paint peeling from the walls reminded Conthan of a Hopper painting. In the painting, a woman lying in a bed exposed her body to the rising sun. Hopper used the awkward colors to create dissonance, an uneasy feeling, while he tried to delve into the psyche of his subjects.

There was a quiet that existed beyond the silence in the room. Just beyond the walls of this makeshift speakeasy, there was no movement for miles. The corpses had been removed from the immediate area, but there was a sense of death hovering over the super powered inhabitants at all times. There had been jokes in the last century that the only things to survive a nuclear holocaust would be Twinkies and cockroaches; so far there had been neither.

He was sitting at the bar, alone, removed from the others. Hopper's painting always tugged at his heart. In Nighthawks, three patrons were at the bar in an intimate setting, two of them appearing to be on a date, but the painting spoke to him about solitude and isolation. He couldn't help but see the figures, so close together, but worlds separating them. Behind the bar, the proprietor prepared coffee for the late-night visitors, and despite their being regulars, he didn't dare ask why they were there.

He felt isolated as his fingers traced the neglected counters and broken cups stacked in front of him. The bar was located in the Danger Zone, and any patrons that had frequented it were long since dead. In the carved initials and embedded stains he connected with the ghosts of a time gone by. If he thought about it, it was as if the people were speaking in the room with him. He tried not to think of them dying during the fallout.

"Nighthawks," came a silky smooth voice.

"The painting was one of my favorites. I always meant to visit Chicago again so I could experience it once I knew something about art. When I was in college, I made a replica of it, and when I was done, I realized life had treated me too well to really capture the pain Hopper must have felt."

"So why did you do it?"

He paused to consider the question. His professor had complimented him on his execution, style, and application of the paint, but nobody had stopped to ask him why. He turned to see Vanessa sitting at the bar. She was wearing her weathered red robe, her blonde hair flowing onto her shoulders, and her collar continuing to hide her mouth as if the garments were built for a telepath.

"I felt isolated."

"Why?"

There had been a time when he was surrounded by friends, receiving the praise of his peers and professors. Despite their admiration, he spent more time alone than with these acquaintances. It wasn't until he met Gretchen that he found somebody who also viewed themselves watching the world like a kid staring through the window of a candy store.

He opened his mouth to speak and paused, deciding the question was far too personal for somebody he had just met. He looked at her eyes, and saw she held no judgement. They reflected a question he wasn't ready to explore. It took him a moment to realize every thought darting across his mind was like words on a page for the telepath.

Why do you ask questions you already know the answers to? he thought.

Her laugh was quaint, soft and short, but sounded as if it was mixed with the distant chime of bells. She pushed her hair behind her ear. "When I was young, I discovered I could eavesdrop on every thought. Nothing was filtered, the good and the bad, the happy, and the sad. What I learned, just because I could hear thoughts didn't mean I was always listening."

He nodded, accepting her answer. He looked at the warped wood underneath his hands. "It never dawned on me, but I never got sick as a kid. I think that's how they found out about Sarah. Up until high school, my foster parents would randomly take me out of school for a week at a time. We would go on vacations and I thought they were the greatest parents in the world. I never questioned why we never went back to the same house, or the same school. We would start new every year."

"They were protecting their child."

"I miss them," he said, imagining his mother's face.

"What happened to them?"

"Drunk driver." He looked at the woman, trying to read her expression. "They weren't my biological parents," he added.

"Family doesn't require blood."

He understood the reference she was making to the others. "How do you make your wings come and go?"

"I can't control a Child of Nostradamus," she admitted, "but I can give suggestions." Out of nowhere, her wings blinked into existence. "I suggest you see nothing but an ordinary woman, you're the one who has to accept the suggestion."

"Why be ordinary? You're beautiful."

Her wings vanished again and she feigned a smile, the sentiment never reaching her eyes. "It is appreciated."

It didn't escape him that she batted away the compliment, not convinced at the sincerity of his words. She turned to the giant window looking out onto the street. "Not all of us have had the chance to lead a normal life. My powers appeared when I was very young. I've known almost my entire life I was different, and while the people who took me in cared for me, there are some scars that don't heal so easily."

"You mean your skin?"

Her eyebrow rose at the comment. "My what?"

"I'm not sure a telepath is allowed to play coy."

"Someday," she said, "I will be ready to tell you. Until then, it is a thought I choose to not hear."

He nodded, understanding her need for secrecy. It was the first time in years he didn't feel he was the kid staring in the window. He tried to ignore his gut. These people with powers beyond the imagination were still strangers to him. Vanessa hiding her secrets was the first real human thing he had observed. He couldn't help but grin at the thought that the only woman he couldn't keep a secret from was the one with secrets. A smile finally reached her eyes. "The irony is not lost on me," she said.

They stood in silence for a moment. She gestured for Conthan to follow. They stepped back from the bar and she closed her eyes and breathed in deeply. She pointed to the seats where they had been sitting moments ago. She repeated the breathing pattern. She rested her hand on his shoulder as she inhaled deeply. She slowly let the breath ease from her lips. As it touched the bar, ghosts began to emerge from nowhere.

Conthan jumped from the sudden bustle of activity in the room. He saw a jukebox in the corner and several sets of young people dancing to music. Behind the bar, two men were slinging drinks down to the patrons waving money. The crowd was alive and by their clothing it was a scene played out years before his birth.

A young man sat next to a beautiful young lady. He cautiously held his hand palm-up on the bar. Conthan felt his heart swell as the woman slowly slid her hand into his. The look on their faces as they stared into each other's eyes told a story that would play out through the decades as they grew old and died in the company of one another.

"What is this?"

"Some places carry such a strong energy," she said, "that even years later, I feel the imprint. When I focus, I get impressions. Every bar stool, counter, and cup tells a story. It's one of the reasons we come here. I can't help but feel that we are this bar's final legacy."

"How do you mean?"

"When we die, the stories housed here along with its patrons die."

"How can I see them?"

"You're not seeing them," she said. "You're currently asleep in a bedroom and I'm in the room next to you."

He didn't try to hide his confused look. "Then how are we here?"

"I could feel your mind reaching out to mine. I thought it best we meet some place we both recognize. It's not often I get to experience peace and quiet like this."

Conthan didn't try to understand. It didn't faze him that Dwayne could shoot lightning bolts or that Skits could do something that made her super hot. It didn't even bother him that Alyssa was able to learn kung fu from a video, or that Vanessa had wings. But the telepath thing, somehow that perplexed him.

They both watched as kids danced and music filled the air. The bartenders did a well-choreographed dance, moving around one another as they flipped bottles and pushed drinks out to the patrons. Vanessa smiled as a young girl twirled about. Conthan noted from the corner of his eye she was watching the girl, and suddenly it dawned on him this wasn't just a memory of the bar, it was the yearning of a woman cheated out of her youth.

"Perhaps Hopper had it wrong," she said calmly. "Perhaps the emotion wasn't meant to be isolation. Maybe the bar was meant to be where lonely souls came to find one another."

Conthan smiled at her optimistic interpretation. "Maybe we really are Nighthawks."

***

The hood over her face smelled of dust and disuse. The cotton was uncomfortable, pulling tightly on her face. She could make out light through the black fabric, but she had no idea exactly what was on the other side. With a few taps from the toe of her boot, she could tell by the echo the room was small.

She began working at the tape over her mouth with her tongue. She forced spit onto the tape, loosening its hold on her skin. As it gave way, she began chewing at it until it was pulled from her face. She pushed it to the side of her mouth and began gnawing away at the hood, trying to pull it from over her head.

There was motion in the room.

"Who's there?"

Jasmine pulled against the plastic around her wrists. As she struggled, the material cut into her flesh. She focused on her skin, searching for any point of contact between her and a denser material. She recognized the plastic, duct tape, and even the fiber of rope around her torso. None of them were a material capable of aiding her escape. Her captors weren't fools.

"Who are you?"

Whoever the person was, they hovered just out of her swinging reach. They were cautious. As the person took a step, she recognized them as a man, perhaps over two hundred pounds. He wasn't wearing shoes; the scrapes of his feet on the pavement told her they were in a disused room, perhaps a basement?

Liquid poured down over her head. She coughed as it soaked through the mask. He was drenching her. She sniffed the air. It was water as far as she could tell; nothing that seemed to be capable of burning.

"If you're attempting your first waterboarding, you're failing, sparky."

The mask was slowly lifted off her face. She had been right; it was the lightning-hurling member of the group. The room looked like the basement of an old building. Behind the human lightning bolt were several massive water heaters. For this many, so tightly packed together, she had to assume they were in a large office building or hotel.

Her captor was barefoot, wearing only a pair of ripped jeans. She eyed the man, studying the expression on his face. He didn't blink, staring straight into her eyes.

"You're going to need to do more than give me a shower, sparky."

His face was stern, but his demeanor gave a general disinterest in her. She didn't let it show, but she was impressed with how well he could hide his thoughts. She followed his skin down to his chest and torso. He was a bit overweight without a single hair on his body. It dawned on her there might be a reason he was half-dressed.

"Rape? Really?" she asked.

He laughed hard enough it sent her back in the chair. The laughter wasn't condescending; he was genuinely amused by her comment. She couldn't fathom what he found so funny. He braced himself against a wall as he continued roaring at the comment. He let it go on far longer than the inside joke warranted. He wiped the tears away from his eyes.

"You haven't got what it takes to get me hard."

"Oh," she said, seeing the joke.

He straightened and took a step toward her. It wasn't the first time she had been captured. It was the first time it had been against her will. It was also the first time somebody had the foresight not to use handcuffs on her or to bind her with wire. She wondered just how much the man knew about her abilities.

"The telepath," she hissed.

"Surprisingly, no," he said. His words were distant. His mind seemed to be occupied, only coming back to the present when he spoke. At first she thought he was daydreaming, going through a memory, but it dawned on her that he was detaching himself from the situation.

"You're going to torture me?"

"Yes."

She could only hope his plan was to beat her. If she was lucky, a pipe or even brass knuckles would prove to be his undoing. If he got close enough, she could even brush against the button on his jeans. Her face went flat as she masked her plan.

He shuffled his foot a little closer. She raised her eyebrow as she waited. He had no demands, nor did he seem like he was in any hurry to begin beating her.

"Normally people torture to get information."

"Not this time."

She had misgauged the man. She expected him to be the big brother of the group. The defender, the righteous one. She had no idea why, but for some reason, for a man who could sling lightning like a baseball, she just assumed he'd be the stoic member of their team. She paused at the thought.

She looked down to his foot. Inches away, the water pooling under her chair worked its way toward the human battery. She looked up, her face showing the first bit of panic.

He smiled.

"What do you want?"

"Revenge."

As the water touched his foot, the sparks flew, rippling along the surface of the water. The electricity jumped from one small river to the next until it reached the water running down her bare legs. She clenched her eyes shut as the first jolt touched her skin.

Jasmine screamed.

253

Chapter Eighteen

May 19th, 2032 9:22PM

"I could start breaking her limbs."

Even though the girl was speaking, Jasmine never broke eye contact with the man in front of her. The girl was more talk than not, her mouth her second most dangerous weapon. He didn't speak at first, letting his sister do the talking for both of them. Instead, he locked her stare, his face showing no emotion.

He kneeled in front of the captive, making sure there was no point of contact between them. "If we were going to resort to torture, Skits, I'm sure I could find a way to make her scream."

Jasmine relaxed her muscles as they continued twitching. She tried to ignore the pain still radiating throughout her body or the darkened burn marks along her legs. He had proved a point.

"She smells like she pissed herself."

Dwayne continued staring at the woman. His straight face gave way to a slight grin. She knew underneath the calm exterior he was far more dangerous than she initially thought. He was more than willing to take whatever measures were necessary to get a job done.

Skits stopped talking to watch the exchange between her brother and the woman. She had no idea what was going on, but she caught the Paladin's eye. The soldier was scared.

"What do you want from me?" asked Jasmine, exhausted and tired of playing games.

"Who's asking the questions?" Skits barked.

Dwayne waved his sister off. He stood in front of the woman, looking down at their prisoner. "You're the infamous powered Paladin. We haven't been properly introduced. We're the Nighthawks, Children just like you."

"Like me? You're nothing like me. You're vigilantes. You think you're above the law. You killed—"

"You've sold out your own kind," Alyssa said, stepping into the room. The Middle Eastern woman walked closer to the others. Jasmine was still unsure what her gifts were. "You've hunted us like dogs. You are not above us, Paladin."

Jasmine rolled her eyes.

"Bitch," Alyssa said, punching her.

Jasmine turned with the blow and looked back at the girl. "Savages," she said. She spit blood onto the floor and flexed her wrists, feeling the plastic continue to cut into her skin. She had already felt the fury of the Middle Eastern girl; she could only assume what the two girls would do if left alone with her. She had a feeling they wouldn't be as controlled as their male counterpart had been.

He leaned in, bringing his face closer to hers. "My sister wants nothing more than to light up her hand till it's red hot. Then she'll take it and slide it along your skin, peeling the flesh from your bones. You'll wish you were dead, but it'll cauterize your wounds almost instantly. You'll live until your heart gives out. So do not test me, Paladin."

She didn't reply.

"I think we understand one another."

"What do you want with me?"

"Why were you after us?"

"I was given orders. I'm a soldier. I do not disobey my orders."

"You came with a jet and two mechs for backup. Nothing about that seems like protocol."

"Humans can't enter the Danger Zone."

"And the mechs?"

She started to talk and stopped, pondering the situation after the fact. It was standard procedure for her to have mech backup if she went into the Danger Zone. Their intel had revealed there was a massive firefight. They had even seen the angel on their surveillance. Even if her entire team had gone, they would also have taken half a dozen mechs. Her cockiness had prevented her from asking why she was underequipped for the mission.

"I…I don't know."

"How long before they come for you?"

She thought about the laser trying to bore through her back. The muscles ached as she thought about them. "I was set up for termination." As she said it out loud, she wanted to scream. If her throat

256

hadn't already been sore, she would have begun yelling. The general had sent her in with obsolete tech. The military had never intended for her to walk out. She had been a sacrifice, tossed to the wolves to show their capabilities.

"I'd terminate you," Skits mocked.

Conthan strolled through the door. As he stepped to the side, Jasmine could see the Angel of the Outlands. She was smaller than expected, almost appearing dainty compared to the others. Jasmine wondered how much of her demeanor was real and how much was the angel affecting her brain.

"She's telling the truth. They were going to kill her."

"Telepath," Jasmine hissed.

"You were sent to be killed," Vanessa explained. "The question is, why? Why not just reach into your head, pull the kill switch, and destroy your brain?"

Jasmine flinched at the obvious reading of her thoughts. "Stay out of my head, telepath."

"Try not thinking so loudly," Vanessa replied, her eyes almost as intense as the man's. "Why not just kill you?"

Jasmine thought about it. At any point they could have pulled the trigger. Even with her powers imprinting the densest material on her skin, her brain was still vulnerable. She played back the battle and tried to think of what would have made them rely on the mechs instead of the small bomb at the base of her skull.

"Me," Dwayne said.

"What?"

"I hit you with enough electricity to light up the

city. What if the trigger broke?" The comment about electrocution didn't escape her.

He made sense. The general would have fried her the first opportunity he got. He supported her as long as she served his purposes. However, he made it well known that he would kill her the moment she got out of line. Jasmine avoided meeting the man's eyes. The irony was not lost on her. The same Child who saved her life was the one threatening to end it.

"The general giving the orders, he sent me on the mission. He's the one who would have controlled what mechs went with me. He's also the first person to offer to kill me. His scientists want to open me up and see what makes me tick.

They all looked at Vanessa. "She's telling the truth."

"What do we do with her?" Skits asked.

"Cut her free."

Skits's arms went up, stopping everybody in the room. The girl put herself between the prisoner and the rest of the people in the room. "She tried to kill us! What's to say she's not going to turn around and try to do it again?"

"The enemy of my enemy," Vanessa said. "I believe Jasmine has every intention of surviving. I also believe she has every intention of killing the man who set her up to die."

"Stay out of my head, witch," Jasmine growled.

"We're her best chance of survival and we're her best chance of revenge," Vanessa said. "Right now there is an entire army wanting her dead. We've been at this longer, she needs us."

"To hell with you." Jasmine spat more blood

from her mouth.

Vanessa stepped up close to Jasmine, who recoiled as she reached out. Jasmine struggled against the restraints. Vanessa grabbed both sides of her head, leaned in, and stared into the Paladin's eyes.

"Out of my head," Jasmine snarled. She recalled the training manual on dealing with telepaths. She tried to fill her mind with useless information. She thought back to math classes and science equations. Without warning her mind turned to the girl from earlier in the day.

Jasmine watched as the girl ran crying down the hallway. The cosmos had played a cruel joke on the child, and now she was an outlaw. Jasmine thought about the general in her ear at that moment, knowing everything that had been said. Her mind turned to the girl, how she should have stayed and escorted her to safety. Now, she would never know if the girl would survive puberty.

Vanessa let go of her head. Jasmine could see the smile in the eyes of the telepath. "That's why you're with us, Jasmine. Each of us has a past filled with questionable moments, but each of them have a common purpose. Somewhere underneath your need to survive, you've found your humanity again."

Vanessa stepped back, ignoring the tears beginning to well up in the soldier's eyes. Vanessa thought of the small girl she had saved. She wondered if there had been anybody in Jasmine's life who tried to save her. Vanessa turned and walked out of the room. "Free her, then meet me in the bar."

Conthan stepped away from the telepath as she passed by, storming out the door.

***

Conthan chased after Vanessa and emerged in the lobby of the hotel. He followed her through the once elegant space and caught the door as she moved at a brisk pace. "What did you do to her?

He had seen her assert her powers, but she had never been so direct in manipulating another person. He knew this was a war and there would be casualties. Somehow this intrusion seemed far crueler than killing another person. He looked at the soldier as she tried to rebuild the walls protecting herself from her own emotions. He couldn't help but think maybe God's creations were not the innocent cherubs he once believed they were.

Vanessa spun around and stared at him. "I do what has to be done. I do what nobody else can do. If that means violating the most sacred of private thoughts, then so be it. My job is to keep those in my ward safe."

He was impressed with her anger. It was the first real emotion she had shown. She had been cryptic, reserved, and even deceitful with her feelings, but this was real. He held up his hands to show his surrender.

"I didn't ask why," he said. "I asked, what did you do?"

Her wings appeared out of nowhere and her skin began to turn a sickly green. He observed, but pushed thoughts from his mind, trying to hide his shock from the telepath. He couldn't ignore it. He could hear her taking deep breaths and as fast as her image shifted, it returned to the golden-haired woman. She could see him staring and it didn't require powers to know what he was thinking. "Conthan…"

"What did you do to her?" he asked, again keeping to the subject.

"She's angry, so filled with rage. I can still feel it in the pit of my stomach. It lingers on me like the smell of cheap cigars. She wants blood." Her muscles relaxed as a calm washed over her body again. She straightened her back and let out a breath, imagining the negativity leaving her lungs. "But it has nothing to do with us. Somebody she tried to help didn't make it."

"That made her break down?"

"She's been forced to hunt her own. Her cause, once righteous, has been twisted until the powers that be buried her so deep she was forced to be a puppet. It was kill or be killed, and the weight of every decision just came bubbling to the surface."

"Harsh."

She turned around and continued to the bar. "This is war."

***

The man stepped up, pulling out a blade. Jasmine flinched as he crouched before her legs, cutting the rope. He made sure the blade didn't touch her skin. Next he stepped behind her and dragged the blade along the rope binding her wrists. It wasn't an hour ago he attempted to kill her. *Now, with a simple command from the telepath, he submitted to her words*, she thought to herself.

"You do whatever she says?"

Dwayne stopped cutting. "We don't follow her blindly, if that's what you're asking."

"How do you know she's not controlling you?"

Skits scowled. Jasmine imagined the anger, the heat she carried, was almost as intense as the plasma she could create. She looked at the other girl and was surprised to see she was calm.

"I owe Vanessa my life," Alyssa said bluntly.

"How?"

"She saved me from slavers," Alyssa said. "If it wasn't for her, I'd be a whore for some rich man."

Jasmine had never encountered people who peddled in Children of Nostradamus, but the military was well aware they existed. Jasmine was impressed with her fighting, but she wasn't sure how that would make her a target for prostitution. She studied the young girl, her skin an off-white. "You're from the Middle East?"

Alyssa nodded. "And I would have been forced to use my powers to adapt to some pimp. So right now, I follow Vanessa. She's done nothing that makes me question her."

"How do you adapt?"

"Visual stimuli."

Jasmine processed the information. She finally understood how the woman was such a keen fighter and why she hadn't been prepared for their first encounter. She must have learned new fighting methods between battles. She might not be able to wield lightning, but the gift was impressive.

Jasmine's hands were free. Her first instinct was to assault the man with the lightning. He wouldn't be able to use it in such a small room with the others present. He would come at her with the knife. The wound it'd make would be a small price to let the metal touch her skin and alter her density. The fighter wouldn't be able to move in the space. Her close-quarters combat skills may prove difficult to overcome on the field, but here, a single hit would quiet her.

Then there was the other girl. Jasmine could already see her hands were glowing blue. "I would kill you before you had the chance to move."

The teen was looking for an excuse to kill her. Jasmine wasn't surprised there was animosity, but the sheer anger in her face was startling. She remembered harboring hatred like that, disgusted with the world for the hand fate dealt. She wanted to be mad, but even the man sending shocks through her body was attempting to protect his people. She wasn't sure she wanted to be a member of the community, but until she got revenge on the people who tried to kill her, she would bite her tongue.

"Truce," Jasmine said.

"So you think."

Dwayne held up his hands. "Skits, back down."

His voice had a commanding tone. Jasmine had witnessed him come full circle in the last hour. He had been willing to trade in his humanity to force secrets from her lips. He had been the lapdog to the telepath, and now, he was the keeper of peace. She was beginning to see this group was far more complex than the military had ever considered. Jasmine eyed the man and the youngest girl and the similarities were obvious. "Siblings?"

Dwayne nodded. "My one and only."

Jasmine continued to think of the general. What she wanted was to see him and his band of scientists nailed to crosses. She rubbed her wrists as she dwelled on how difficult it would be to break into a military base and target one man. They would have revoked her access already, considering her a threat to national security. It wouldn't be impossible, but it might as well be. In front of her, she had the tools to make it happen. The telepath, the teleporter, the heavy hitter and the stealth—between the entire group, they could achieve it. At that moment, she realized why they worked so well together.

"My gear?" she asked.

Dwayne shook his head. "We brought you something a little less…" he pointed to the rags on the small table "…tactical. We appreciate the change of mind, but nobody calls us fools."

Jasmine was discovering this operation wasn't filled with mindless, rogue Children of Nostradamus. She began to wonder how the group had been brought together. It was unusual for so many to gather in one location, let alone stay together. Up to this point the largest "nest" had been four. The small troupe had spent more time fighting amongst themselves than the Paladins. This group, however, seemed to be a delicate balance of personalities and abilities.

Alyssa opened the door out of the basement.

"Study us all you want, Paladin. You're getting your free pass. Next time you cross us, we'll kill you."

Jasmine was sure they'd try. "We all adapt," she warned.

She pulled the sweatpants over her jumper and then the hoodie. There was no material on the clothing for her to sync with her powers. Dwayne tossed some sandals on the floor. "Welcome to New England."

She slid the sandals on her feet and tucked her hands into the pouch of her hoodie. The stairs led to a small office and then the lobby of an old hotel. She was surprised to see the interior was in relatively good condition. Outside of the building the street wasn't nearly as well kept. Cars were littered about, flipped over, all of them scorched reminders of the many fires that broke out in the city. Solitude wrapped around her. The sense of emptiness was palpable in the air, tasting of sorrow and loss.

"You live here?"

"The Danger Zone is the only place humans can't follow us. For now, at least."

"Mechs?"

Dwayne pointed down the street. A solitary mech stood there, its legs severed, looking like they were sliced with a hot knife. She could see the scorch marks across its body. She was impressed with the constant defense these Children must be employing to stay alive. "Frequent?"

"Not anymore," he said. "We assume they realized they were sending them to be destroyed and the government couldn't accept the cost anymore."

"Now we're more worried about another bomb."

Jasmine heard rumors there was a project being developed that would yield the impact of a nuclear bomb, but not the fallout. The military had halted it at the start, unsure of what was causing the powers in the first place, scared their technology could exacerbate the situation. Now it was on a shelf waiting for somebody to discover it again.

"We know about the bomb," Skits said through gritted teeth.

That startled Jasmine. "How so?"

"Do you really think we're the only ones?" Dwayne asked, looking back at her with a smirk.

Jasmine observed the many windows of the surrounding office buildings. She was surprised by this small contingent. It was difficult to believe that there were more of them. "How many?"

"We were nearly a hundred a year ago," he said. "Your people either captured or killed the rest of us."

She flinched at the "your people" comment. It was becoming obvious they saw her as the personification of the government. She had once been proud protecting the American people from the threat of powers. At some point, she realized she was perpetuating a holocaust.

She opened her mouth to apologize, but stopped as they reached the bar. Her training as a soldier buried her emotions deep. She returned to analyzing her captors.

"Welcome," Vanessa said.

Jasmine was shocked to see the woman sitting

there. Unlike before, her wings were gone and a normal, calm, average female was seated at the counter. The young man was sipping coffee from a mug with a broken handle.

"What the fuck," she mumbled under her breath. She felt like she had stepped into a twisted reality. They were in the middle of an abandoned city, left uninhabitable by a nuclear bomb. These were some of the strongest Children of Nostradamus she had ever encountered, and there they were, having dinner. The sight of the man taking a swig of his coffee, his pinky almost extended, made her realize there was indeed something wrong with the world.

"Dwayne," Vanessa said, her voice a smooth steady calm, "would you mind firing up the generators? Some food for our guest might make her a bit less hostile."

"Who cares about her?" Skits interjected.

"While I don't condone her decisions," Vanessa admitted, "I'm not sure what any of you would have done in the same situation. But now she is here as a free woman. Let her see if the food tastes better without a collar."

"Stay out of my head, telepath."

Conthan held up his hand. "As the former newest arrival, let me say, it gets easier to ignore her. She can't shut it off. Just don't think of porn."

Vanessa shot him a dirty look. Jasmine didn't need to know their backstories to know there was a freshness about Conthan. While the others looked seasoned, and in the case of the man, weathered, the boy was green. He still held an optimism in his eyes the others didn't. Jasmine almost felt sorry for the innocence that would be lost and replaced by a cold distance. It was only a matter of time. It was what you did to survive.

Jasmine sat down on a stool. "So what is this operation?"

Vanessa looked from Jasmine to Conthan. "We're the Nighthawks, so I've been informed."

"Great," Jasmine said. "I'm living a comic book now."

"We came here for sanctuary. When we came together, we started trying to save as many Children of Nostradamus as we could. We will fight and kill for our safety, but for the most part, we simply want to live."

"Peaceable," Jasmine scoffed. "You killed almost two dozen guards yesterday at the facility."

Skits barked at the woman, "And how many of ours have died at the facility?"

"They were saving me," Conthan interjected.

"Why you?"

Conthan reached into his leather jacket and pulled out a sheet of paper. "I was given a note that told me to see somebody at the facility. My powers only manifested a couple of days ago and I was hoping for answers."

Jasmine gawked at the marbled paper. She didn't dare open her mouth at the sight of the crumpled sheet. It was similar to the one delivered to her at the barracks.

"You've received one too?" Vanessa asked.

Jasmine ground her teeth at the intrusion. "Yes."

"What did it say?"

"Told me to hesitate."

There was a stillness every time Vanessa stopped relying on her physical abilities and focused on her talents. Jasmine could only assume she was attempting to tear from their psyches every bit of information they had about the letters. It dawned on her there was an irony dwelling on the telepath's abilities while having her mind read.

Despite trying to dodge the thoughts and keep Vanessa from knowing what happened, she couldn't stop thinking back to the girl. She had hesitated just as the letter had told her. She had unknowingly played into the psychic's trap. What was worse, Jasmine was certain the girl was currently being taken into custody and nothing had changed.

"What happ—"

Vanessa held up a hand to halt Conthan. She made contact with Jasmine and could see the thanks written in the woman's sad eyes. For a mind reader, it was always a question of what should be discussed and what should be shared in quiet misery. Jasmine did not want to talk about it and Vanessa knew better than to disclose personal trauma to the rest of the group.

"Several of us have received such letters," Vanessa admitted. "By some grand design, they have brought us together. Conthan's put him in the right place at the right time. Dwayne's led him to me."

"Why would a murderer send us these?"

"Eleanor was a powerful psychic. Our associate, Dav5d, theorized she was only surpassed by Nostradamus himself. Dav5d is able to predict probabilities on an astronomical scale. Turning his powers toward the events that lead to these letters, he had a theory that Eleanor was bringing us together for a greater plan."

"This isn't a comic, telepath."

"Vanessa, please," the angel said. "We are well aware. But for some reason, the collection of these powers has created a pivot point in a way that even Dav5d cannot predict. Eleanor brought us together because she thought we, each of us, were the keys to bringing about a brighter future for all."

"We're six people."

Jasmine noted the woman's smile as she referred to them as a group. She could hear the whispers from the newcomer's mind. The soldier wasn't aware, but her thoughts were similar to each of theirs. It wasn't always revenge, but each of them needed the others. Jasmine's need wasn't as pleasurable as the rest, but at least it was there.

Conthan chimed in. "We're six people with some serious juice."

"You can barely use yours," Skits poked.

"People, please." Vanessa eyed them both.

"Sorry," they said in unison.

Jasmine waved her finger in the air. "No, wait. Eleanor attempted to put a bullet in the president. Don't you think that there might be something less righteous behind her motives?"

"Even Dav5d couldn't understand why she might want to kill the president, a woman who employed her, taken her in, and been her confidante for years. We assumed that Eleanor's abilities had stymied Dav5d and prevented him from unraveling her intent."

Jasmine knew the look on the angel's face was hiding more. "But you have a theory."

"The Warden said something that may have been the clue, the very reason why we are all together."

"And?"

Vanessa gave a slight shrug. "Somehow, the president is involved with the Warden."

"Everybody knows that the Warden was a friend of the president. He worked at the White House when Eleanor attempted to assassinate her. He became the head of the president's detainment procedures when the Children of Nostradamus began emerging. Later she had the facility built and he was placed in charge."

"The Warden is a Child," Vanessa said.

Jasmine's raised eyebrows gave away her surprise. She found it hard to believe the president, a woman who hated the Children of Nostradamus so much that much of her public relations was dedicated to their eradication, would incarcerate them under the watchful eye of the Warden. However, she thought, having that many powered people in one place could make for a threatening army.

Jasmine could see Vanessa and she knew every thought crossing her mind was betraying her. She had to ask, "What about your letter?"

Vanessa shook her head. "My letter told how to find Skits."

"Thanks for that," Skits said.

"It didn't tell you how to find the others? Or what role you played?"

"It didn't have to. As a child, Eleanor convinced

271

the president to spare my life."

Chapter Nineteen

May 20th, 2032 12:12AM

Dwayne held on to two jumper cables and summoned his powers. Conthan covered his eyes to block out the bright light. Sparks shot out in a dozen directions as the current worked its way through the wires into the batteries stacked together.

"It's easy when I've been keeping an eye on things," Dwayne said with no strain.

"You have to do this every night?"

Dwayne laughed. "I wish, more like every few hours."

"How do you sleep?"

"I keep a wire attached through the night to act as a ground. Otherwise I'd either build up and let loose or I'd start sparking and set a fire."

"Wow," Conthan said, "your powers kind of suck."

"It seems that just about everybody has some weird downside to their power." Dwayne flexed his muscles, forcing the current into his hands. He was

273

elated at the sensation of his powers traveling down his arms. He closed his eyes and enjoyed the euphoria. "But, I can make lightning. Dude, I'm like Zeus."

They both laughed. Dwayne pushed the last of the electricity through his hands and slowly closed access to the reservoir of power in him. He dropped the cables and sat down on a large piece of equipment. He motioned for Conthan to join him. "So how are you handling all of this?"

Conthan opened his mouth to answer but bit his tongue. Dwayne gave the guy a moment to process what must be an uncanny amount of emotions. Since Dwayne had seen the kid for the first time at the gallery, his world had been a constant struggle. Unless he had been unconscious, this was the first downtime he had in days.

"Yeah, it's all cool," Conthan said, trying to play it cool.

Dwayne cocked his head to the side with a raised brow. "Barely keeping it together, huh?"

"Another telepath?"

"You're a kid," Dwayne said. "You had your entire life ahead of you. Could have been a firefighter or some weird shit. Now"—he waved to the dingy storage room—"you have this to look forward to."

"Yeah," Conthan admitted. For a moment, he thought he could feel the radiation bombarding his body. Vegetation in the Danger Zone fought to stay alive, but after seeing the Outlanders, he could only imagine what it was doing to his body. Despite the potential for sterility, the world hating him, and their rogue mission to stop a conspiracy that ran deep through the government, he was processing the total collapse of his world fairly well.

"So how are you handling it?" Dwayne asked again.

Conthan let out a long sigh as he thought about how to say it. "It's a bit much. If I was back home, I would probably be sitting in a deserted warehouse with a bunch of bohemians drinking beer. If I was feeling particularly productive, I might be working on some art. If the guys could see me now..." He trailed off.

"Not sure what they'd say?"

Conthan nodded. "I guess I'd be worried they'd think I was a freak. But they would probably think it was cool. They'd ask a thousand questions. They'd seem okay with it. But really, what normal person could be okay with watching a guy tear through space? I'd be just as worried if they were okay with it."

"It's hard letting go of who we were."

"Gretchen..." He laughed. "She'd be all about it. She'd find some way to put me on a pedestal in her gallery. She'd pimp me out; she'd be jealous I got some cool power."

"She struck me as a bit of a wild one. She'd fit in."

Conthan raised his eyebrow. Before he could ask, Dwayne filled in the blanks. "We were there the night it happened. We're the reason more soldiers didn't come after you."

"Eleanor," Conthan whispered. "She really did think of everything."

Dwayne nodded. "I think of her as a guardian angel."

"I'm okay with it until I think of my past." Conthan turned back to their earlier conversation. "Then I think, I'm barely in my twenties and I'm a wanted felon for absolutely nothing."

"You did kill a guy," Dwayne pointed out.

"I've killed several guys," Conthan said, remembering the men he murdered.

"Self defense."

"It doesn't make it any better."

Dwayne shook his head. "It won't get any easier. And if you find it does, then we're going to need to have another talk."

"There is part of this that feels right, though. I mean, I really had no path in life. I had some spotty parts of my history and this kind of explains all of them. So there is an upside, I guess."

"But…"

Conthan frowned. "You've been hanging out with Vanessa too much. Her mind reading tendencies are rubbing off."

"Yeah, it happens."

"But I feel kind of useless. I'm basically a taxi driver for you guys."

"From what Jasmine said, if it wasn't for you, we'd all be dead."

"I guess."

Conthan shoved his hands in his pocket at the awkward silence. "What was it like when you found out you were a Child?"

Dwayne examined Conthan for a moment. "Wasn't much different than your own story. I ran away from home because I didn't think they could handle it. I had to learn to survive on my own. Every day I traded a little piece of my humanity to stay alive. Eventually I found the Danger Zone and then Vanessa discovered me."

There was the quietness again. There wasn't a noise except for the two of them. Dwayne could tell Conthan was still unsure of how friendly he could treat their relationship.

"It takes time. Your powers emerged a few days ago and already you've managed to find a few ways to make them useful. When I first lit up, I nearly blew up the car I was sitting in. I almost electrocuted an entire bus full of people and I set my parent's house ablaze. So far, you're doing pretty good by my measure."

Conthan smiled at the remark. "Thanks."

"Want some advice?"

"You're going to give it anyways."

Dwayne gave him a sour expression. "You and my sister are going to be the death of me."

He continued. "You need to be in control of your abilities, not the other way around. They're a force of nature, and if you let down your guard, they'll try to take over. We've all had that moment that we lose ourselves in our powers. You'll learn to find your limits, and when you do, you'll always want to rage against that boundary. You'll learn as you go."

"I feel like a liability right now."

"I won't lie, we weren't thrilled about you joining us. You're a kid, you've got no training, and why would we want somebody like that watching our backs?"

"Thanks…"

"Let me finish," Dwayne interjected. "If it wasn't for you, we wouldn't have gotten to Vanessa fast enough. You serve a purpose with this troupe, just like me or Skits do. We need the heavy hitter, we need the brute force, we need the level-headed one, and we need the seasoned fighter. Everybody is playing a role, and we just needed to adapt to the new guy."

Conthan mulled it over. The group wasn't so different than the artists he drank with night after night. The man in front of him understood a dirty secret Conthan hadn't known he was carrying. Something in that fact felt like it was fast-tracking them to friendship.

"I appreciate that."

Dwayne nodded. "You'll eventually fit in. Give it some time. You should have seen when Skits and Alyssa first met. I had to tear them off one another. But from my point of view, I'm glad to have you watching my six."

"And tomorrow?"

"We're going to go in guns blazing. We're going to do everything we can to save some people. I don't know what it'll be like."

"Do you think we can trust her?"

Dwayne stared off into nothing for a moment as if he was recalling a distant memory. A moment later he was nodding his head with confidence.

"She needs us if she's going to get revenge. As long as we serve a purpose for her, she will do the same for us."

"That sounds pretty messed up."

"The enemy of my enemy and all that jazz."

Conthan stood up and Dwayne gave him an awkward male-on-male hug. As they separated, a spark snapped against his skin, stinging his cheek. "Jesus."

"I'm going to empty out again. Go get some sleep, tomorrow is going to be a chore."

Conthan nodded and exited the small room. The batteries were in the service area of the basement. Three stories above them, a king-sized bed awaited him. He oddly looked forward to the cold shower in his en suite bathroom. He turned to the stairs and paused. He grit his teeth for a moment and the icy sensation coated his skin. He stepped into the portal, delighted his powers answered when he wanted them.

***

Jasmine imagined herself on the beach as a kid. The sensation of sand wedging itself between her toes was real. The smell of salt water assaulted her nostrils and for a moment she felt a calm come over her body. For a moment, she wasn't an adult being forced to side with Children of Nostradamus. For a moment, her baggage washed away and she was innocent again.

She breathed in and out, letting each exhale steal away the tension from her body. She had found it difficult to start this session, the stress creating a knot between her shoulders. She was convinced the telepath was listening to her every thought, waiting for her to somehow betray them. Now, she let her mind go quiet, focusing on the nothingness in her thoughts. Her muscles relaxed and she found her spot, the one place where she felt at peace with herself. In the distance, she could almost make out the faces of her parents.

She opened her eyes to shadows under her door. She wondered if it was Dwayne coming to try another round of shock therapy. The shadow didn't move and she then assumed it was one of the younger Children, unsure of how to proceed.

"Come in," she said aloud.

The door eased open. Conthan peeked around the corner. Once he noticed her on the floor, he didn't speak.

She eyed him. "Checking on me?"

"I'm not entirely sure."

She studied the kid. He was wearing a pair of ripped jeans, a soiled t-shirt, and a weathered leather jacket. He could have been any young man, but something about his face was starting to tell a story that would harden with age. She could tell by the way he kept his hands in his pockets and tried to avoid eye contact, he wasn't like the others. "You're new."

"Yeah," he mumbled.

"You're the kid who killed the Corps soldiers at the art gallery."

He gawked. Was she the only one who knew what happened? He obviously hadn't thought she would know what started this journey for him. "He was going to kill me. He had already killed another artist there."

"So you felt it was better to kill than be killed?"

The heat crept up his face until his cheeks were red. "No," he spit out, "he shot at me, and then he was dead on the ground."

"Fight or flight reflex," she said. "Not too shabby."

"I didn't do anything to him."

"But you ran."

"Everybody knows what happens to Children of Nostradamus." His eyes started to burn a hole in her. "What you do to them."

She nodded. She had seen judgment like this before. She thought to the young girl earlier that day who had accused Jasmine of betraying them. For a long time, she would ignore the accusatory looks, but she couldn't shake the girl from her mind. "You're not wrong."

"Why?"

"My motives are none of your business."

"Why hunt down your own kind?"

Her eyes narrowed as she stared at him. "Fight or flight," she said as if it answered any questions he could have. "If it comes down to me or somebody else, it won't be me that dies. You have to be concerned with yourself. It's every person for themselves."

He looked ready to spit back a retort but stopped. He was tense, maybe even angry. There came a moment in his contemplation of her answer that his body relaxed. She was surprised to see it, usually people would tear apart her desire to survive. There was a brief moment when the look on his face softened, and she looked away, refusing to accept his pity.

"Don't fuck us over tomorrow," Conthan said with no aggressive tone to his voice. Before she could retort he added, "I've got your six."

Jasmine's anger tingled along her skin. Her powers reached out to find materials to mimic. As he spoke, her emotions turned to anguish. She tried to take a calming breath but she could feel her emotions welling to the surface.

"Why?" she asked simply.

"Somebody had faith in me not too long ago. Figure it's only right to have faith in you."

"You're using me just like the Corps, don't try to act righteous."

"They used you, Jasmine," he said. "We're relying on you. There's a difference. Without you, we all go down. We need you and you need us. It might not be friendship, but it's..." he thought about his word choice, "it's an alliance."

There was an awkward moment between them. He gave her a slight nod and backed out of her room. The door clicked as it came to a close. She was alone again, and now she let her emotions flow over the surface. Tears rolled freely down her face.

She didn't like that her emotions were getting the best of her. If for no other reason, it made her look weak, and that was not a word she used to describe herself. She reached behind her head and her fingers pass over the small bump at the base of her skull. For a decade, she had been fearful somebody would flip the switch and she'd die for no other reason than the cosmos selected her to be different.

"Freedom," she whispered.

Despite the word and its grand possibilities, she

felt that she was entering one prison after another. She was a free woman and could do whatever she wanted, but now she was a liability and the government wouldn't stop until they reacquired her. The rest of her life consisted of hiding from the authorities. Even with that thought, she smiled; at least now she could decide how and when she would die. It wouldn't be at the hand of her jailers. Now she could wrangle ahold of something in her life.

The kid had a point. When she had told him "truce," she hadn't been lying. He had saved her life. She owed him a debt. It was the first time she owed somebody for an act of kindness. She would pay her debt and then she could begin to figure out what she wanted to do with her life.

"Freedom," she whispered again, letting the taste of the word linger in her mouth.

***

Vanessa stood in a room with no visible walls, the entire scene bathed in white light. In every direction she could see as far as the eye would let her. She was kneeling on a floor, reciting a lengthy prayer. She held her hands together, rosary beads draped between her fingers.

"A praying angel," said a voice. "Don't you think it's a bit too cliché even for you?"

"How are the survivors?" She never looked up from her prayer beads.

"We met with the remaining Outlanders at the rendezvous. They are terrified after waking up to a slaughter. Some of them remember snippets. They are discussing the shadows that murdered their people. They understand it was a telepath."

"This is their hell."

"It is better to keep them in the dark. Let them be confused. It prevents them from being angry until we cross the border."

She attempted a smile. The smile became authentic as she stared into his eyes. "How are you, Dav5d?"

"I'm asleep in the back of a van with three other people." He laughed. "I'd be sleeping better if Victor's elbow wasn't wedged into my shoulder blades."

"Have you made it to Canada?"

"Almost," he said. "We found the border we intended to cross was host to more guards than we imagined."

"Will you be able to make it?"

He nodded. "We may have to travel on foot, but that doesn't seem to bother anybody. Except for Victor, he would complain if we were at a five-star resort. Twenty-Seven has spoken at length about her encounter with you before the meeting. It seems you have had a lasting impression on her."

With an image of her in mind, Vanessa could sense Twenty-Seven was sleeping in the front seat of the van. Her hand dangled over the front seat, only inches from a gun she tucked away in case of emergency. The woman was resilient; they would need her as they began to plant roots in the north.

Dav5d stood in the room without walls, his thick jacket hiding most of his frame. His face was neutral as usual. She found it impossible to hear his thoughts. He was the one person she couldn't read like a book; it was both a blessing and a curse. She finally asked, "And how are you?"

"I am well. I have already figured out that pending an anomaly in my predictions, we will make it across with no difficulty, even accounting for Corps interference. They will not spare enough forces to render us immobile."

He reached down and brushed the back of his hand across her cheek. Their encounter contradicted all logic. She could hear his mind dissecting their interaction. She wasn't really there, but he couldn't help but enjoy the sensation that his brain falsely registered. He knelt down. "How are you doing?"

"I am tense."

She rested her face against his hand. Even across the many miles her skin remembered his touch. She could feel the warmth radiating from him.

"The Warden is a telepath. His power is…" she searched for the word "immense. He was able to force his will upon so many that…"

She watched as he studied the arch of her eyebrows and the slight pause between blinks. He could deduce her thoughts almost as fast as she could have them. He was painfully aware she was fearful of what was coming. His thoughts echoed in her mind. "You're not sure you can win?"

She shook her head. "No. Worse. I see the appeal of his power."

Dav5d seemed genuinely surprised by her remark. His thoughts went back to being a whirlwind of mathematics, probabilities, and connecting information. She looked down as his hand wrapped around hers, squeezing. For the briefest of moments, all she sensed was his confidence. "You see a warped possibility."

She nodded.

"The difference is you know you're seeing a reflection. You can see the mangled version of yourself staring back at you."

Her silence let him ponder the situation further. He could see it was weighing on her more than he would expect. He searched for words to comfort her. "You're not him, Vanessa. You know right from wrong. You are ethical, humble, and underneath even the most ruthless decision I've seen you make, there is compassion."

The smile across her face was accompanied by pained eyes. She stood and took several steps backward, putting distance between them. Dav5d watched as she transformed. The feathers of her wings dissolved, until there were only scales.

Her pupils began to fade, morphing from circular orbs to something almost snakelike. Her skin's milky white flawlessness was replaced by a dark green. In place of her golden hair there was a thin mane of equally sickly strands.

She wrapped her arms about her torso, hugging herself as her body shook. He did the only thing he could think of. He stepped forward, reached behind her head, and kissed her. As his hands slid to the side of her face, her hands reached about his back, cautious and hesitant. She clutched him, pulling him closer. Her teeth were sharp against his tongue, almost as sharp as the nails digging into his shoulder blades. Pain didn't slow him.

He could access every bit of processing power offered to the human brain. His mind was the fastest computer known to mankind. She could hear alarms going off in his head as her body pressed against his. He understood the reality bringing them together was a fabrication of her abilities. His gifts alerted him to the falsehood, but her skin, her embrace, and her beating heart were more rewarding. She nearly gasped as the thought became clear as words. It was the first moment since his power awakened that he ignored facts.

He pulled back to see her face. Her eyelids opened slowly revealing the yellow rings around her irises. He stared into them and smiled. "I've been waiting."

She smiled back, exposing her elongated canines. "I know."

"Why now?"

She lowered her chin, avoiding the eyes analyzing her every word. "I've spent my entire life fighting"—she spread her wings out wide—"this. I look in the mirror and see a monster looking back at me. But…" She took a deep breath. "I'm not a monster."

"You're beautiful," he whispered.

She couldn't help it, her insecurities drove her powers to reach into his mind. She could sense the coursing river of his consciousness. She was shocked she could hear his thoughts, and each of them brought her back to this moment. He was admiring her, soaking up the beautiful woman before him. She could hear each word echo through his mind, and she was embarrassed she couldn't accept them.

"Read as much as you want, Vanessa," he said. "Right now, there's nothing more important than this. This very moment."

She witnessed herself through his eyes, and she was amazed to see he wasn't focusing on the image she had forged for herself. Her heart swelled; it was a moment of acceptance she hadn't expected, even from the man she had grown so fond of.

"I'm sorry," she whispered.

"And that's what makes you better than him. You're strong, Vanessa," he said with a confident, firm voice. "You thought this void that Eleanor couldn't see beyond revolved around Conthan. But what if this entire time, it's been you? You've brought us together. You've led us. You've been the anchor that has kept this, us, safe. Vanessa, without you, we would never have been."

Had she been capable of crying, the tight feeling in her heart would have caused her eyes to begin leaking. She let out the faintest of smiles and embraced him again. "Dav5d," she whispered in his ear, "you've been my anchor."

"I've always known your secret, Vanessa," he confessed. "I couldn't *not* know it. I've waited for you to confess this for yourself."

"Thank you."

"Sleep, Vanessa. Tomorrow will be a challenge for you. But no matter what happens, know that I'm here. I will always stand beside you, angel," he said with a coy smile.

He stepped back and as fast as they had come

together, she was in a bed alone. She was lying on her stomach, her cheek resting on a rolled-up blanket. She held out her hand and saw milky white skin again. She relaxed her mind and the tension in her body washed away, and with it, the telepathically manufactured pigment of her skin. She stretched her hand, examining her fingertips, each end more akin to claws than nails. Staring at the green of her arm, she thought of Dav5d embracing her.

"If you believe…"

***

Twenty-Seven gripped the gun under the scat. She let her thumb inch up the stock until the safety gave a faint click. Her eyes opened slowly. She inspected the immediate area without moving a muscle. Snoring came from the back of the van in a symphony drowning out Mother Nature.

She lifted the gun to her chest. Her left shoulder ached. Dav5d had performed surgery on her. The bullet was removed without issue and he said she'd mend quickly. The pain intensified as she tensed her muscles, sitting up slowly, not making a sound.

The van was dark and only the moon illuminated the area around it. Nearly two dozen had met at the rendezvous, battered and beaten. She was surprised to see so many. For some reason she expected them to all be killed by the terrifying force that took them over. The survivors whispered about dreams they had and the reality they awoke to, the massacre of their loved ones, scared it might happen again.

Gripping the gun, she knew the boogie man wasn't really there; he was miles away, and with a thought he could reach them. His power was chilling, somebody who could turn friends against one another so quickly. More frightening, a man that could rob your body of its independence.

"We're alone," Dav5d whispered.

He was some sort of genius. He had no social skills to speak of, but she liked him. His awkward ways were endearing. He spoke in facts and would analyze things out loud. It made the other Outlanders nervous. She found him to be a relief. If only the men in her life were always so straightforward.

"I'm scared."

"That's appropriate, considering the trauma you recently sustained both mentally and physically."

She smiled. He had no idea he was doing it. "Where are we going?"

"We will be in Canada tomorrow. I will introduce you to Elias and Jessica."

She pushed the safety on and quietly set the gun back on the floor. Her hand rested on the weapon as she tried to get comfortable again. Once she found a spot that kept her shoulder from hurting, she whispered to Dav5d, "Who are Elias and Jessica?"

"Children of Nostradamus. They ushered several of our younger wards to Canada to keep them safe from the government. They have begun a small community for Children. They will help get you situated. You'll have a home that will not slowly kill you."

There was a long pause as she thought about

what it would be like to have a home again. She only stayed a couple days with the Outlanders. But the hotel had seemed more like a fortress than a home. There were no humans she found herself bonded to. Her thoughts moved from the Children to Vanessa, the angel who had saved her.

"May I ask a question?" Dav5d asked harmlessly.

"Yeah."

"Do you know your role in the bigger picture?"

She started to respond and found herself at a loss for words. She had been a prisoner. She had been a wayward, lost soul. She had been rescued. She had been united with kindred spirits. She was in the midst of fleeing to their Valhalla. She shook her head. "I haven't the faintest."

"What did Eleanor say?"

The psychic. The woman had started her on this path. Twenty-Seven gripped the gun tighter. The cool metal reminded her of the lock on the safe her husband kept. With a few words, a long dead woman changed her entire world. "She freed me. She gave me the ability to make choices again. I'm still figuring out where it'll take me."

"You will discover it in time."

"Did Eleanor send you a letter?"

"Yes, each of us have been influenced by Eleanor's letters."

Twenty-Seven wished she could remember her letter word for word. There was something in the woman's tone, in the very way she curved her letters that showed sympathy. Twenty-Seven knew Eleanor understood her situation, perhaps far more than she cared to admit.

"I think she only gives letters to the people who need them, those lost on their journey. Eleanor must have known you existed. Maybe she wrote somebody else a letter because she knew you'd find your own way?"

The silence hung in the air for several minutes. Twenty-Seven wanted to say more, but she didn't know how to explain herself. She had been at her weakest and Eleanor had raised her up. She wondered if Dav5d was forging a path that did not need Eleanor's input.

"Thank you."

She grinned as she closed her eyes. He might be the smartest man alive, but she was certain it was only the teachings of a determined mom that forced his thanks. He meant it as much as he could, but he had no idea why two words could alter a person's mood so much.

"You're welcome."

Chapter Twenty

May 20th, 2032 6:27AM

"Seriously? There must be more guards," Dwayne said, looking at the crude map in front of them. They all huddled around the table, inspecting the sheet of paper on which Jasmine had drawn the complex. Small x's littered the map, showing the most likely locations of the security guards.

"Did you see more? And there will probably be fewer because somebody slaughtered half the detail."

Dwayne stared at Jasmine, reading the anger on her face. "Fine. What about mechs? They must have a good detail to deal with the more hostile powers in the facility."

Conthan watched as they went back and forth, arguing out the plan. It was obvious that Dwayne wasn't used to taking orders from somebody so aggressive. As much as he was attempting to take the backseat during their planning, Jasmine wasn't used to being questioned by her subordinates.

"There will be at least a dozen synthetics."

"Dammit," Dwayne hissed.

"Two nearly killed us last time," said his sister. They all turned to Skits. "What? I'm all about kicking some ass, but I would like to make it out alive."

"Where is their remote outpost?"

"Not at the facility. All synthetics are controlled from a base in DC. There is no way we can infiltrate their computers."

"Where's Dav5d when you need him?" said Alyssa.

"We fight through," said Dwayne. "Where are we going to find the Warden?"

Conthan pointed to the map. "I think that's where his office is. Should we take him out first? What about the guards?"

Jasmine shook her head. "If he's a telepath like you say and he can control that many humans, then the guards will be operating under his direction. After exposure to him for so long, there's a good chance he has their powers under his influence."

"He does," Conthan said. "Sarah was completely vacant."

"See?" she said. "We need to get in and free who we can. If we can take out the Warden, consider it an additional perk."

"There will be Paladins," Dwayne added. "I can't imagine them letting their most valuable target loose."

"Holy shit," Alyssa said.

They all looked up to see Vanessa walking toward them. She was dressed in one of the black tactile uniforms they had confiscated on a raid. It was rare to see her not in her robes, but it was the exposed skin making them stare.

Dwayne's lip curled. It was hard to work with her for so long and not suspect she was hiding something. Even with her serpentine wings stretched out on either side, he was glad to see a darker battle with herself had ended. The nails on her bare feet clicked loudly as she approached the table. He wanted to inspect her more closely, but he turned back to the map. "Vanessa, your thoughts?"

Thank you, Dwayne.

I'll admire your complexion after we win.

Then let's be sure we win.

Jasmine lacked any of Dwayne's tact. Her mouth gaped at the gargoyle-esque woman standing beside them. She began to speak. Vanessa held up her hand. "Jasmine, your expertise will be extremely useful, but let us do what we do best."

Jasmine got quiet for a moment, an action not lost on the rest of the team. "Your thoughts?"

Vanessa nodded to her. "We will need to coordinate this flawlessly. We get one chance and the moment one of you missteps, you have to realize it will be the death of all of us."

"He'll know we're coming," Dwayne said.

"Leave the Warden to me."

Conthan wanted to say something witty. The woman next to him was one of the most amazing things he had seen. He thought to the grotesques that lined the walls of churches, protecting its patrons. While she wasn't made from granite, he did see a comparison between her and the stone gargoyle's mission. She wasn't fearless, nor was she ruthless, but she was taking the burden of leadership and he admired that. He listened to her talk about where each of them would be located and how they would attack.

"Conthan," she said, "this all depends on you…"

Chapter
Twenty-One

May 20th, 2032 6:59AM

"Let me guide you," she said, her voice just a whisper. "Remember why you are doing this. Sarah is counting on you."

There had once been a small stage for live performances in the bar. The old wood was peppered with the stains of many dropped drinks. Conthan stood face to face with Vanessa, rotating his shoulders, trying to loosen his muscles. The others stood nearby, waiting for Vanessa to activate Conthan's abilities.

Conthan relaxed the moment Vanessa's hands rested on his forehead. Her skin was cool to the touch. There was strength in her hands and an uncanny amount of restraint as she gently rested her hand on his brow. The hair on his arms stood out straight as he listened to her thoughts.

A tingle rushed through his body. He clenched

his fists instinctively as the sensation intensified through his arms and then chest. The spot in the back of his mind locking away his abilities flared to life. The darkness that controlled his portals looked for an escape as the pressure built. He stared into Vanessa's eyes and let her ease the panic washing over him.

"We have faith in you," she said aloud.

Her thoughts began to consume his. He couldn't make out specific words, but flashes of memories assaulted his senses. He focused on her eyes, thinking about how much he trusted the woman. He knew she would do whatever it took to keep him safe. Now that he was one of her people, he knew she would risk her life for his.

"You're going to be exhausted. Alyssa is going to stand guard. I will do what I can to protect you from here."

He nodded. "Do it."

His powers flared without any direction. His fists both opened wide. He could feel the portal open, the darkness calling to him, attempting to consume him. He was beginning to understand Dwayne's warning. There was something alluring about losing himself to the grandeur of his own abilities. He wondered how strong he was to resist a drug constantly at his beck and call.

A stray emotion from Vanessa washed over him. The anxiety from a dangerous situation left his mind as quickly as it entered. The portal was open and like before, it beckoned him to create a sister void tying the two points together. Unlike before, he didn't let his powers force open a second portal. His mind raced from his body and he felt as if he were flying over a great expanse. The wind rushed by his imaginary self. The hair on his physical body began to stand on end.

Not quite a telepath, Vanessa's voice whispered in his head, *but there is more than meets the eye to your powers.*

The research facility sped toward him at an uncanny speed. He closed his eyes as his body penetrated the giant wall. His projected self slowed, but still moved fast enough that every living person remained frozen.

"Don't let your powers control you," Vanessa coached. "You are the master of your gifts."

In a blink of an eye he stood in front of a massive machine. There was no sound, just the still image of mammoth metal contraptions all around him. He released the tension in his hand and a portal appeared in a dark corner of the room. He could see guards frozen in time, and behind each of them, a shadowy figure.

"Don't worry about him," she said. "I will take care of that."

Another moment passed and he was standing in the control room. Two figures sat at a large computer. He stepped back and opened another portal. His powers worked in tandem with his wishes, no longer resisting his control.

"One more, Conthan," she said.

He stood in a small room with Sarah sitting on her bed. Behind her, the same shadow caressed side of her cheek. His chest clenched with anger as he realized the Warden had tainted her like he had the

Outlanders. He wanted to reach out to her, but knew he was hundreds of miles away from his friend.

The rushing sensation as he returned to his physical body was so fast it was deafening. He opened his eyes and Vanessa smiled at him, her canine teeth showing under her lip. "Good work, Conthan."

His muscles fought to keep him standing. She looked to the others. "Godspeed, Nighthawks," she said confidently. "You know why we fight."

Vanessa rested a hand on Jasmine's shoulder as she prepared to walk through the portal. "Fight for a young teenager," she said.

Fight for your penance.

"Out of my head, telepath," she said.

From here on out, I'm in all of your heads.

Dwayne took Skits's hands and stepped into one of three portals in the bar. The moment he passed through, Conthan felt the tug and he closed the rip in space. Jasmine tapped one of the bands on her wrist and the air vibrated as she grunted. She buckled over for a moment and then staggered upright. "Remember our quid pro quo, angel," she grumbled as she vanished into the portal.

Alyssa grabbed Conthan's hands and they crossed the threshold through the remaining void. It was like every other time; as they touched the black void, only a fraction of a second passed. The darkness sapped all the heat from their skin. Before he stepped through the other side, the pressure on his head began. They emerged on the other side, the power raced out of his body and as he tightened his muscles, the last two portals vanished.

"Holy shit," he said as he collapsed to the ground.

***

Alyssa could feel the air rush by her head before she saw the fist causing it. It was like a club smacked her across the face, knocking the spit from her mouth and drawing blood. It only took a moment before her abilities surged, assessing the environment and the immediate threat. Her body adapted.

Alyssa ducked beneath the next clumsy punch and kicked out to push the woman backward. Her assailant was covered in bones just like Conthan described. Alyssa hooked her arm around the woman's slow moving fist, immobilizing her arm. She moved quickly, striking at the back of the bony woman's leg, knocking her to her knees. Alyssa reached back to punch the woman and realized there was no vulnerable area to attack.

Before Alyssa could react, the woman's rigid skull slammed back, knocking the wind out of her lungs. Alyssa assessed their environment. The cell was ten by ten feet with only a bed, while a solid metal door blocking their exit. Alyssa grunted as she backed against the wall. Sarah spun about and pulled back for another punch. Alyssa sidestepped the blow and gasped as the bones in the girl's hands chipped away at the solid brick cell. "Damn, chick."

She looked down to Conthan taking up valuable square footage on the floor. Then she jumped up on the bed and put two feet between her and her assailant. She looked through the room and realized that other than a bed, there were no furnishings to use to her advantage. She had watched plenty of close combat videos an hour ago, but none prepared her for an enemy she couldn't hit. Her muscles reacted, dodging one punch, evading a knee to the chest, and throwing another oncoming hand out wide.

"Conthan," she said, "when you're done throwing up, I wouldn't mind help with your friend."

She heard the fist connect with the brick again. She could continue to dodge the woman and evade the direct force of her blows, but even blocking the attacks was going to take a toll on her fleshy body.

Alyssa put her foot on the woman's chest and threw her back, knocking her over Conthan's puking body. She ripped the sheet off the bed and spun it around into a long narrow band. "Let's improvise," she said.

The bony girl clambered to her feet, ignoring Conthan, and lunged at Alyssa, who used the sheet to wrap around her attacker's wrist. She ducked beneath the outstretched hand and pulled it up behind the woman's back. She kicked at her knee again, knocking her off her feet and rendering her immobile. She grabbed the other hand and was surprised; despite the bone husk encasing her body, there wasn't more strength than a typical Child of Nostradamus.

She wrapped the sheet around the other hand and ripped off another strip. Using her knee to hold the woman down, she bound her ankles and tied the restraints together. The woman continued to struggle. "Jesus, you've got some fight in you."

Alyssa grabbed Conthan and helped him stand long enough to sit on the edge of the bed. "Now that your girlfriend is done trying to kill me, we wait."

He nodded. She tried to hide the worry on her face, but she could see Conthan was feeling the same thing. "It's up to them now."

***

The cold penetrated her skin. Being tough as steel, Jasmine was used to not feeling the outside world. She shivered as the heat siphoned away from her body. She emerged from the portal to see two men standing with their backs to her. The control room wasn't very large; had she been any bulkier, it'd be a tight fit. The computers overlooked a massive bay window showing giant turbines two floors below.

She closed the distance between them and punched as one guard turned. Her fist connected with his jaw. His bones crunched under the weight of the blow. Despite its force, she couldn't feel the impact through her epidermis.

"What the…"

She kicked the other man, knocking him over a chair in front of the control panel. He reached up for the computer and she grabbed his hand, snapping his wrist. She realized he was attempting to start the automated defense systems. He didn't care to alert the humans in the facility, no, she knew that with the Warden in charge, they were already aware something was amiss. The moment she walked through the portal the vile telepath was beginning to infiltrate her thoughts.

She kneed the guard in the face, destroying his jaw and leaving his still frame on the ground. As she turned, another guard in the doorway caught her attention. The bullets connected with her skin and impaled themselves, unable to penetrate her hide.

Before he could fire another round, she grabbed the gun, breaking the barrel. She clutched either side of his body armor. Her arms strained as they adapted to the uncanny amount of weight from her epidermis. While her skin could mutate in the blink of an eye, it took the rest of her body a few moments to increase her muscles.

He lifted his leg, pulling a knife from the side of his boot. His enhancements allowed him to slam the blade into her neck with twice the strength of an average man. The blade bent as it glanced off her skin. He dropped the knife in astonishment.

"Seriously?" she mocked.

She dragged him into the computer station and hurled his body. He smashed into the computer, leaving a dent in the sparking screens. Jasmine grabbed the door and pulled it shut. She broke off the handle to prevent outsiders from entering. She turned her attention to the man scrambling to his feet.

His face grew vacant. There was a moment when she wondered if he was receiving messages from central command. It dawned on her the only person contacting the guards was the Warden. His eyes followed her, but he didn't make any move to remove himself from his throne on the computer station.

"I didn't expect to see you again, traitor."

"I owe you a serious ass kicking," she said.

"So much fear underneath all that bravado."

She slugged the man's face with a closed fist. His head barely moved at the blow. The machines inside his body were hard at work augmenting his strength. She grabbed him by the neck and leg and raised him above her head, then brought him down over her knee. The man's body went limp as his spine snapped. She hurled him against the wall. "Stay out of my head, telepath!"

She almost felt bad for killing him, a pawn in the Warden's game. The body didn't appear human as it lay on the control room floor folded in half. As she began to think of him as a man, she pushed aside the thoughts. Everybody who died today was in the hands of the Warden. The pressure at her temples increased. She could tell the telepath was attempting to touch her thoughts. She wanted to see his body crumpled on the floor like the guard.

Keep dreaming, bitch, the voice echoed.

***

Dwayne scooted up against the wall. Skits followed suit, her elbow brushing up against his body. They both watched as the portal vanished. Dwayne took stock of their surroundings. They were in a small alcove on the second floor of the football field-sized room containing the generators. The metal grates underneath their feet showed large hoses and wires connecting to three large turbines.

His body vibrated. Underneath layers of insulation and metal, an uncanny amount of electricity called to him. He dared a glance around the corner and could see several guards talking amongst themselves. Two stories higher was the control room where Jasmine should have landed.

He looked his sister dead in the eye. "Follow my lead," he mouthed.

"Make it interesting," she whispered.

He grabbed her by the shoulder. "I'm getting us out of here in one piece."

Her hands started to flare blue. "Time to feel alive, brother."

He shook his head. He couldn't help but smile at her gusto. His sister was ready to take out some pent-up anger on anybody who crossed them. It wasn't too long ago he had rescued her from a facility far too similar to this. When he had found her, she was full of rage, and now, from the gleam in her eye, he could tell she had become better at hiding her feelings than dealing with them.

He wasn't going to get in her way today.

The charge built within his body, the imaginary battery he stored underneath his heart started to overflow with electricity. His powers were desperate to be unleashed and fought to escape his body. He had held off draining his powers. He knew he'd need every ounce of electricity he was capable of generating. He was sure it was his imagination, but he could almost feel his cells working in overdrive, attempting to meet his demands.

The heat radiated from Skits's hands, the space

around her arms dancing back and forth in a haze. She flexed her muscles and her powers surged through her body, intensifying until they distorted the air. She clenched her fists and the plasma ignited. The sleeves of her shirt vaporized, leaving burnt edges near her shoulders. The liquid fire dripped from the space around her hands, hitting the ground and burning through the metal grates.

She stepped back as her brother held up his fists. The neon pink hair on her head began to stand up. She took another step back as small arcs of electricity jumped between his fingers. He pushed his palms outward and the sparks turned into rampant chains of lightning, striking any exposed metal. The loud snaps in the air alerted the guards there was a problem.

A bolt of lightning crashed into the closest generator. The sound of tearing metal filled the massive room. The lightning continued to hammer away until it found its way inside the opening. The large machine sparked from his violation. Small explosions started to go off until the generator ruptured, forcing it to power down.

"We've got incoming," Skits said. She began a circling motion with her hands. As she spun them around quickly, liquid fire hovered in the air, creating a large disc between her and the firing guards.

Dwayne grunted as his internal battery neared depletion. Two of the three generators were powering down. He had one last target. His body was on fire as he spread his hands wide, lightning casting out in wide arcs, landing on steel walkways filled with guards and slamming against the final generator.

The men skidded to a stop and backed away from bolts striking the walls near them. Skits ducked, letting him having a clear shot at the guards. His lightning slammed against the first few men, launching them over the railing. The remorse he felt for killing was replaced by a momentary victory against the Warden.

"Synthetics." Skits pointed behind him.

Dwayne weakened the bolts shooting from his hands and focused on the walkway. A minor sting raced along his back, something he had learned to ignore in his hands. His shirt erupted as a chain of lightning left his shoulder blades and hit the first oncoming robot.

"New tricks, huh?" Skits said.

Her feet were moving, her boots thumping along the steel grates, launching her into a sprint. One of the synthetic humans fell to the ground under the weight of Dwayne's lightning. She jumped up just as the bolt stopped. She pushed harder, the heat making her palms sweat. The blue light around her forearms turned white and the liquid fire began to shape into a blade from her fist.

She punched down, surprised at the resistance of the metal in the machine. She let the weight of her body push her forward. Inch by inch the metal gave way. She reached out, grabbed the mech's neck, and focused on intensifying the power in her hands. Its head fell.

"I'm on fire," she yelled.

Another synthetic clutched her neck, preparing to

hurl her over the railing. She grit her teeth, forcing more heat into her hands. She grabbed onto its arms. The plasma pulsed from her body, melting the joints. As she pulled away, the shoulder of the synthetic opened and the small laser snapped upright. She jumped on the synthetic and grabbed the weapon case, the metal in her turning malleable and soft, solidifying on the shoulder of the machine.

The synthetic attempted to bat at her with its club-like arms. She laughed hysterically. She grabbed its head with both hands and pushed until there was nothing but a misshapen metal skull.

"We're coming for you next, government peeps."

She turned to Dwayne as he motioned for her to help him. He pointed over his shoulder at the several guards firing in his direction, pinning him inside the small alcove. She started to fire her powers to life until the lights suddenly went out. He could see his sister's body lighting up the metal walkways. He could see the smile on her face as she shook her arms, letting her abilities turn off. The room went very dark.

"Time for payback," she said, moving toward the gunfire.

***

The cool tile under her body helped relax her muscles as Vanessa sat cross-legged on the floor of the bar. She rested her hands on her knees and began her breathing exercises. She recited a prayer as she breathed in and out, asking God to watch over her friends as they tried to save their kind.

"I pray you were right, Eleanor."

She thought of the Warden and said a prayer for her upcoming encounter with him. She didn't ask God to protect her from the malicious man. She instead asked her creator to let her walk away from the encounter confident in her convictions. She had spent so much time in silent prayer as a child, convinced God had abandoned her. She had come to believe she was alone, a child of a more nefarious deity. A calm washed over her body, and she was certain she was being watched by the same angels she had envied her entire life.

"Warden," she said in an exhale, "today we test whose conviction is stronger."

The light from the windows vanished and she entered into what she referred to as her war room— the dark space inside her head where she worked with the others so often, helping them learn to control their powers. Here, she was the master of her domain and capable of expressing her abilities to their fullest potential.

Staring back at her was a reflection of the angel. While she was beside herself with joy at Dav5d's acceptance of her real self, a sense of doubt clung to her. The angel was an identity she forged many years ago, a sort of armor she created to protect herself. Emphasizing her chest, a breast plate was shaped tightly to her body, and sheathed at her hip was a fiery sword. She stretched her feathered wings out wide and her robe fell away, caught on an imaginary gust of wind.

"Even though I walk through the valley of the

shadow of death…" She watched as her body began to glow brighter. "I shall fear no evil."

She turned away from her reflection, and off in the distance, a mirage of the research facility awaited her. Dark clouds hovered overhead, a pestilence and gloom radiating outward from the structure. She knew it was her mind explaining the presence of the Warden. She took her first step toward the large cube and the distance shrunk to nothing. The image of the bar became a distant memory as she reached to her hip and drew the sword. "I shall not fear his evil."

Chapter Twenty-Two

May 20th, 2032 7:12AM

Dwayne pressed himself against the wall, just out of sight from the guards. The red dots stayed fixed; the soldiers showed their training by not letting the laser sights bob to and fro. They held their fire, waiting until he dared to jump out into the open. He didn't have to see their glowing eyes to know they had ocular implants. This moment, they were seeing shades of green, using what little light existed inside the facility to illuminate the battlefield.

He tried to remember the layout of the room. There was a catwalk leading to the guards, and another in the other direction headed toward the maintenance room. He contemplated making a run for it but knew they would land at least one shot. He thought of trying to jump over the catwalk to the floor below, but could only imagine he'd break his legs and die a victim.

"Skits," he said into his headpiece, "I'm pinned down."

"I've got you, bro," she said, huffing into the microphone.

A flash of light lit up the room. Then darkness. More light. Then darkness. Bullets fired off into the distance. He watched as the red dots on the wall began to shake and sway from side to side. There was another clap of light and then more darkness.

"You're a genius," he said.

She ran past him, flashing more light and then falling down to the walkway, hugging the metal grates. Dwayne spun from his hiding spot and held out his hands. He launched a barrage of lightning in short bursts at the guards. He could see two of them stumble and fall and the rest began backing up. "We need to get out of here."

The glass shattered twenty feet above the guards. A shadow jumped from the second story and landed on the catwalk. The steel groaned as part of the walkway ripped away, bending toward the ground floor. "Reinforcements have arrived." He could hear the excitement in his sister's voice again.

***

Jasmine leaned against the window overlooking the generators below. Bullets flew toward a flashing light further down the maze of scaffolding. As the room became visible, she counted almost a dozen guards below, shielding their eyes from the blinding flare. She couldn't resist smiling at Skits's genius.

"Night vision doesn't work in the light."

A bolt of lightning felled two of the guards. The rest were using the edge of the massive generator for protection. She stepped up onto the computer and punched the glass, sending shards raining down on her soon-to-be victims.

She jumped through as a bolt of lightning lit up the room. She hit the catwalk and the metal gave under her feet, breaking the supports and nearly sending the walkway to the level below. She gripped the railing, stopping herself from falling to the wiring underneath. Jasmine pulled herself forward, stepping onto the platform level with the guards.

The guards were masked in darkness, but their eyes glowed a dark green. One held up his gun, pulling the trigger, and bullets caught her in the chest and neck. She didn't flinch at the little biting glances. She moved forward, grabbing the first man within reach. She hurled him backward, knocking over his companions. Before he could gain his footing, she caught his hand and hurled him over the railing.

She didn't try to assess the damage. She balled her fist and began swinging wildly in the dark, hoping her punches would connect with any of the humans. Her fists sunk into soft flesh. She grabbed onto whatever she could and threw him to the floor below. She paused as the emergency lights flooded the room, casting an eerie red glow on the survivors.

Three guards lowered their guns. Each of them straightened to the point where Jasmine could tell something was different. "You cannot kill us," they said in unison.

"Fucking creepy," Skits said as her hand flashed blue and plunged into the back of the two closest guards.

The last guard reached for his sidearm and pulled it up to fire. Jasmine stood there, waiting, uncaring if the shot connected with her body. He pulled the trigger and the gun flashed a bright red. The beam seared into Jasmine's shoulder. She staggered backward, hissing at the sharp pain near her collarbone.

"What the hell?" She went to one knee on the ground, trying to push away the pain radiating through her shoulder.

Dwayne reached out, grappling for the gun. The guard pulled the trigger and the laser connected with Dwayne's sternum. The heat of the beam seared his skin as the light dissipated before touching his body. He gasped in anticipation of the pain of a killing shot. His gasp turned to a loud groan as his back arched in pain.

Jasmine did a double take as Dwayne's eyes lit up red. His muscles tensed and she swore she could see red lightning coursing through his body just beneath his skin. He flexed his hands, the sparks jumping around his skin not their typical white and yellow. She wondered if he was capable of siphoning more than just electricity.

Skits thrust her hand into the guard's side, the fire burning through his body and turning his heart to mush. She pulled her hand back and shook off the flames. "The talking thing has gone from creepy to fucking annoying."

One of the guards on the ground below called out, "Only my pawns."

Jasmine looked to her comrades. "What does that mean?"

"Something worse?"

"We need to get to the Warden," Jasmine said.

Conthan's voice sounded over the earpieces. "We have trouble in the cell blocks."

"Can you teleport?" Dwayne said, holding his ear.

"Not yet," he said.

"Alyssa?"

"I'm good." She gulped loud enough they could all hear. "I hate to admit it, but we need Class I support."

Dwayne looked to Jasmine. "Do you know how to get there?"

She shrugged.

Their earpieces made a loud cracking sound and turned to static. They each flinched at the pop. Dwayne pointed to the far door. "We might as well keep moving. Sitting here isn't helping anybody."

"The Paladins will go to the holding cells first. They'll make sure the prisoners are contained and then they'll begin sweeping the rest of the facility."

"Best get moving, then," Skits said.

***

Conthan grabbed the door to hold it shut. He leaned in with his body weight, wedging his foot by the base. "Who the fuck would open the doors?"

316

"Who do you think?"

"At least this wing is low security," Alyssa said.

Conthan staggered backward as somebody hurled themselves against the door. It swung open and Conthan was staring at a woman with short-cropped hair. He waited for her to burst into flames or shoot lasers from her eyes.

Alyssa pushed him aside and punched the woman in the face, knocking her to the ground. "They're Class III's. Their powers are going to be almost all passive. We can rumble our way out of here."

Conthan pointed to Sarah, her legs and arms bound behind her back. The girl was struggling against the makeshift rope around her rocky limbs. "What about her?"

"We'll come back for her. I can't do my thing in this small room."

Alyssa bolted from the holding cell. Outside, a circular room's walls were covered in doors similar to the one she had just exited. The red safety lights made it difficult to see, but she was sure all of the doors were opened. She backed up to Sarah's cell, as more Children began to emerge from their cells.

"When you can teleport," she said, "get us out of here."

He was impressed with how fast she ducked a blow from a man. She proceeded to sidestep and grab a body. She rolled backward, taking him with her. She landed on top of him and pinched his shoulders, rendering him paralyzed. "A fight where I can't hurt people." She groaned as an elderly woman grabbed onto her vest. "Not fair."

Conthan wrapped his arms around the middle-aged woman clinging to Alyssa and tossed her backward onto the floor. She hit the wall and slumped down, not unconscious, but not in any shape to continue her assault. "Do we fight?"

"If it's us or them," she said, pressing her back against his, "you better choose us."

Alyssa spun her head as a fist connected with her jaw. She rolled with the punch, reached out to block the upcoming hit, and only found empty air. She resumed her position behind Conthan and found there was nobody else standing in the room with them. "What the hell?"

She grunted as a foot pounded into her stomach. She grabbed at the air and found the invisible appendage. Spinning it, she watched a man appear out of thin air. She gave him a swift kick to the gut, ensuring he would stay on the ground.

Conthan tumbled to the ground as a larger than normal woman struck him. He grunted as he rolled to a stop. "Help."

"Have you never fought?"

He coughed back in response.

She stepped on Conthan's back and jumped, bringing both fists down on the woman's head. The woman staggered, shaking off the blow. Alyssa stepped back out of reach of her elongated arms. She started to charge at the massive woman but a man grabbed onto her shoulder. She used the momentum to turn around, grab the man who seized her and launch them at the large woman.

"Conthan, if you don't help, I'm going to kick you next."

Conthan sucked in air, gasping loudly. He rolled over just in time to see the large woman hurl a body against the wall. She drew back her leg to kick Conthan. He scurried out of the way as quickly as he could, barely escaping the massive club-like limb. Her foot rose again, ready to slam down on his head.

There was no tingle. There was no controlling it. He reacted. The woman's foot vanished into a circle of black. It emerged above her head. As she tried to crush him, her foot drove downward onto her own head. She toppled to the ground. He clenched his fist, a symbol of closing the voids, and he watched as the dark circles vanished.

"Good," spat Alyssa. "Keep making yourself useful."

"We have to get them out of here," Conthan said, gesturing to the bodies littering the ground.

"Let me ask nicely if they'll stop attacking us and march in a single file line."

The remaining Children in the room froze. They turned toward Conthan and Alyssa. "We are many."

"Oh, shut the hell up," Alyssa yelled back at the voices.

"You cannot…"

"Kick your ass?" she continued to yell.

"Alyssa…" Conthan pointed to a man standing perfectly still. "What do you think is happening?"

"Who the hell knows anymore? Telepath shit gets weird."

The Children were all wearing white pants and white shirts. The room had a sense of sterilization to it. They stood motionless, as if they fell asleep standing. Alyssa grabbed Conthan and helped him to his feet.

"It's Vanessa," he said.

"How do you know?"

"Do you know of another telepath that can fuck with people's heads?"

He ran back into Sarah's cell. She was catatonic, unblinking as she stared off into space. He got down on his knees and shook her shoulder. "Sarah, are you in there?"

He leaned in closer to her face, trying to see her eyes in the dim red light. His hand rested on the only spot on her body with exposed skin. "Wake up, Sarah. It's me, we're here to rescue you."

"Conthan…"

"Alyssa," he yelled. "It's her."

"We've got bigger problems."

Conthan turned to see a bright light coming from the other side of the large room. Alyssa slid into the cell and grabbed the door, throwing it shut with a loud bang. Conthan watched as fire flooded the area and the temperature began to rise. The clothing of the standing Children caught fire, but none made a motion to stop from being engulfed.

"It's a pyro," Alyssa said with a look of horror.

***

His eyes were fixed on something she could not see. His large frame was partially hidden by an even larger desk. For a moment, she almost wondered if he was dead, his body unmoving as if he wasn't inhaling. She could only imagine controlling so many people required more concentration than he let on.

The distance between them vanished and she was standing on the other side of the desk. He paid her no attention. This was not her first time waging war on another person's psyche. Each instance before, the person had been hysterical, almost mad in their approach. He almost seemed serene. She had never met somebody so calm when she entered their mind.

In the office, standing near the only door, were two guards. She had no desire to infiltrate the minds of humans, but something about the two guards appeared missing. She reached out with her fingers, her thoughts gently grazing theirs. She pulled back her fingers, clutching them as if she had been shocked. Where she expected a collection of the human experience, she found the two guards were vacant, thoughtless husks.

She squinted, trying to focus on the two sentries standing watch at his door. She could normally touch their minds and see their faces from their own self-perception. Where there should have been faces were only two blank heads with twisted smiles. She drew back, avoiding their empty souls.

The small office looked like any other would, down to the desk, the chairs, even the paperwork strewn across his desk. However, as the room ended, where walls should have been there was only darkness. It appeared as if the platform on which they stood was hovering in a perpetual black void.

She started for the sword hanging from her hip, her hand resting on the pommel. She reached over with her other hand, creeping it along her stomach until she gripped the handle of the sword. She drew the massive piece of metal in a single fluid motion and held the sword in front of her with both hands.

She wasn't alone. She couldn't hear anybody, but it would be impossible for a telepath as strong as him to move without being felt. His movements should be as loud as boots dragging across gravel. She reacted, spinning just as a shadow emerged from the darkness. The shadow's weapon clashed against hers as he begun to laugh.

"Did you think my body would be so primitive, angel?"

The telepath's psyche consisted of dense smoke, wisps radiating outward from the human-like figure. His mace pressed against her sword. The weight of his body behind the weapon was nothing more than his determination, she thought. She could only imagine a man this cocky had reasons for such an inflated ego.

"More arrogant than I expected," she said.

"Here, arrogance is strength."

She turned her sword, catching the smoky weapon hard enough it made her arms vibrate. Each blow possessed more power. She knew they weren't physically confronting one another and the weapons at their disposal were only symbolic representations of a battle between their minds, but she could already see he was far more versed at this than she. The faint delight she had experienced when she found another living telepath was replaced with seething anger as she pushed his club away from her body.

"You radiate weakness," he said, slamming the mace into her sword again.

She knocked aside his blow and jabbed with her sword, thrusting it through the shadow. As the blade pushed through the thickness of the smoke, she twisted it, savoring her victory. She paused when the expression on his face turned to a smile. His laughter mocked her attempt to slay him.

The shadows making the man dissolved away into nothing. She pulled the sword back and stared at the spot where he had been standing. Before she could register the action, she spun around, sword out, knocking away an axe-like shape. She brought the sword back around and pushed a long spear out wide, deflecting it from connecting with her body.

"You've practiced, angel," said an echo of voices.

Where there had been one attacker, the smoke split apart into two, both identical to the first. She took several steps back from the smoky figures. She watched as wisps moved between the humanoids, as if they were conjoined by black tendrils. She cursed herself for being enamored by another telepath. She cursed herself for not anticipating how adept he would be. Where he had power, she had cunning and speed. She dug her heels into the imaginary ground. There was no way he was leaving alive.

She dropped into a crouch and spun on the ball of her foot. Her wings stretched out, slicing through legs of smoke. She carried her momentum forward, standing upright, passing her sword through both figures. She didn't hesitate as she sensed another body lunging at her. She ducked, letting whatever weapon it held cut above her back. She dropped to one knee and brought her sword back, sinking it into the flesh of another shadow.

Her physical body would be sweating, aching from the conflict, ready to see it over. Her mind, however—her mind craved the fast-paced stimuli; here she could fight indefinitely. She turned to see another figure. Before she could lift her sword, tendrils of smoke grasped her face. The sensation was as real as if a person pressed their hand against her skin, but as the tendrils flowed across her face, she could feel a pain spreading through her body.

"You're a child to me," said the voice.

She cried out as the pressure behind her eyes began to swell. The sword fell from her grasp and she reached out to scratch at the hands around her face. Tendrils of smoke emerged from the tips of his fingers and began to seep into her skin. The pain intensified along her spine. She could sense his strength, his will, beginning to penetrate her mind.

The room blurred and she was standing in a large church. A man she had long since buried was standing over her. His black clothes and white collar reminded her of the horrors she used to endure. She had the urge to run, fleeing her tormentor. The aisle led to the altar, a cross with Jesus Christ hanging above it, his head wrapped in a crown of thorns. The rose window should have let in an ethereal light, but now it stood dark, a symbol of the church for her so many years ago.

As she attempted to move she could feel her legs, solid as stone, holding her hostage in this nightmare. She tried to will away the heaviness, but found her limbs refused to cooperate. She flapped her wings in a panic, hoping she could remove herself from this nightmare.

"Demon spawn," came the priest's chalky voice. She wept the moment he spoke, saying words she heard day after day for years. At any moment she would feel the sting of the belt across her back, making welts and splitting her alabaster skin. She closed her eyes and tried to will away the man and his instrument of retribution. Cries began to pour out of her mouth at the first of many strikes he forced her to endure. She shivered at it, biting her lip so she wouldn't cry out loud again.

"I cast you out," the voice boomed.

She gasped at the sting of another blow from the belt. Her eyes clenched shut as her hands hid her face from the evil man. The smacking of the belt in his hand told her he was debating on how many strikes she would need to be cleansed. The sound of footsteps worked around her until the man was standing directly in front of her frozen self. She dared to peek through her fingers. Where she expected to see the priest staring back at her, another smoky figure grinned. Her mind was a swirl of confusion, memories mixed with the present.

As the belt came flying toward her face again, she reached out and grabbed the piece of leather. She shot up from her kneeling position and lunged at the man. She took him to the ground and began to claw at his face. The rage consumed her as she continued to rake her talons against his face. Finally, the man's body went lifeless below her.

She sat up and saw the image of the priest, still,

his body void of life. She screamed at the memory. The screams returned, echoing off the massive stone walls. Tears ran down her face, dripping onto the corpse. She lifted her hands, looking at the silky smooth skin. As she wiped away her tears, she smelled his aftershave, a musky scent she couldn't wash out of her pillows.

She wailed. Her scream turned primal as she purged her lungs of the musk wafting off his body. The man had been her tormenter for so long. When the pain became too much she always reminded herself she was better than him. Now, as she looked down at his glassy eyes, he had won.

Laughter came from the shadows of the massive cathedral. She tried to find the source until she saw the man below her, his bloodied body laughing. Where his bloodshot eyes had been, they were replaced with dark eyes with red halos. "So much potential and yet you're lost to your own fears."

She grabbed his shoulders and slammed his head against the ground. She continued screaming with each blow. She slumped to the ground, exhausting herself. The remnants of laughter still filled the air. "This isn't me."

"But it is…" He let the next word hang on the tip of his tongue. "Demon."

Chapter
Twenty-Three

May 20th, 2032 7:26AM

Jasmine looked at the door and saw how its many latches fed into the wall, keeping it secure. She grabbed one and began to pull it back. She grunted at the strain but was elated that the metal was bending. She ripped it off and then began on the next. A moment later she hurled her body against the door and it flew open.

"Holy shit," Skits said.

"That's one impressive bitch," Dwayne said.

They ran down the corridor and came to a large door. Jasmine gave it a firm punch but pulled her fist back, shaking it off. "It's denser than any other metal I've seen in this place."

"This door shouldn't be here. Dav5d's blueprints didn't have anything blocking our way. It should be a straight shot to the Warden."

"Can you open it?" asked Dwayne.

327

"You took out the main power. Auxiliary power will be up shortly, I'm doing what I can." Jasmine pulled open a small panel next to the door and examined the wires. "Maybe we can—"

They all turned as the loud clank of footfalls stomping down the hall grew louder. Jasmine cursed under her breath. "Synthetics."

She put her hand on the door. Even through the dense epidermal layer of her skin, her powers let her sense the metal under her fingertips. Her abilities flared to life, the cells of her body mimicking the metal. The pain rippled through spine. She buckled over and fell to her knees, gasping loudly as her skin transformed.

"What did you do?"

"My skin," she said through gritted teeth, "mimics density of what it touches."

Dwayne reached up to one of the emergency lights above them. "Sounds painful," he said as he ripped open the panel.

"It is," Jasmine said, forcing herself back to her feet.

Dwayne pulled the wires out and electricity jumped from them onto his hand. He covered the end of the wires and leaned his head back. A smile spread across his lips as his eyes started to spark. "Ammo."

The first synthetic marched around the corner. The human-like figure held up its arms. Both palms flared to life as lasers rapidly fired. Skits ducked behind Jasmine, who didn't flinch as the lasers pelted her body. Where the laser had penetrated her hide before, now, with the new metallic skin, she couldn't even feel the red beams pelting her.

Jasmine laughed. "That's what I'm talking about."

Her muscles strained against the weight of her skin. It felt as if she was moving through water and her body was finding it difficult to cooperate. The stinging sensation of her abilities still coursed through her as muscles adapted to the newest synched material.

The synthetic was joined by another and the lasers began to intensify as they sank into Jasmine's flesh. "Stupid machines."

The first robot grabbed her arm and tried to pull her to the ground. She flexed and found that she couldn't even feel the touch of the machine. The other grabbed her head and tried to spin her neck. She felt the tiniest tug. She laughed. "What are they trying to hide back there? Nobody puts in doors like that unless they're trying to keep people out."

Dwayne stared in amazement as she crushed the skull of one robot and tore the head off the other. "She's crazy."

"My kind of woman," Skits said.

"Do we help her?"

Skits kinked her neck to the side. "We slaughter them."

Jasmine reached up, snatched at both of the guns producing bursts of light, and ripped them from the synthetics. The robots clung to her, trying to drag her down to the ground. They punched at her midsection but the loud thuds didn't bother Jasmine. She freed an arm, grabbed one skull, and began to squeeze. The dense material under her hand resisted. Her powers avoided mimicking the material, favoring the densest metal they had ever absorbed.

The skull was crushed in her grip. The other machine braced its legs against the wall and pushed, knocking Jasmine backward. As they landed, her body dented the grates beneath her. She couldn't begin to imagine how much her weight had increased.

The machine was reaching for her head and she could feel its claws scraping along her face. It finally settled on attempting to wedge its thumbs into her eyes. She grabbed its hands and tried to pull it free. She was fully aware, after numerous experiments by her previous employer, that her eyes were not affected by her powers.

She was about to scream when she saw the blue light severing the machine's head. She could feel the distant heat, but was more shocked by the brightness so close to her face. She looked up to see Skits standing over her. "Stop hogging the fun."

"You're crazy."

"Damn straight."

"Holy shit," Dwayne said, staring down the long corridor to where another twenty synthetics marched toward them.

He ran back to the panel, examining the exposed wires. Jasmine stood between him and the synthetics, using her body as a shield. Dwayne reached into the panel, grabbing at wires and pulled until sparks started to jump his arm into the control box. The plastic around the wires melted and the panel lit up for a moment.

The large blast door began to open. A loud groan filled the room. The door only split a little more than a foot before coming to a halt, freezing into place.

"Best I can do," Dwayne said.

"We'll take it," Skits said, panicking as she looked at the robots over her shoulder.

Skits easily slid into the gap and Dwayne wiggled his way through, swearing he'd diet if they made it out alive. Jasmine started to claw at the doors but found that her stiff skin made it impossible for her to fit.

She grit her teeth and imagined a layer of light clinging to her skin, then shattering and falling away. The searing sensation throughout was uncanny. She had never converted from such a dense material; her body was giving up as the room began to spin.

"What's happening?" Skits asked.

"She's turning off her powers."

Skits grabbed Jasmine's arm through the gap and pulled. Jasmine's skin became malleable. A second later, it was as normal as Skits's. Skits tugged harder on Jasmine's arm until she slid through the split doors.

Jasmine screamed as a laser skimmed across her forearm. She fell inside the doors.

Dwayne pushed to the side of the parted door. "It's an elevator," he said as he poked at the buttons. Unlike the panel on the outside, this one reacted. He slammed it, forcing the motors above them to fire to life.

Skits's hands lit up and she forced the plasma to

spear through the skull of a machine trying to crawl through the gap. Jasmine recognized the fatigue washing over the girl's body. As soon as the adrenaline faded, she would be unconscious. Jasmine continued to be impressed with how hard each of her acquaintances pushed themselves.

"Die," she screamed.

She punched into the chest of another mech. Their bodies resisted as the flame around her hands faded. She grit her teeth and began growling. She tensed every muscle in her body and her hands flared one last time. The two machines in the gap melted enough that they were permanent fixtures, blocking the remaining robots.

"Smart," Dwayne huffed.

She hit the floor. "I have my moments."

The room began to shift and then drop downward. "This part of the facility has its own power," Dwayne said as he braced himself in the corner of the elevator.

"What's that mean?" Skits asked.

"We're about to find out."

"If you get me killed…" Jasmine gasped.

There was a moment of silence. Jasmine winced from the pain in her ear as Alyssa screamed into the communicator. "Pyro."

Dwayne reached up and barked into the device, "We're nowhere near you. You and Conthan are on your own."

Skits had her back against a wall as she slid down into sitting position. "We're so screwed."

***

"We're going to cook alive," said Alyssa.

"I'm sorry, do you have a better idea?"

"Teleport our asses out of here."

Conthan looked from Sarah to Alyssa. He realized they were counting on him. He backed up against the far wall and clenched his fists. He thought about the darkness at his control, trying to focus on the part of him that stored this awesome power. There was a dull ache at the base of his skull, making it difficult to find that tingling sensation.

He looked up at Alyssa in dismay. "Nothing."

"Focus harder," she barked.

"No," he said, "I mean it's like they never existed. I've got nothing"

Sarah looked to her friend. "What do you mean, Conthan?"

"Your boyfriend can rip holes through space and time but not when it's absolutely necessary."

Sarah looked at him. "You're one of them?"

"Us," Alyssa corrected.

Conthan could see the sweat beginning to drip down Sarah's exposed cheek. Her eyes were judging him. He didn't need to be a telepath to know she was asking herself why she was locked up and he got to be free. She was having difficulty not letting the sorrow creep onto her face.

Conthan looked away from her. He couldn't handle seeing her disbelief in him. He would let her be angry when they were far away from here. He knew it was up to him. He clenched his fists tighter, his nails digging into his palms. He looked at his hands in disbelief. "Gone."

They could hear laughter from outside. "Why can't you teleport, Conthan?"

Alyssa looked at the door as it continued to glow red. "It's the Warden. He must be doing something."

Conthan understood Jasmine's hatred. "Damned telepaths."

Alyssa's shirt was starting to soak through. A continuous stream of sweat fell from her brow. "We're going to die."

The two women's eyes connected for a moment, a glance that spoke volumes. Sarah stood, clenching her fists, the bones scraping against one another. Conthan turned back and forth between the two women. Alyssa could see past the exoskeleton to Sarah's eyes, the woman signaling toward the door. She turned to Conthan and then back to Alyssa, giving her a nod. Alyssa knew what she meant, protect him, at all costs.

Sarah moved toward the door.

"What are you doing?" asked Conthan a moment too late.

Alyssa lunged, swiveling behind him and holding him in a deadman's lock. He tried to wrestle free out of instinct, and knew there wouldn't be any way he could break away from the girl. He saw Sarah reach for the door.

"No!"

Sarah looked over her shoulder for a moment and pushed the door open. The wave of flame washed over her body and she held still, letting it char her exoskeleton. She covered the small portion of her face with no bone and took a step into the oncoming inferno.

"No!"

Alyssa dragged Conthan to the floor and held on to him tight. He wasn't fighting her. He continued to yell at the top of his lungs. He felt Alyssa let go of his arm and all he could do was reach out toward his best friend. He watched as the flame poured around her until it came into the room, forcing him to turn away.

Alyssa watched in silence as the woman she just met was engulfed in flames. She could make out the girl's outline as she moved closer to the origin of the fire. She had read about pyros. She knew they were deadly with the ability to generate flame. She had never heard of one able to control it like this. Her shadow pushed onward toward the source.

The flame vanished for a moment. Sarah swung her arm out wide, slamming into a figure a dozen feet outside their small room. The man fell to his back, his body covered in smoke and still smoldering. Alyssa saw the spark start on his arm, and then his entire limb was engulfed and fire spread to the rest of his body.

"No," she whispered.

The fire wrapped around Sarah and the girl vanished into the flickering flames. Alyssa watched, horrified, as she fell on top of the man and began to bring her fist back. The slow action showed how much pain she was in. She never screamed. She brought it down, connecting squarely with where the man's face would have been. She did it one more time, and as fast as the flames had begun, they vanished.

"Sarah," Conthan said, calling out to his fallen friend.

Alyssa didn't stop Conthan as he crawled out from under her. He was at Sarah's side in moments. She grabbed the torn sheet and ran out to them. She patted down the girl, extinguishing the small flames still burning through what little fabric she was wearing.

Conthan ignored the pain in his hands as he rolled Sarah over. The bones covering her body were blackened. Her chest was fractured in multiple places, revealing where skin should have been beneath. He could see her face, both eyes closed, the skin as black as ash.

"Sarah." His tears landed on her skin, making a hissing sound as they made contact.

"Conthan," Alyssa said, pulling his hands off her body. Conthan swung his hand out, knocking her backward. He tried to touch his friend and he could feel the heat still radiating from her body. He waited for her to open her eyes. She lay there unmoving.

***

Jasmine's jaw was slack as she listened to Conthan mumbling in disbelief about his friend. Dwayne's eyes were closed, his face expressionless as they listened to Conthan's pleas. Skits on the other hand, her hands were already starting to burn blue again, and Jasmine could see the anger beginning to appear on her face.

Jasmine pressed the button on the elevator, hoping it would open. "I'm in a room with a Child who is about to go berserk," she said in a flat manner. "Let her exercise some grief."

The doors hissed and began to part. The girl vanished through the crack before they were fully open. The flare of her hands could be seen inside the dark room. Dwayne followed her out and Jasmine could hear the snap of the lightning as they began fighting.

Jasmine stood up and reached for the metal band on her arm. Her powers went into motion and she felt the pain, the surge, and the change in her skin. The weight of her body increased and she took a single step forward, trying to follow her companions out of the elevator shaft.

She walked out of the doors and found Skits huffing and puffing. The girl turned and looked at her teammate. Animalistic rage was painted across her face. Jasmine knew the signs of pain. Skits was in the midst of a break and she couldn't blame the young woman.

Dwayne turned to the massive room and waited for any other opposition. As he walked further into the space, lights began to flicker high above. It was huge, the length of several football fields. He paused to take in all of the spaces filled with machinery, half-built mechs, giant stasis tubes, and dozens of huge crates. "What are we seeing?"

"I have no idea," said Jasmine. A dozen men littered the ground; unlike the men earlier, these weren't soldiers. The white lab coats and computer pads scattered across the floor reminded her of the government scientists always trying to experiment on her.

Jasmine walked into the bay. Three-story tall ceilings made the space look immense, and the scatterings of machinery seemed out of place proportionally. She walked up to a series of tubes towering above the ground and realized she was staring at people trapped inside, suspended in liquid, masks attached to their faces.

"What are we looking at?" Dwayne asked.

"Didn't Conthan say his friend was covered in bones?"

"Yeah, she has an exoskeleton," Skits huffed.

Jasmine pointed at a man suspended in the liquid. Bones creeped up his leg, looking awkward as the rest of his body was still pink flesh. Near his shoulder, several spikes protruded through the skin. Jasmine looked down at the various controls and then to the others. "I know what this is."

"What?" Skits asked in a hoarse voice.

"They're grafting powers onto humans."

"What?" asked Dwayne.

Jasmine pointed to the man. "That's Conthan's girlfriend's power."

"Couldn't it be that somebody has the same power?" asked Dwayne.

"How many lightning hurlers have you found lately?"

"Point made."

Jasmine looked at the next tube and saw the outline of a human body in the liquid, but found that the actual person was impossible to see. The regulator clung to his face, forcing oxygen into his lungs. It caused his chest to rise and fall as if he might still be alive. The last tube was empty, and the floor in front of it was drenched.

"We're not alone."

Skits hands came back to life. "I've got this."

"This place is massive, it could be hiding anywhere," Dwayne said.

"How often does somebody bad get out and run away?" Skits said with a maniacal sneer on her face.

Jasmine turned to a series of computers blinking and coolant fans grinding away. She sat down in the chair and felt it creak under her weight. She took off her gauntlet and set it down next to the computer. She looked for a port to access and finally grabbed a small wire on the wristband and fed it into the computer. The download bar appeared on her gauntlet.

"Jasmine," Dwayne said with a hushed tone, "I think we are so fucked."

"What?"

She looked into the darkness at the far end of the bay. The lights began to flicker to life. Housed at the end were at least twenty people, standing, unmoving. Jasmine narrowed her eyes, trying to focus on the figures. "They look like synthetics."

"Those are people," Dwayne said. "Outlanders, to be exact."

"Holy shit," Skits said. "They've been experimenting on powers and humans?"

Jasmine turned to the others. "Were you wondering why the most heavily sealed part of the facility had no guards?"

Dwayne watched as each of the limp bodies twitched. Their hanging heads shot upright, their backs straightening. "Not anymore."

***

Vanessa wept over the bloodied corpse, the tears streaming down her cheeks, landing on the priest's face, mixing with the crimson. She paused at the sensation and wiped them from her cheek. She turned her head and saw the feathered wings stretched alongside her body. Confusion began to set in. "This isn't real."

The scene had reset itself and she could see the priest standing in front of her once more. She listened to him scolding her, calling her a monster. She looked up and to the man and she could see the reflection in his eyes of her blonde hair and alabaster skin. "It's not real."

He drew back the belt, preparing to strike her. She reached up and grabbed his wrist and felt him try to wrestle away from her. She stood and held the man's arms, grasping them with all her strength until the man was kneeling, submitting before her.

"You're not real."

The substance of the priest vanished and all that was left was smoke. The belt she had come to fear lay on the ground. Without the man, all she had were the memories of the pain it caused her. She remembered the day he had cast her out and the rage she felt toward him. She had contemplated killing him for decades, but she had turned her back on that life. She had forged a new existence. Now she practiced the words the women of the church had instilled in her.

"I shall fear no evil."

She whispered it out loud, thinking of the

Warden, the man she had come to stop. She reminded herself of the Warden sitting behind the desk. She realized that, as she murmured the prayer, it wasn't the Warden she feared.

She looked at the massive rose window of the church, shining light down on her. She had always felt close to heaven in this spot, letting the light wash across her skin. She looked to her side and saw a young woman sitting in the pew, her blonde hair and alabaster skin resembling her own. She smiled at the woman. Sincere blue eyes pierced Vanessa's camouflage. She remembered the moment she had looked upon that woman. She had wanted to be her in all her perfection. That was the day she forged herself a new identity.

A shadow formed behind the woman. She could smell the repulsive stench of the Warden even in a world without senses. The shadow pulled the woman's head back and slid a blade along her neck. She wanted to cry out, but she reminded herself that nothing was real.

"I'm not real," she whispered to herself.

"You'll relive this moment for the rest of your days, angel."

She started to laugh at her moniker. She had been called that for so long she had begun to embrace the name. Even the Warden couldn't see past her conjured exterior. She knew none of it was real, and she decided it was time to let the mirage fade away.

She knelt down, focusing on the skin holding her body together, the constricting flesh she had woven about herself. She flexed her muscle and the image began to tear away. As she stood up, she knew the shadow was seeing her, the real her, for the first time.

She opened her hands and the claws at the tip of her fingers extended further outward. The shadow was staring at her, and for the first time, no laugh mocked her. She had surprised the man. She roared as a sensation in her gut revealed access to a power she had long since hidden away.

Vanessa turned about in the church and with that motion she was standing in the Warden's office again. She could see the man now. Instead of staring off into space, his eyes made contact with her.

She had his attention.

The world vibrated around her as two shadows appeared out of thin air. Before she could see them with her eyes, she was already turning toward one, claws stretched out, raking against the unknown substance. Her hands sank into the shadow, and as fast as it appeared, it dissipated. She continued the turn, swiped her hand across the neck of the second shadow, and watched it vanish.

The Warden was standing now. She felt his presence. Unlike the shadows he commanded, he was a solid object in the room. She jumped on the desk and reached forward to rake her nails across his face. He caught her arm. There was strength in his hands, a confidence in the way he stymied her approach.

The moment they touched, a rush of emotions and thoughts flooded her mind. They were more different than she had worried. Hers was a wild energy, free for the first time. His was like a rock, solid and unmoving. He pushed back and her body hit the ground and skidded to a stop. His form moved through the desk, closing the distance between them.

"Even now," he said in his calm, deep voice, "your power means nothing to me."

She screamed at him and lunged again. She could sense his movements before he made them, and for the first time she felt her claws rake against his face. The flesh was soft but malleable. She had struck the man, finally doing harm.

He didn't respond to the gashes across his face. The blood began to well up and slowly ooze down his cheeks. His eyes were unmoving, focused on the woman huffing and puffing in front of him.

He remained motionless as the pressure began to build in her head. It was as if a cement block was thrown against her torso, and she rolled backward. He was no longer using his avatar to assault her; he was relying on the abilities of his mind.

"No," she said firmly as drops of blood began to emerge from her nostril.

She willed herself to stand again, pulling her wings in close to her body. She could see the green skin on her hand and she began to push back against his intrusions. There was a moment of relief. The pain of hiding for years behind a mask caused her emotions to build. She embraced their overwhelming nature. The man in front of her threatened her way of life and the people she called her family.

The Warden's avatar was thrown backward. He

remained standing, but it was as if he were fighting against gale force winds. The more he resisted, the more Vanessa became enraged and her emotions continued to fuel the invisible storm.

"Power you had never imagined, angel," the man said. "I had so hoped you would join me."

With the slightest swipe of his wrist, it appeared that the storm calmed. Vanessa's anger subsided and she realized he was beginning to influence her more. He started to invade her mind. Even with her newfound confidence, she found herself facing an adversary with the ability to make her submit against her will.

***

"Conthan," Alyssa said in a hushed tone, "we need to get out of here."

Her companion held his best friend in his arms. She could tell by the heaving of his body he was sobbing. She didn't dare reach down and touch him again. "Conthan, we really need to get out of here."

He looked down at the charred remains of his friend. She tried to imagine what he was going through, but even she couldn't understand his guilt. Today, he had come to save her, and instead, she had saved him. The result had cost her life. He looked up through the tears to Alyssa standing there. Her face reflected the sadness in his eyes.

He laid Sarah's head back down onto the ground and took a moment to memorize her face. The pyro's corpse lay next to his dead friend. The Warden had constructed this situation. She watched as the sadness on his face turned to rage. The Warden was at fault for this.

She didn't see him gesture to call his powers. The portal simply opened in midair where he had navigated the maze to teleport before. He stood up and looked to Alyssa. "He's going to die."

"Who?"

"The Warden."

He didn't wait for a reply as he stepped into the frigid darkness.

Chapter Twenty-Four

May 20th, 2032 7:38AM

Dwayne pushed Skits behind the metal incubators while sheltering himself behind Jasmine. Her body responded to the thud of each bullet. She leaned forward, holding her arms at her side, deflecting as many as she could.

"We need better cover," Dwayne said.

"You think?" Jasmine yelled back.

He stepped to her side and let loose a bolt of lightning. The charge hit one of the metal men, which staggered backward. Dwayne flexed his arm and could feel that his internal battery didn't have enough energy to continue launching manmade bolts of lightning. He started preparing to jump behind the large tubes when he saw the black circle open mid-air.

"Incoming," he yelled.

They were stepping right into the line of fire. He

pushed the last of his charge out through his palms, offering what little cover he could. He saw Alyssa come out of the portal and grabbed her, pulling her to the ground.

Skits grabbed her brother's hand and pulled him behind the tubes. They all watched as Conthan stood in front of the portal. The expression on his face betrayed his cool demeanor. The flushed red skin showed his anger.

"Get to cover," Jasmine barked.

Dwayne could see the vacant look on his companion. He was staring off into space, his mind altogether elsewhere. Jasmine stepped in front of him and spread herself wide with clank after clank of bullets pelting her hide.

"Conthan, run," she yelled.

The sound of metal scraping across Jasmine's skin got louder. Dwayne could tell Conthan was lost. He watched them hide, but there was a disconnect between what he was seeing and how he was reacting. Dwayne could only imagine Conthan was still focusing on his dead friend.

Beyond Jasmine a dozen synthetic soldiers were holding rifles, firing in his direction. The energy tore itself from Conthan's body and without thinking about it, the void ripped through several of the oncoming soldiers. Dwayne could hear the pain in Conthan's voice as he yelled. His muscles must be on fire as he strained to open the portal from inside the torsos of the human robots, Dwayne thought.

He growled and a scream erupted from his lips. Dwayne recognized what was happening, Conthan was losing himself to his abilities. The voids burst out of the waists of several soldiers, swallowing their upper halves. Conthan's mind raced as time began to slow down. His powers needed to expel the robots.

His arms were on fire. The blood in his veins burned and only got worse as he let the portal find its other end. The upper bodies of half the robots came raining down on their companions, who stumbled under the assault.

Skits ran forward. Both her arms were blazing blue fire. Conthan was startled back to reality as Jasmine leaned forward and began chasing after the girl. Dwayne knew it might be their last chance to rally.

Jasmine grabbed on to the neck of the closest soldier and raised it into the air. Before she could slam the body back into the ground, a flash of light blinded everybody in the room. Lightning hit her skin, reflecting off her body and spreading out into a web across the soldiers.

Dwayne held on to the piece of shrapnel wedged into an outlet. Electricity poured into his body and as quickly as his body could absorb it, he hurled it at his teammate.

Jasmine reached back and with all her strength, thrust her hand into the soldier's chest. She worked her fingers into the breastplate as sparks shot between her and the robot. Her hand pushed past the metal chest as the skin ripped away from its upper body. The machine went limp in her grasp.

"Warn me next time," she yelled.

She took the machine and slammed it into the

next closest robot.

Dwayne hissed as his skin began to burn. His internal battery was full and it was only a matter of minutes before it forced its way out of his body against his will. He took a staggering step toward the battle.

"Conthan," he said as he walked past, "get Alyssa out of here. This is out of your league."

Conthan held up his hand to protest but Alyssa grabbed him by the shoulder. "They're just soldiers. We're after the Warden."

Dwayne saw even the mention of the man made Conthan's blood boil. He clenched his fist and the massive portal vanished. Alyssa's jerking on the man started to turn more manic.

"This is for Class I's to deal with," she said.

Alyssa tugged at Conthan and he began to run behind her. Dwayne followed close behind, stopping to hurl volleys of lightning at the machines. They passed large tubes and moved toward the far end of the massive bay. He couldn't help but feel dwarfed by the scale of the room. It was the size of a warehouse hidden inside the facility.

Alyssa paused long enough to see cages sorted on either side of them. "Oh my god," she gasped.

"What?"

She stopped running and pointed toward the cages. Inside were dozens of people. They were all wearing body suits, lined against the bars hoping to get a look at what was causing the commotion. Dwayne clapped his hands together, sending out wave of bolts, striking the floor around Jasmine and

Skits, giving them a chance to start falling back.

Alyssa turned as light flashed. As the room lit up, her jaw dropped at the sheer number of captives.

"Who are they?" Conthan asked, confused.

She shrugged. "If they're in cages, then they're friends of ours."

"How can you be sure?"

She yelled at the people, "Any of you crazy killers? No? Okay, let's get you out."

"Please," one of the women said, "let me go."

"How'd you get here?" Conthan asked.

"They took me in my sleep."

Alyssa looked at the woman. "What's your power?"

The woman's eyebrow rose. "I'm human."

"You're all human?"

"Some more than others." She pointed to a man in the next cage.

Conthan moved closer and could see that the middle-aged man's face was covered in scars. His eyes glowed a faint red in the darkness. "What happened to him?"

"They've been trying to give us powers."

Alyssa turned to the woman. "Who?"

She grabbed the bars. "Whoever took us. Please, let us out."

Dwayne saw several faces he thought might be former Outlanders. Each of them pressed themselves against the bars, reaching through, begging for escape. He couldn't imagine leaving them here. Even if they had been criminals amongst society, nobody deserved this kind of treatment.

Jasmine stormed past them and ripped off the

first lock. "Project Chimera," she said. "I thought it was a rumor."

The captured woman stared in disbelief as the door opened. She examined Jasmine, her savior, whose skin looked as if it was cracked in several places. "Who are you?"

"A convert," Jasmine said. "Is it safe to release everybody?"

She nodded. "They just want to go home."

"There is no more home for you," Jasmine said. "You'll be hunted like Children of Nostradamus now."

Dwayne nodded in agreement. He knew Jasmine was right, there was no way they could be free again. At best, they'd be hunted and captured again, at worst, they'd be slaughtered. After a moment, he wasn't sure which was the worse scenario. "We can offer you sanctuary in the Danger Zone."

"They're not powered," Jasmine said.

"They're dead without us," Dwayne replied.

"We're not babysitters." Jasmine gave him a stern look, trying to relay their purpose to him without saying it.

"When did this become a 'we' operation?"

She stopped fighting him.

Conthan followed a row of cages until he saw a small form outside the prison, lying curled up on the floor. He walked closer to the mumbling man. Conthan took off his jacket, wrapped the man in it, and picked him up.

"What now?" he asked.

Dwayne looked at all the people behind him. "We can't just run out of here."

"A transport," Jasmine said. "There must be one."

"Can you fly it?"

She nodded.

"We have to hurry. The Corps are going to be all over this place."

"I'm not leaving," Conthan stated firmly.

"We can mount an attack another day. We have to save these people."

"What about Sarah?" asked Conthan.

They all got quiet.

Conthan handed the man to Jasmine. Dwayne knew the look on his friend's face. There was nothing left but revenge in the young man's eyes. "I have unfinished business."

Dwayne watched as his companion fell through a portal in the ground and vanished. As fast as it happened, the portal closed into nothing.

"We're going after him, right?" asked Alyssa.

"His fight is with himself," Dwayne said.

Chapter
Twenty-Five

May 20th, 2032 7:48AM

Vanessa could feel his hands pressing at her temples. His mind jabbed at hers like a red hot poker. Each time she warded against his attack, more pain shot through her body. She tried to let her avatar vanish and fade back into her physical self, but the Warden held her mind on the battlefield, refusing to let her leave.

"Angel," came his deep voice. "Why would you want to leave before the fun begins?"

She could only resist at this point. The inevitable was about to happen. His fingers felt like liquid as they seeped deeper and deeper into her mind. She was well aware attacking him had been a mistake and that her hubris was going to kill her.

"When your will is broken," he said, "I can only imagine what amazing things I can accomplish with another telepath."

"You," she hissed, "talk too much."

His body tensed and the darkness began to retreat. She could see the Warden's office again as his assault let up.

"It seems the two I hoped to enjoy have come straight to my door."

Vanessa realized he wasn't talking to her. She looked out of the corner of her eye and without being able to actually see it, she knew there was another presence in the room.

***

"It seems the two I hoped to enjoy have come straight to my door."

Conthan's chest was heaving as he stepped into the Warden's office. He could see the man standing at his desk. "I'm going to fucking kill you."

Conthan lunged at him and was surprised by how fast the large man moved. The Warden stepped to the side and grabbed Conthan, slamming his head against the desk. Conthan didn't have to feel the blood running down his cheeks, he could see the splatter across wood's surface. The Warden flipped him over on the desk and his sneer was inches from Conthan's face. "Did you really think you could win this fight?"

Conthan tried to punch the man but his hand was inches from making contact. He opened a portal and reached through it, feeling the chill of the darkness. The exit appeared behind the Warden. Conthan's fist connected to the back of the man's head. He punched twice before the Warden threw him off the desk against a bookcase.

Conthan closed one portal to open another beneath him. He fell through and dropped behind the large man. Conthan wrapped his arm around his thick neck. "I said, I'm going to fucking kill you."

***

The pressure against Vanessa's skull began to ease. She clawed at the Warden's face and he staggered backward. She could sense Conthan in the room. She tried to work with the kid to fight the same man on two battlefields.

"Angel," he said, cupping his eye, "this changes nothing."

She stepped in to slash with her hand and he grabbed her wrist. He bent it backward, and had it been in the physical world, her bones would have snapped. She brought her feet up to his chest and pushed off against the large man, launching herself backward. She used her wings to stop her momentum and reached down to the imaginary belt at her waist. The familiar handle of her sword made her smile as she drew the weapon. "This ends now, Warden."

She charged in, the sword held straight out in front of her. She expected to feel it slide into his abdomen, but she looked down to where he had caught it between his hands. She saw the mocking smile on his face.

"Submit," he said through gritted teeth.

With the single word Vanessa felt his mind invading hers again. Memories of her childhood flashed by, and in each, he was standing there. She gasped as he pushed further into her past. The memories were beginning to distort until his presence was in all of them.

***

Conthan's back slammed into the floor. He was looking at the Warden upside down. The large man's face was purple as he sucked in oxygen. The veins on his neck and forehead were beginning to protrude. His gasps turned into grunts.

Conthan tried to suck in air but his lungs refused to cooperate. The Warden turned, walked over to his desk, and pulled out a small gun. He stumbled as he walked forward and he landed on his knees, looking down at Conthan.

"Child," he said with a raspy voice, "you either submit, or I exterminate you."

The gun pointed at Conthan's temple. The metal touched his skin and dug into his scalp. The anger on the man's face was palpable. Conthan realized as he was staring into the killer's eyes that he was about to die.

Remember Sarah.

Vanessa's voice touched the edge of his thoughts. He clenched his fist and felt the pain course through his tired body. Sarah was dead. He repeated it over and over in his head as the pressure continued to build behind his eyes.

"This"—the portal opened—"is for Sarah."

He reached into the portal and felt the exit tear open inside the Warden's chest. He pushed through into a second portal that exited just in front of the Warden's face. It took several blinks for him to grasp what the boy's power had accomplished. Mere inches from his face, his heart thumped one last time. The organ was draining of blood as Conthan squeezed it tightly.

"That's how you win a fight, asshole."

Conthan opened his hand and the heart landed next to the Warden's face. He pulled his arm through the portals and strained to shut them. He could see into the man's eyes and realized the man had only been giving him part of his attention.

Conthan looked around the empty room. He could feel her nearby.

"Your turn, Vanessa," he mumbled.

***

Vanessa was looking at a nun's face. Another memory. The young woman was holding Vanessa's infant self out in the rain. The small cardboard box beneath her contained a blanket. She could see the kind woman's face, her soft eyes absorbing the sight of the baby's demon-like skin and reptilian wings.

Standing behind the woman in black and white was the Warden. He was staring at her, examining the small child with wings with a twisted smile. He started to reach for her when his hands froze. He brought them back to his chest and clutched at his shirt.

"Feeling a little shaken?" asked Vanessa.

Standing in his office again, she could see

Conthan holding his still heart. She turned the sword, loosening the Warden's grip and plunging it into his chest. She knew the vacant look of a dead man. He tried to reach for her, but she turned the blade and a guttural groan left his lips.

The sword slid through his body until the hilt pushed against his chest. She sneered at the man. "You pissed off the wrong people."

One of Vanessa's taloned hands let go of the sword and grabbed the Warden's face. She pushed with every ounce of her being and felt his mind begin to crumble. She weaved through the broken images until she found one of a frail man sitting on the couch with the president. He smiled at the woman. She waited to see if he was exerting his will over her. By the touches and hushed tones, she knew the president was free of his will.

Vanessa looked more closely at the image of the man sitting on the couch and could see physically there was no way he was the Warden. She pushed harder at the disguise to unravel the web of deceit. Her mind focused on the Warden, the large bulky man behind the desk and slowly, his image faltered and she could see the older man in his place.

Her mind retreated as she looked at the wavering image of the Warden. It suddenly dawned on her that he was more similar to her than she anticipated. Where she was a master of projecting disguises, the older man had literally grappled and taken control of the host known to her as the Warden. She could see the image of the Warden fading to reveal the frail man from her memories.

He looked up from under his heavy eyelids and

smiled at Vanessa. "We're not so different, you and I."

"We're nothing alike."

***

Conthan rolled out of the way of the falling corpse. He forced the portals closed as he tried to choke down air. He jumped as two men he hadn't seen in the room before collapsed on the ground. Before he could stand up, he felt a presence nearby. He attempted to force his muscles to move, but found they were sluggish. He took the pistol from the dead man's hands.

He sat up slowly to see Vanessa standing in front of him. He knew without asking she wasn't physically in the room with him. His voice squeaked as he spoke. "We won."

"Not yet."

"What now?"

"Follow me."

She reached out her hand. He reached out for her. "You're not here."

"Do it."

He took her hand. The moment they connected he could feel the echo in his mind. He was looking through his eyes but he was a passenger in his own body. Vanessa was in control, showing him her memories.

"The Warden is alive."

It was a flash, but he could see the memory of a frail old man on the couch with the president. He had no idea how she was doing it, but he had come to expect weird when it came to Vanessa's powers. He saw the man's face as he bantered with the president.

He looked down to his hand and could feel Vanessa's mind resisting him. He let out a low growl as he realized he had murdered a puppet. He thought he had given Sarah the justice she deserved. He looked at the portal in front of him. "Don't get in the way, Vanessa."

I can find him.

"No need."

Conthan started to step into the portal and time seemed to freeze as his powers searched for an exit. His mind raced looking for a destination in which to open another void and provide passage between the two points. His other self soared outward from the facility.

Vanessa was still connected to him. Her guiding hands helped provide stability to his outward journey. He moved as fast as his thoughts could take him until he saw the transport vehicle flying away from the facility. As he soared closer to the vehicle, it shimmered for a moment and turned invisible.

Before he realized it, he was stepping out of the portal into the middle of the transport. He saw Dwayne's shock and disbelief. "You're alive."

Dwayne attempted to take his hand. Conthan vanished and reappeared behind the lightning wielder. "What's going on?" asked Dwayne.

Conthan continued walking past several refugees until he reached Skits. She sat holding a blanket around an elderly man. She looked up just in time to see Conthan raise his hand with a small gun.

Bang.

They all jumped from the volume of the gunfire. It was done. It was over. The battle had been won. Conthan was barely aware he was falling as Dwayne tackled him. "What the hell?"

Conthan felt his body strike the metal floor. Only a few feet away, Skits was covered in blood. Next to her, a frail old man with a vacant look in his eyes and a twisted smile on his lips. It wasn't a question that the frail, decaying body in front of him was the real body of the Warden.

He let the gun drop from his hands as the world grew dark.

Epilogue

"Feel better?"

Conthan jolted upright. He looked up into Vanessa's serpentine eyes. His head and muscles were on fire. Just across the street from Vanessa, the darkness gave way to a large church. Seeing the gargoyles perched on its spires, he couldn't help but think Vanessa was amongst her kin.

"I hear each and every thought."

"Your burden to bear," Conthan said with a devilish smile.

She took his hand and pulled him to his feet. He had no idea where they were. The street seemed to be vacant, but unlike their residence in Boston, it appeared to be perfectly preserved. He wiped his eyes to shake away the last of the fuzzy edges. "We're not in Boston, are we?"

"He's not the sharpest amongst you, is he?"

Conthan turned, expecting to find Jasmine, but was surprised when the space in front of him was empty. Jasmine emerged from a veil of shadows next to a decrepit building, almost as if by magic.

"Somebody has to be our Class Zero."

Dwayne appeared from nowhere along with Skits, smirking. "I'm going to start having power envy."

"As the only Class III here…" Alyssa's voice echoed from nowhere. One moment the space was empty and next the Middle Eastern girl was in front of him, taking a bow. "Can we just agree everybody has their place?"

Dav5d appeared behind them. "Ahem." He cleared his throat. "Two Class IIIs."

Conthan turned to see Vanessa standing there, her wings flared out wide. He was amazed by how massive she seemed, the appendages spanning twenty feet. He touched his own face. The sensation was different, like moving his foot while it was asleep.

"We're not in Boston?"

"We're not even in the same room," Dav5d confessed.

"Telepath voodoo," Jasmine said.

Skits punched Conthan in the arm. "That's for getting villain blood on me."

"Sorry," he said. "I was kind of raging there."

"I hadn't noticed."

Dwayne patted him on the shoulder. "Feel better?"

Conthan thought of Sarah, her beautiful smile and her carefree laugh. It came to him in waves. He would never see her again. He looked at Dwayne and shook his head. With a whisper he replied, "No."

He could feel the warmth of Vanessa standing

next to him. She rested one of her hands on his other shoulder and gave a concerned smile.

"That is why you were worth saving."

"What now?" asked Jasmine.

Conthan jumped in. "The Warden wasn't the person in charge of the project."

"Who was?" asked Jasmine.

"The president," said Dav5d.

"What?" they mumbled.

"He was put into place by Cecilia Joyce, the president. If you ever asked if Eleanor was a precog with good intentions or bad, we have confirmation. Eleanor wasn't a killer, she was trying to prevent the future we were born into."

"But we've had several presidents since."

"What if the president had been replaced by a shapeshifter all those years ago and Eleanor found out? What if she knew exactly how things would pan out?"

Vanessa nodded as each of the eyes turned toward her. Conthan finally asked what they were all thinking. "What if the darkness she spoke about has yet to happen?"

There was a pause before Dwayne gave Conthan a nudge with his elbow. "Nighthawks for life."

Vanessa looked off into the distance, behind her newfound teammates. Conthan followed her eyes and could see the dark clouds just on the edge of where the city street vanished. He suspected the rumbling storm was a reaction to Vanessa's state of mind. He watched as a cloud lit up. He knew the darkness had yet to descend upon them.

Acknowledgments

I must acknowledge the many people involved in bringing this book to fruition. Thank you to the Metrowest Writers, Amelia, Chris, Cristina, and Ken for your feedback, support, and guidance. I always need people to kick me in the pants and chug coffee with me. Thank you to Catie Joyce and Jessi Robinson for being faithful beta readers and giving me the feedback I needed to hear even when I wasn't ready. And thank you to the New England Horror Writers and Chris Philbrook for answering a thousand questions and helping me get one step closer to my dream.

About the Author

I'm high school graphic design and marketing teacher, at a large suburban high school in Massachusetts. Working as a high school educator and observing the outlandish world of adolescence was the inspiration for my first young adult novel, "Suburban Zombie High."

My inspiration for writing stems from being a youth who struggled with reading in school. While I found school assigned novels incredibly difficult to digest, I devoured comics and later fantasy novels. Their influences can be seen in the tall tales I spin.

I took the long route to becoming a writer. For a brief time, I majored in Creative Writing but exchanged one passion for another as I switched to Art and Design. My passion for reading about superheroes, fantastical worlds, and panic-stricken situations would become the foundation of my writing career.

I participated in my first NaNoWriMo in 2006 and continue to write an entire novel every November. Now I am the NaNoWriMo Municipal Liaison to the Massachusetts Metrowest Region. I also belong to a weekly writing group, the Metrowest Writers.

Facebook:
https://www.facebook.com/writeremyflagg

Twitter:
http://twitter.com/writeremyflagg

Website:
http://www.remyflagg.com/

Printed in Great Britain
by Amazon